SHIELDED

LISS BREWER

Cover design by GermanCreative

Author photograph by Melissa Stampa

© 2020 Melissa Stampa

✽ Created with Vellum

For my love, you changed my life.

CONTENTS

CHAPTER 1

He would come again tonight. He came almost every night. Rosie wriggled under the covers, burying herself until only her eyes and auburn curls poked out, hoping to hide. An army of soft toys surrounded her, Big Bear, a worn giraffe, the white bear with the fuzzy fur Grandma June had given her at Christmas. Clutched tightly under her arm was her favourite teddy, Pinkie, threadbare, and missing its nose. *If I go to sleep very quickly,* she thought, *I won't be awake to see him.* But sleep eluded her, and fear kept her awake. *I could call out. I could call out to Mama.* She wouldn't hear though, Rosie knew. Their house was a duplex, two houses side by side, fitting together in a neat rectangle. It was old too, her mother had told her, and built by an old man, who had lived on the other side with his wife when he was young. His wife had been moved to a nursing home when she got too old to manage the stairs, and later she had died, leaving the old man alone. When he had passed away - on the toilet, her mother had whispered, making Rosie giggle - he had left it to the nursing sisters who had cared for his wife. The nursing sisters rented it out, just this side of the duplex, the Old Man's half remaining virtually untouched. Mama had taken her over there in search of a soup pot, unlocking the door with a large key that Rosie thought looked like a key for a castle door. Photos sat covered in thick dust; books remained on the bookshelves. Mama had gone into the kitchen, and Rosie had wandered the rooms, opening a jewellery box and pulling out strands of brightly-coloured necklaces. She had placed them back and thought how odd it was that these were their things, all neat and in their places. The woman's makeup sat on the dresser, and Rosie had popped the lid of the compact, drawing pleasure from the way the top sprang open like a jack-in-the-box and stared at the rouge that had once coloured the dead woman's cheeks. Rosie had covered a fingerprint on the mirror with her own, smaller than the one left behind. She felt an odd tilting of reality, as though the past and present had folded over on each other - and the strangeness of how little of ourselves is left behind when we die. Mama had found Rosie holding a large leather bible she had picked up from the table in the bedroom and said, "You can take it if you want, Rosie. I'm sure he wouldn't mind. The sisters should have cleaned this place out and given all these things to charity."

So, Rosie had, tucking the Bible under her arm. Mama had helped herself to a pot. *And now*, Rosie thought, *he must want them back.*

He never made a sound. Rosie never heard him at all. But if she kept her eyes trained on the doorway, sooner or later, he would come. The first night had been the night they had taken the Bible and the pot, and Rosie had been lying awake in her bed with just Pinkie for company. Her room was large, like all the rooms in the house, with wide glass doors that folded like an accordion, and Mama never shut them. Mama's room was beside hers, and a large covered verandah ran past them both. Across from Rosie's room was the bathroom, and then the kitchen, before the house took a sharp right angle and led to the dining room, which led on to the lounge. The lounge was where Mama was now, where she would never hear if Rosie called out. Rosie knew this because the first night she had screamed, and Mama had not heard and not come. He came from the right, as though he was walking from the kitchen, and walked across the verandah, heading towards Mama's room. Always the same way. He had white tufts of hair that stuck out from under a hat, a long-sleeved yellow button-up shirt, and brown pants. The first night, upon seeing a man walking past her room, Rosie had let out an ear-piercing scream, and he hadn't even glanced at her - just continued walking past her room until he was out of sight. That was when Rosie remembered the photos in the duplex next door, and knew who she was seeing.

Now Rosie couldn't sleep because she knew, soon enough, the Old Man would walk past again. She felt uneasy in her tummy and hugged Pinkie closer. She didn't think he knew she was there. He didn't look when she screamed - never looked around at all, just that same walk, staring straight ahead, every night. Despite this, Rosie was terrified that one night he *would* look, and they would lock eyes, and in Rosie's mind, that would be *the worst thing*. Some nights Mama would stay and read to Rosie until she fell asleep; those were the nights Rosie loved best because he never came when Mama was there, and once she was asleep, she couldn't see if he did. Mama's body would be warm and soft beside her, and she could curl into Mama's arms, fear melting away. Tonight, Mama did not read a story, and now Rosie was waiting for the Old Man. She felt him before she saw him, goosebumps rising on her arms, and then there he was, walking past her room in the shuffling gait of the elderly. Rosie held her breath and waited for it to be over.

CHAPTER 2

Twenty-five years later.

Rosie lifted the camera to her eye, "Honey, can you hold Daddy's leg? He might try to run away!"

The little girl in front of her giggled, holding on to her father's leg tightly, leaning her head against his thigh. Rosie pressed the shutter, click, click, click. That tactic always worked for toddlers who hated being posed.

"Thank you for being so patient with her," the little girl's mother said from where she stood slightly behind Rosie.

"It's no problem," Rosie answered. "Honestly, ninety percent of shooting small kids is following them around and waiting for the shot."

"What's the other ten percent?"

"Grass stains on my knees and leaves in my hair," Rosie laughed and tugged a rogue leaf out of her auburn curls.

"Well, you've been great with her, she doesn't usually

warm to people so quickly," the mother said, smiling towards her daughter.

Rosie stood, removing the camera strap from around her neck, "I think we are done here. I'll be in touch later this week with proofs."

Rosie said her goodbyes and began to pack the camera into its bag. The sun was low in the sky, but the air was warm, autumn air still holding on to the last traces of summer. As soon as the client's car drove down the dirt road of the state forest they were shooting in, Rosie felt the smile slip off her face. She lay down on the grass and turned her face to the blue sky, closing her eyes and stretching her arms out to the side. Above her, the tips of the hoop pines slowly rocked as a gentle breeze caressed them. The forest was her favourite shooting location, comforting and familiar, despite the fact it shot a keen slice of pain through her because this was the first place she had taken Ben to for a date, six years ago. They had picnicked in this exact spot; maybe she had even sat right where she lay just now. Ben had been thrilled by the little hideaway, as were most of Rosie's clients. Tucked up a dirt road that looked uninteresting, and framed by row after row of hoop pines, most people never bothered to travel up it and see what lay at the end.

Rosie had found it by accident years ago when she was driving by it one day and became enchanted by the way the light fell at the end of the road. This was when she had first really fallen in love with photography instead of just flirting with it. She had taken her camera with her everywhere, continually stopping and shooting things she had never really paid attention to before. Suddenly, it seemed the whole world was more interesting. *Had the sky ever been that colour before? Were the Autumn leaves always so vibrant? Was there anything more magical then peach blossoms bursting forth from bare branches in Spring?* That day Rosie immediately slammed the brakes on and lurched across the road, slowly moving towards that light at the end, stopping once midway along to take a shot of the way it fell. When she arrived at the end, she realized the road swung to the right, and around the corner a little way, it opened to a clearing with an old wooden shed whose purpose was long forgotten, and two large jacarandas. On the day Rosie first found them, they were in full bloom, raining their purple petals onto a lavender carpet. Rosie had nearly whooped out loud at the find. She had spent an entire afternoon there that day, shooting it from every angle until she returned to the car giddy with excitement, jacaranda blooms caught in her curls, her hazel eyes sparkling with joy. When she had taken Ben here, he made jokes as they went up the dirt road about Rosie taking him somewhere to bury him, but when he had seen the clearing, he was as breath-taken as she had been the first time.

Rosie's phone vibrated in her pocket and broke her from her thoughts. She removed it and looked at the caller ID on the screen. Her mother. *Damn it.* She was going to be late to get Lucy again. Shoots always ended up running longer than she anticipated, and her mother panicked when she was left with Lucy too long. Rosie didn't like to lean on her mother too much, she was so fragile, but she didn't know what else to do; she couldn't afford after school care. She jogged to her little blue Corolla, put her camera bag on the seat beside her, and turned the car on.

"Happy anniversary, Ben," she whispered. "I miss you."

She put the car into gear and drove out of the forest.

<hr>

Rosie pushed open the door to her mother's house to find her standing in the lounge room, wringing her hands.

"You were late," Kate complained.

Her mother's watery blue eyes were filled with an afternoon of anxieties that would never come to pass. Kate saw danger everywhere it seemed. Every headache was meningitis; every mole was skin cancer. Every time Rosie was late, she came in to find her mother beside herself, entirely sure Rosie had either died unexpectedly in a car accident or decided to skip town without leaving so much as a note. This trait had not been helped when eighteen months ago Rosie's husband had indeed not returned home when, for reasons unknown, he had lost control of his car, on a perfectly straight and well-paved road in good weather, and wrapped it around a power pole. Ben had died on impact. Now it seemed Kate was sure that in the same way that Ben and Rosie had been inseparable when he was alive, her daughter would certainly have followed him in death every time Rosie was more than five minutes late.

Rosie suppressed a sigh, "I know, Mum. I'm sorry. It ran a little longer than expected."

Lucy came barrelling into the room from the little sunroom where the toys were kept.

"Mama!" she cried, launching herself into Rosie's arms.

"Hey, baby! How was kindergarten? Did you have fun?" Rosie buried her nose into Lucy's dark curls and breathed in the scent of her daughter. If she closed her eyes and tried hard, she could almost still catch a faint whiff of the baby scent of a smaller Lucy trapped within her locks.

"I made a necklace," Lucy said and pulled back to show Rosie a strand of dyed pasta threaded on to a string that Lucy was wearing around her neck, with all the pride of a necklace of precious stones.

"It's beautiful, Luce. You should make me one next time," Rosie set her daughter on the floor. "Why don't you grab your bag so we can head home and Mama can start dinner."

Lucy scurried off to collect her things.

"Thanks for minding her, Mum," she said to her mother. "I know it's hard for you, but I really appreciate it. I'll look into after school care again soon; I just need to get back on my feet."

Losing Ben had been hard in ways Rosie could not even begin to express. The absence of him in their bed, the quiet of just her and Lucy at home without his laughter booming through the rooms - but in practical ways, it had been an adjustment too. Suddenly, she had been thrust into single motherhood and forced to navigate her way alone financially, and in caring for her daughter. She and Ben had never had a lot of money, but half of 'not a lot' was basically nothing. She had stayed in their old home as long as possible, but when money began to run out, she went seeking cheaper rentals. She had moved with Lucy to a smaller house a few suburbs away in Olive Wood after staying with Kate for a month - an exercise that nearly drove them both to insanity. Kate had wailed about that move, though, because despite the rather innocuous-sounding name, Olive Wood was a neighbourhood that had gone to seed decades before. Its inhabitants were a melting pot of cultures; the hardworking poor smashed up next to drug addicts whose nightly rows with their spouses or housemates punctuated the night. Amongst these, were the elderly who had lived there for years and either couldn't afford housing in the safer neighbourhoods, or were too stubborn to move. Kate had begged Rosie to reconsider, even offering for Rosie and Lucy to stay with her permanently, an offer that Rosie knew would have been disastrous with her mother's near neurotic OCD and anxieties. Still, Rosie had appreciated the offer, it was one of the few times Kate had shown any maternal instinct in the last two decades. For the most part, Rosie had been lucky in Olive Wood. She rented a small two-bedroom on Wattle Street for less than half the price she and Ben had been paying in Clayton Hills. But between the funeral expenses and moving house, she had ripped through almost all of her and Ben's savings – something they had been putting away in the hopes of saving for their own home. As of that morning, Rosie had precisely $438.47 left in her savings account, which, she thought to herself, probably made her one of the more affluent residents of Olive Wood.

Lucy came back into the room, carrying her water bottle and a small purple backpack. "Come on, sweet pea, let's get you home," Rosie ushered her towards the door.

Kate followed them to the doorway and watched them walk out to the car. Rosie knew her mother wouldn't step over the threshold; she hadn't left the house in more than five years.

"You want me to bring in your mail?" Rosie called, the box was stuffed with junk mail flyers.

"No, that's okay," Kate sang back. "I'll get them later."

Despite her complete avoidance of the outside world, Kate always pretended it was just a temporary situation that would end tomorrow.

"Lucy, go give Nanna those brochures," she whispered to Lucy, who obediently skipped down to the letterbox, pleased with her job. Kate accepted the mail with praise and a kiss, and Lucy came back down the driveway and climbed into her seat. They waved goodbye as Rosie backed out, Kate closing the door; no doubt bolting it before Rosie had even made it down the driveway.

Traffic moved slowly on the drive back to Olive Wood; everything northbound was congested as usual. Lucy chatted in the background, "Liam said that Jacob ate his boogers, but I haven't seen it, so saying that is just mean, isn't it, Mama?"

Rosie fought for concentration. *Was the red car planning to merge or just keep the blinker on,* she wondered.

"Mama?"

"What was that?"

"I said, it is just mean for Liam to say lies about Jacob."

"Yes, that's very mean," Rosie confirmed. The red car still wasn't coming across. Rosie looked in the rearview mirror, traffic was really banked up. Finally, her lane began to pick up the pace, and Rosie pressed gently on the accelerator.

"Mama?"

"Yeah?"

"Can you get my bag?"

"No, Luce, I- "

The red car began to merge just as Rosie came up beside it, she tapped the horn in a polite beep and swore under her breath as the red car swerved back into their lane.

"Sorry, Luce, what did you want?"

Rosie tilted the rearview mirror to see Lucy in the back-seat, but Lucy had forgotten her request and was looking out the window towards some cows in a field. Rosie fixed the mirror and sighed. *Finally, some peace*, she thought with a smile. She looked up in time to see the red car coming across again, crushing her side mirror and scraping down the bonnet's side, pushing her on to the shoulder of the road with the sound of metal screaming.

CHAPTER 3

Rosie gripped the wheel as she slid on to the grass beside the highway. For the first time in her life, she was grateful for the banked-up traffic, which meant she was going far slower than the speed limit. Even so, the car bounced and jolted as they pulled to a stop, and Rosie tasted blood as her teeth found her lip. She sat there for a second, shaking and gasping, and watched as the red car continued up the highway, slipping between traffic and out of sight. She tried to see the license plate but found her eyes blurred, and she realised she was crying. Ben. *Ben.* God, this could have been so much worse. What if she died and left Lucy alone? What if she lost *Lucy?* Lucy! Rosie whipped around in the seat, cringing at the slight tweak in her neck. Lucy looked at her wide-eyed and still.

"Baby, are you okay?" Rosie said, trying to keep the panic out of her voice.

Lucy drew a shaky breath and nodded, "I'm okay, Mama."

Rosie reached out and patted Lucy's leg to assure herself that her daughter was still there, whole and unscathed.

"What happened?" Lucy asked.

"Just an accident, honey. We are both okay though; we are going to be fine."

"Is our car okay?"

Rosie groaned, "I'll have to get out and check. Will you be okay for a few minutes?"

The last thing she wanted was for Lucy to be standing beside the highway with all the cars going past. Rosie let out a breath and slumped back into her chair, closing her eyes tightly. She could *not* tell Kate about this; she would lose her mind. She needed to find her phone. *Did the police need to be called?* Rosie rubbed her hands through her hair and turned to look for her handbag.

A woman was sitting beside her in the passenger seat.

"Jesus Christ!" She shouted and reared back, smacking the back of her head against the glass of the driver's side window.

She was gone. There was no one there. *Of course there was no one there; it's a trauma response or something.*

"Mama!" Lucy cried from the backseat, frightened by Rosie's outburst.

"I'm okay, honey, I'm sorry. I just got a fright. Mama's okay."

Even so, Rosie glanced tentatively at the passenger seat again. Empty. *I am losing my damn mind.*

Lucy pointed out the window, "Look! It's Mr. St Clair. He will help us."

Rosie turned to see a black Ute had pulled off the road a little way up, and James St Clair walking towards her. Rosie met James earlier in the year at kindergarten orientation; his daughter Violet was in the same class as Lucy. The girls became fast friends, and she and James frequently took them to the play centre on the weekends. It was on one of these playdates that Rosie discovered James was a framer, and she had been using him to frame her works for her ever since. She tried to open her door, which resisted at first but then gave, with a shriek of metal that made Rosie grit her teeth.

"Hey! Are you ladies okay?" James called as he got nearer, holding his hand up to shield his eyes from the sun.

Rosie quickly wiped at her cheeks, brushing away her earlier tears, and nodded in response, "We're okay. I can't believe he didn't stop. I don't even know what happened."

Rosie stepped back to survey the damage, half the side was scraped up, her door bent inwards, the mirror long gone, and her driver side headlight was hanging half out of its socket.

"I hope you're insured," James said, letting out a low whistle.

"I am - but if I don't have the other driver's details won't I have to pay the premium?" She bit her lip, wondering where she would ever find the money to outlay on the premium and still keep a roof over her head.

James stopped in front of her, "Violet and I saw the whole thing. He was completely erratic, not your fault at all. I don't have a dashcam, but I got the license plate. I don't know if that helps?" He handed her a napkin with his neat handwriting on it.

Rosie folded it carefully, trying to stop her hands shaking, and put it in her pocket, "It does. Thank you."

James leaned into the car, "Hey Lucy, are you alright? You had a bit of an adventure just now!"

Rosie left James and Lucy to have a chat while she

searched the passenger seat side for her phone. James looked at her, "You better call the police, Rosie. I can stay with you if you want?"

Rosie waved him away, "No, please don't. I don't want Violet to have to sit here for goodness knows how long until this is sorted. It's okay."

"You sure?"

"Yes, absolutely. Thank you so much for stopping."

He smiled, "Not a problem." He leaned forward to wave to Lucy and began walking back to his car.

James got into his seat and turned around to face Violet, "You doing okay back there?"

She nodded, "Is Lucy and her Mum going to be okay?" She asked.

James and Violet had been behind them on the way out to the hardware store when they saw the accident. Only a few moments before, he had mentioned to Violet that it was Rosie and Lucy's car. Violet had been trying to guess where the pair were going, each guess becoming more ridiculous - the zoo, England, the moon - and then the red car had abruptly put an end to that. Violet had gasped, then wailed, and promptly burst into tears. James had pulled off the road as much to console his daughter as to check on the Parkers.

"They will be, it was only a little accident," he told her, to alleviate her fears.

"Why didn't the other car stop, Daddy?"

"They're supposed to, princess. They did the wrong thing."

Violet craned her neck to look back at Rosie's car as James moved slowly forward, lurching back into the traffic.

"*I* would stop," she said.

James smiled and wondered not for the first time how Violet could be so *good*. It certainly wasn't genetic. His family was made up of privileged, self-absorbed narcissists who drank themselves into early graves. And Violet's mother... well, she wasn't winning any prizes for Mum of the year. Amelia was a junkie who skipped out when Violet was five months old, and not sent so much as a postcard since. The only family Violet and he had was his sister Brooke, and his Uncle David, both miraculously unscathed by the St Clair curse of booze and ego. Violet, however, was kind and empathetic and honest - almost to a fault. She saved him before she was even born. A rainy autumn day when he and Amelia were both nursing hangovers after a three-day bender and finally realised Amelia's might be more than just the vodka. He knew he needed to sober up, and Amelia said she did too. For the next year, they had played house; he had gotten a job for the first time in his life, cut up the credit card attached to his family account, and tried to be a caring partner to Amelia.

The first time he made anything, it was a carved wooden duck for Violet. He had sanded it carefully, oiled the wood, and attached small wheels to the bottom of it so it would move along the floor. When he held it in his hands, he felt like the timber had come alive, as though it told *him* what it wanted to be. Amelia stayed clean for a while after Violet was born, then the occasional night out drinking, which led to weekends where she would come home still high - and finally, there was a week where he had no idea where she was. By the end, James had gone beyond worry and was furious. When she finally walked in the door, he had yelled, and she had screamed, and he had - god, did he *really* grab her? Squeezing her arms tight as though he could *just wake her up, goddamit*, and she had slapped him - hard - clawed him really, her fingernails raking his cheek. He rubbed at that spot now, as though he could still feel it there like a brand. Amelia had blown out of the house and out of their lives, barefoot, taking nothing but her bag.

Violet never asked about her mother, not once - not ever - and James was grateful she seemed content with the little family he could give her. James didn't tell anyone about that fight, he couldn't, he was so ashamed, and he had never felt more like his father. He kept thinking she would turn back up, the next day, next week, next month, and he would apologise. But Amelia stayed gone. She had no money, but that never seemed to be a problem for Amelia, she found friends wherever she went. She was *a real fun girl*, that's what Brooke called her, and not always nicely. But Amelia *had* been fun, and gorgeous; he had called her Snow White because she had hair so dark it was almost black, and pale skin that never tanned, and never freckled. Her smile, *man*. It did him in. Violet had the same smile, but on Violet, it was pure sunshine. The older she got, the more she looked like James, the same chestnut hair, soft brown eyes, and olive skin... but every now and then, Violet would pull a particular expression, and it was all Amelia - like she was right there in the room. He would marvel at how something like that had to be genetic. Amelia hadn't stuck around long enough for Violet to mimic the face Amelia pulled when she was reading or the way they both twined pieces of hair around their fingers while they watched television. Every time it would stop him in his tracks, and he would just think, there she is, there's Amelia, after all.

CHAPTER 4

Two hours later, Rosie finally pulled up in her driveway courtesy of a taxi she couldn't afford. She thanked the driver and helped Lucy out of the car. Rosie's car had been towed away to the mechanic, and tomorrow she would have to organise a hire car which, thankfully, was covered by her insurance. Rosie realised reluctantly she would have to tell Kate as there was no way a five-year-old would stay quiet about an accident. After the initial shock, Lucy had been quite excited by police officers, a tow truck, and a taxi ride that included a trip through a takeaway drive-thru as a special treat for Lucy being so patient. Now, Lucy carried the box containing her meal to the door, having already retrieved the toy car from inside the moment it was handed to her. Rosie fumbled in her bag for her house keys, juggling Lucy's kinder bag, her handbag, her bulky camera bag, and a small cola she didn't trust Lucy to hold in the back of the taxi.

"Come on, Mama, my hand hurts from carrying all this," Lucy called. Rosie gritted her teeth and latched on to the keys in the depths of the bag.

"Okay, hang on," she unlocked the door and flicked on the lights, releasing Lucy inside, where she raced into the lounge room and turned on the television.

Rosie dropped all the bags on the floor just inside the door and gave Lucy her drink. Groaning she reached up to massage the tender spot on her neck, her whole body ached as the tension of the afternoon slowly ebbed away. Leaving Lucy happily eating fries, she headed to her room to get out of her clothes and into something baggy and comforting. Rosie pulled on sweatpants and an old t-shirt of Ben's that she had stolen when he was still alive and able to complain about it. Then, pulling her hair into a messy bun, she padded back to the kitchen in her socks. Rosie opened the fridge and surveyed the contents before heading to the pantry, where she ate crackers out of the container, away from Lucy so she wouldn't have to explain her questionable dinner choices.

"What a shit day," she said aloud to the pantry.

No response. She sighed and put the crackers back before opening the fridge and taking out two beers.

"Hey, Luce?" She called.

"Yeah?"

"I'm just going to grab the clothes off the line, okay?"

Rosie waited three seconds but was unlikely to get a response from Lucy when she had both chicken nuggets and cartoons to keep her occupied. She headed back out the door and into the backyard.

The air had a crisp bite to it now that the sun had set, and the wind played through the chimes hanging by the back gate that joined Rosie's yard to the one next door. Rosie stood there for a moment and closed her eyes. For once, the neighbourhood was silent except for the distant sound of a train's whistle. Rosie opened the gate and cringed as the hinges complained. From the dark, she saw the red glow of a cigarette's cherry burn bright as the smoker in the shadows took a drag.

"It's a bit early for your nightcap, Rosemary," remarked Mr. Thompson. Rosie's elderly neighbour was sitting on a wooden bench seat under a large eucalyptus. He scooted over to the side so Rosie could sit beside him, and she collapsed into the chair and handed him one of the beers. Mr. Thompson reached into his shirt pocket and shook out a cigarette from the packet inside, passing it to Rosie with his lighter.

"Well," Rosie said, as she lit it, "it's been a really long day."

Rosie had met Mr. Thompson the week after she moved in. She was standing in the backyard looking at the stars and letting the breeze dry her tears when she suddenly got the feeling someone was watching her. She looked towards the fence, where she came face to face with a six-foot-tall, hair-covered man and gasped, tripping over her feet in an effort to get away. Across the fence, someone began to laugh.

"Tiny won't hurt you, love," came a voice. "He is a gentle giant."

Tiny turned out *not* to be a hairy man, but an Irish Wolfhound with an ironic name, and the voice belonged to Mr. Thompson who came outside every night to smoke his cigarettes. Mr. Thompson had the vain hope that in smoking outdoors, his daughter wouldn't realise he hadn't quit when she stopped by each day to check on him. Rosie and Mr. Thompson bonded over missing their spouses, a dislike of the neighbour across the road, and their mutual love of Tiny, who was just now butting his head against Rosie's shoulder to encourage her to begin pats. Rosie began to fill Mr. Thompson in on the day's events, and he expressed comfort and outrage at the appropriate intervals.

Mr. Thompson took a sip of his beer and patted his hand on hers, warmly, "Cars can be fixed, love. The important thing is that both you and your little girl are safe."

Rosie squeezed his hand and nodded, "It is."

"Go inside and give her a hug from Tiny and me."

Rosie leaned over and kissed him on his weathered cheek, he smelled of tobacco and Imperial Leather soap and reminded her of her grandfather.

"Goodnight, Mr. Thompson," she scratched Tiny behind the ear. "Goodnight, Tiny."

"Goodnight, Rosemary," Mr. Thompson said.

Rosie went inside to find Lucy sitting on the carpet with a small army of cars, constructing a highway, and ushered her into a bath and pyjamas. She tucked Lucy up in bed, and read her three stories before Lucy's eyelids drooped; a toy car still clutched tightly in her fist. Rosie could barely keep her own eyes open long enough to brush her teeth before sliding between her sheets, and falling asleep the moment her head hit the pillow.

"Mama."

Rosie's eyelids fluttered and opened, and she found herself staring into the wide blue eyes of her daughter. *Jesus, what time was it? It was still dark.*

"Lucy?" she sat up, groggily. "What's wrong, honey? Did you have a bad dream?"

Lucy was standing in her pyjamas, a ragged, patched cot sheet under her arm that she had taken for a security blanket at one-year-old, and was rarely apart from.

Lucy shook her head and leaned closer, "Mama," she whispered. "There's a girl in my room."

All Rosie's sleepiness vanished at those words.

She kicked at the sheets to free her legs, "A girl?"

Lucy nodded. *Shit.* Kate's protests about the unsafety of Olive Wood played through her head. She wished she had stayed in Clayton Hills. She wished Ben were here.

Rosie put Lucy in the bed and whispered for her to stay there. She crept out of the room and headed left up the hallway towards Lucy's bedroom, fear making her break into a sweat. *It's probably nothing, stop it. You're acting as neurotic as Kate. It's probably just shadows in her room.* But Lucy had never been a scared child; she was unnervingly confident - a trait that Rosie envied because she had always been shy and timid at Lucy's age. It was Ben that Lucy took after. Ben, who could have a conversation with anyone and make them feel as though they had been friends for years. Ben, whose laugh had won Rosie's heart. Ben, who was gone. And now Rosie was alone, sneaking through her own house towards a mystery girl in their daughter's room with nothing but Lucy's novelty flashlight - that now Rosie thought about it, she had no recollection of picking up. Lucy was never the kind of kid that complained about monsters in the closet.

Lucy's bedroom door stood ajar, and Rosie tentatively peeked into it. Empty. There was nowhere for anyone to hide, there was no space under the bed which was taken up with built-in drawers. There wasn't even a closet in this tiny room. She let out a breath she didn't realize she had been holding in a relieved whoosh, and padded back to her bedroom where Lucy had fallen asleep in her absence. Rosie slid in beside her daughter and curled her body around Lucy like a comma. She could stay here tonight. Rosie closed her eyes and tried to sleep, matching her breath to the steadiness of her daughter's, forgetting that Lucy had not been the only Parker to see a girl where there wasn't one that day.

The following day, Rosie had spent three hours on the phone to the insurance company and the car rentals organising pick up. She then caught yet another taxi down to collect the car. *More money*, she thought woefully. Lucy had gotten the day off of kinder by default. That night they had made a picnic in front of the television before Lucy drifted off to sleep in Rosie's arms. She carried Lucy to her bed, rousing in the night to Lucy once again claiming she had a visitor in her room. Rosie had dutifully gone to check the room before allowing Lucy to stay in bed with Rosie again for the night. Rosie had woken the next morning, teetering on the edge of the bed, Lucy splayed out like a starfish, taking up three-quarters of the space.

"This is gonna get old real quick, kid," she had muttered before waking Lucy up to get ready for kinder and heading down to the kitchen to get breakfast started.

Rosie slid the plate of toast in front of Lucy, careful to move her sheet out of the way of the jam. Washing the sheet was always a nightmare, Lucy sitting dolefully in front of the machine watching it roll along with the water, and Rosie holding her breath, hoping that it wouldn't fall apart. Lucy immediately pulled the sheet back towards her, and Rosie sighed.

"Remember, Mama has a shoot again this afternoon, so you have to go to Nanna's after kindergarten. The kindergarten bus will drop you off."

"I remember," Lucy said around a mouthful of toast.

"Don't talk with food in your mouth, Luce."

Lucy swallowed, "Mama, how come Nanna never walks out to the bus? She always just waits at the door."

Rosie groaned inwardly, she knew she would have to have this conversation with Lucy at some point, she had just hoped it wouldn't have been when she was five years old.

"She's just scared, Lucy. She doesn't like going outside."

"Ever?" Lucy's eye's widened in surprise.

"No, not ever. Eat your toast, peanut."

"Will you make sure the girl is gone?"

Grateful Lucy had let the subject of Kate go, Rosie was momentarily stumped as to what Lucy was talking about.

"Who?"

"The girl. The one in my room."

"Oh!" Rosie said. "You mean the girl you saw last night?"

Lucy nodded.

Rosie sat down across from her daughter, "Baby, I told you. There was no girl. You might have had a bad dream. Or sometimes, in the dark, it's easy to see things that aren't really there."

Lucy eyed her, sceptically, "She was there."

"She wasn't. I looked last night *and* the night before, and there was nothing in your room but the things that are supposed to be."

Lucy picked up her toast and ate it quietly.

Rosie glanced at the clock on her phone. They were going to be late. She hastily pulled Lucy's hair into a ponytail and grabbed her handbag.

"Come on. You are going to have to finish the toast in the car. Put Sheet in your room."

"I could take him and leave him in my kinder locker?" Lucy asked, hopefully.

"Sorry, peanut. You know the rules. Sheet has to stay here, how would you feel if we lost it?"

Lucy's mouth dropped open in horror, and she immediately got up and ran her sheet to the safety of her room.

Rosie did a quick mental sweep of the house, remembering windows and doors she had shut and locked before she ushered Lucy out the door towards the car. Mr. Thompson was at the garden next door holding a fistful of weeds.

"Morning, ladies!" he called and waved his free hand. Tiny sat placidly beside him.

Lucy raced over to the fence, standing on tiptoe to see over the top.

"Tiny!" She called.

Lucy waved the dog over who bounded towards her, tail wagging.

She pulled a small corner of toast crust from her pocket and whispered, "I saved you some."

The large dog delicately took the crust from the little outstretched hand and gulped it before giving Lucy a lick of appreciation. She squealed with delight and ran back to Rosie.

"That dog loves her more than he loves me," Mr. Thompson complained, good-naturedly. "How is your new ride treating you?"

He nodded towards the silver hatchback rental car in Rosie's driveway.

"Amazing," Rosie said. "I'm going to be sad to give it back. Reckon they would swap for a beat-up Corolla with air conditioning that barely works?"

Mr. Thompson laughed, "Can't see why not."

Rosie helped Lucy buckle herself into her car seat - brand new, another expense, but one Rosie didn't begrudge paying for once - and placed Lucy's kinder bag on the seat beside her.

"Do not start eating your lunch or pulling things out of your bag on the drive," Rosie pre-emptively reprimanded her.

Lucy looked back at her with a face of pure innocence and shook her head. In the gutter across the road, a man sat scratching himself and muttering, wearing a strange assortment of clothing in varying states of disrepair and dirtiness, his greying hair dark with grease. He kept shooting sharp glances at Rosie before looking away again.

Rosie got quickly inside the car.

"I have got to get out of this neighbourhood," she muttered, pressing the lock button for the doors.

The drive to Lucy's kindergarten took twenty minutes through crawling traffic. The traffic though, was nothing compared to the worst part of the trip for Rosie, when two streets from the kindergarten she was forced to drive straight past her old house. Lucy would always crane her neck to look, but Rosie resolutely stared straight ahead and gripped the steering wheel.

"They have a swing set," Lucy might remark, and Rosie would say nothing in response. She didn't want to think about other children playing in the backyard where she and Ben had watched Lucy play. She didn't want to think about another family in her kitchen, another man in Ben's office, another couple kissing under the same roof she had been under when her life was both blissfully perfect - and then horribly torn apart. Today though, Lucy seemed distracted and said nothing.

Once parked, Rosie led Lucy into the brightly-coloured building where Lucy spied Violet at the sandpit and ran off instantly. Rosie sighed, left to put away Lucy's lunch box before she tried to coax Lucy back over to her for sunscreen. All the other parents had left, the Parkers were perpetually late.

Finally, Rosie escaped back to the car, mentally checking off a list of things she needed to do that day. She had to get to the grocery store, and she needed to replace a memory card that Lucy had taken from her camera bag and ruined.

"I made a playdoh toaster, and this was the toast!" Lucy had announced.

Rosie had badly lost her temper, lecturing Lucy about not touching work things. Lucy had cried silently throughout this tirade until Rosie looked at her and realised how small she still was and was instantly awash with grief. *If I hadn't been editing for so long, I would have noticed*, she had reprimanded herself. Then she reprimanded herself for feeling guilty about working when she was just trying to make ends meet. Rosie's best friend Dee called this The Mother Guilt Paradox. Even though Dee had no children of her own, she felt very strongly about how she would parent if she had children one day, a trait Rosie found both amusing and infuriating depending on the day. Dee said that mothers felt guilt about absolutely every situation; working mothers feel guilty about being away from their children, stay at home mothers feel guilty about not financially contributing.

"You can't win, Rosie, honey. You may as well own the guilt and drink some wine," Dee had announced over herbal tea one day, months ago.

Thinking of her friend, Rosie abruptly turned left instead of heading right towards the supermarket. She followed tree-lined streets until she pulled into a driveway as familiar and comfortable as home to her. Rosie did not have many friends growing up; she was quiet and shy, content to walk around as though invisible most of the time, but for reasons unknown to Rosie, the vibrant pixie of a girl had taken to her. She and Dee had been friends ever since. Dee had moved to Rosie's primary school when they were nine years old, not long after Rosie's mother had inherited property and a large sum of money that would effectively put an end to Kate's attempts to work ever again.

Kate had been flirting with the beginnings of agoraphobia

then – it had been slowly but surely taking hold for a few years, beginning when Rosie's father, Frank, had left them when Rosie was five years old. Most days, Kate could still be relied upon to leave the house for simple tasks like grocery shopping or to buy Rosie's supplies for a school project. Still, even when Rosie had been a child, it was apparent that her mother was slightly different to other school mums, who seemed warm and stable. Her mother's oddness only increased Rosie's shyness, desperate to blend in where her mother stood out like a sore thumb because of her eccentricities.

Dee Stanley was Rosie's complete opposite in almost every way. She had wild, untamed white-blonde hair, lively wide green eyes, and was slight and small for her age. She reminded Rosie instantly of the fairy in a book Kate used to read to her before she became unwell, and all her energy was needed for herself. Where Rosie was quiet, Dee was loud enough for both of them, and when Dee was around, it felt like the spotlight was so focused on whatever Dee was doing that Rosie could sit pleasantly in the shadows and just observe.

Dee was brought into class on the first day of term. It was a winter so cold that even in South-East Queensland, the children were bundled in tracksuits and beanies. The school had a lax uniform policy; the students were mostly just required to wear the school shirt, even if it was hidden under a sweater or jacket. The classroom was awash with multi-colours that day. Dee's mother was accompanying her, along with the school principal Mr. Locket, who struck fear into the heart of Rosie, despite never having spoken to him at all. He was short and skinny, with cropped white hair and a polished bald circle on the top of his head. Even on this bitterly cold day, he hadn't bothered to don anything extra than his usual dress shorts with long socks pulled carefully to his knees. His arms were covered in thick hairs, and his voice was alarmingly loud for such a small man. It was widely rumoured he had a closet full of canes in his office, and should anyone be called up to him, he would allow the child to choose which cane they were to be struck with. No one Rosie knew had ever actually seen these canes, or been given this as a punishment for poor behaviour, but everyone accepted this rumour as absolute truth.

Dee's mother looked exactly like a grown-up version of Dee. That day both of them were wearing tie-dyed pants with wide legs and oversized handspun, hand-knit jumpers. Later Rosie would learn that Dee's mother, Meg, had spun the yarn herself on a wheel that sat permanently in their living room. All of Rosie's childhood memories of Meg smell like freshly washed wool, an unpleasant smell in itself that Rosie found oddly soothing.

The teacher introduced Dee and asked for a volunteer to help her navigate her way around the school that day. Hands shot up from hopeful little girls all over the classroom, desperate to investigate this new creature in their midst, but the teacher Miss Bower had called out, "Rosie? You'll help Deanna around today, won't you?"

Rosie had flushed a deep red in embarrassment at being singled out and had no choice but to say yes. Dee slid into the seat beside Rosie and leaned over, tugging gently on one of Rosie's curls and said, "Hey? I like your hair. It looks like a sunset."

Rosie, who had suffered merciless teasing her whole schooling career for her red hair, had looked up from her desk and into Dee's warm eyes and smiled. And just like that, they were friends.

Rosie pulled the car to a stop in front of an old house with peeling clapboards and a yard that could only be described as organized chaos. Rosie could kill a cactus, but it always seemed like Dee could touch anything green and make it flourish. The path up to the house was made of uneven stones, spotted here and there with dandelions that Dee refused to pull, she insisted that a weed was 'just an unappreciated plant that can grow in the most offensive of environments.' The small porch held herbs in an eclectic collection of containers, basil waving from brightly painted tin cans and mint that was spilling from an old work boot. Just as Rosie rounded the corner to go up the small set of stairs the screen door was thrown open with such enthusiasm it hit the side of the house and began rebounding back towards the woman that launched herself out of it.

"Rosie!" Dee exclaimed.

She always had a way of greeting a person as though they hadn't seen each other in years and were returning home like the prodigal son.

"Come in! I just put on the kettle."

Rosie embraced her friend, and Dee showered her with a

flurry of greetings, 'how have you been,' 'I love your hair,' 'how is Lucy.' They moved through the living room and into the kitchen, the heart of Dee's house. That day Dee was wearing a long wrap-around skirt in a bright paisley pattern, and a black singlet top with the Cheshire Cat printed on it, her waist-length chaotic blonde waves had been pulled back into a loose braid that hung down her back like a rope. Usually, Dee was the sort of person who left her hair free around her; if it was pulled back, it meant she was baking. Amongst her many talents, Dee was a fantastic baker and made cakes and pastries for local offices, functions, and an expensive vegan coffee shop in the city. Dee had had wild success with her business, 'Dee-licious', and the kitchen was the only part of her old family house she had renovated.

Dee was one of six children that had grown up in this house after they moved to the area - and the only one to still be living there with her mother, Meg, who was a yoga teacher and still stunningly beautiful at sixty-five. The other Stanley children had scattered to the wind like seeds, each one still making the trek home each Christmas to fill the house with a vibrancy that Rosie found fascinating. Growing up, their house had always been full of homemade cookies, side by side with takeaway pizza boxes, cats and handmade quilts. Once, when Rosie was twelve, Meg had tried to sneak a sheep into the backyard.

"It will make excellent wool for my spinning," she had said.

A horrified neighbour had contacted the council, insisting it was relocated, citing regulations about farm animals and noise complaint issues. For Rosie, whose own mother was withdrawn, and whose house was one of quiet order and boredom, being at the Stanley's was like seeing in colour for the first time. Between Dee's house and her grandparents, she barely went home at all.

"I'm sorry to interrupt your baking," Rosie said, sitting at the old farmhouse style dining table.

Dee waved her hand in the air, dismissing it, "Please, I always like seeing you. Besides, I can bake while we chat, and you could always help me pack boxes."

Dee slid a cup of herbal tea across the table to Rosie, "It's lemon balm, I picked it this morning."

Rosie stared at her cup, ruefully, until Dee sighed and took it back, "Fine, I'll drink it. I'll make you up a black tea with sugar and milk. Happy?"

"Very," Rosie said, gratefully.

Dee was always trying to press various herbal teas on to Rosie, patiently explaining the health benefits of the concoctions. Rosie preferred her teas like a confection, sweet and milky with no health benefits except for comfort. Soon, they sat across from each other with steaming cups in front of them.

"It's really too hot for warm drinks," Dee said, lifting her braid off her neck. "I should have made iced tea."

"I don't mind the heat. We'll be complaining about the cold soon enough," Rosie said.

Dee launched into a running description of her week, phone calls from her sister, who was due any day with her first baby, and Meg's latest obsession with coconut oil. She recounted her interactions with 'the cute but horribly boring barista' that worked at the vegan coffee shop. Dee told the story with her whole body, a one-woman re-enactment of people and conversations until Rosie felt she had shared all of the same memories.

"I don't know, Rosie. Maybe I could date the barista, but I'm worried I would fall asleep mid-conversation and only resurrect when he removes his shirt. I used to think I was somewhat attracted to people based on their personalities, but he is so pretty that I am now deeply concerned about my ethics," Dee sipped at the tea. "Anyway, enough about me. How has Lucy been? How are you?"

Rosie filled Dee in on her recent accident and the red car that had left the scene, "Luckily, James got the license plates for me."

Dee reached across the table and took her hand, "Oh, Rosie, that must have been so scary." Her eyes filled with sympathy, and Rosie knew they were both thinking of Ben.

Rosie sighed and closed her eyes, "I miss him. I still miss him. It's been almost a year and a half, and I just thought... Sometimes, it is just having someone to halve the burden with. Or share something cute that Lucy did with."

Dee nodded, "Having a partner."

"Exactly."

Dee stood and took her mug into the kitchen, "Rosie, I am always here to share the burdens and the joys, you know that. But have you considered dating?"

Rosie could not have been more shocked, "What?"

Dee came into the doorway, holding her hands up in surrender.

"Don't shoot it down straight away. I'm not saying you need to get married tomorrow. I'm just saying someone to go out with once in a while that you can have fun with, someone who could inject a tiny bit of sunshine into your life. It doesn't have to be serious. You could even get laid," Dee joked, raising her eyebrows, a curve of a smile on her lips.

Rosie laughed out loud despite herself, and put her head in her hands.

"You have got to be joking," she groaned. "I think I'm done with that."

"Done with what? Sex? Don't swear at me in my house," Dee laughed.

Rosie sat up and drank the last of her tea, "Honestly, I haven't even thought about it since Ben. I don't even have any male friends except Mr. Thompson."

Dee tapped her fingers on her chin in mock thought, "There is Roger?"

"Roger?"

"The guy that mows your lawn," Dee said.

"Do you mean Trevor?"

Dee waved her hand, dismissively, "Sure, Roger, Trevor, whatever."

"He is about sixty-five and married."

"Hmm, okay, not Trevor then. What about Tim? The kinder bus driver?"

"Tim is gay and has a husband."

Dee leaned on the table and said, "Or... James, maybe? Neither sixty-five, nor married, nor gay *and* married."

"James is..." Rosie began.

Dee held up her hands, questioningly, "James is... what? Perfectly fine?"

"I just don't think I'm ready," Rosie said, finally.

Dating had never even occurred to her. She felt as though that part of her life was done, and she had been okay with that.

Dee sighed, "It's okay not to be ready. But, just think about it, okay. You deserve some fun and happiness and something easy in your life."

"Sure," Rosie agreed, to put an end to the conversation.

Dee began preparing icing for cupcakes sitting on the bench where she had left them to cool, the radio playing softly in the background.

"You want me to help you pack the iced ones into boxes?" Rosie offered.

"That would be great, thanks."

They worked in assembly line fashion for a few minutes, the radio presenter coming on and making mention of the hot weather for this time of year. "...unpleasant weather today for those out searching for a sign of Hannah Avery after she failed to return home after drinks with friends three nights ago, the discovery of her handbag in an alley not far from the club prompting fears for her safety. Police have yet to comment on whether this is related to the disappearance of Madison Brown, Tiarna Hunter, and Charlee George, all missing from the city area in similar circumstances in the last three years- "

"Did he say Hannah Avery?" Rosie asked suddenly.

"Yeah, haven't you heard? It's been all over social media."

"No, I have only been online to check my emails. I shot a wedding five months ago and that was the bride's name. Dee, do you have a photo?"

Dee eyed Rosie strangely and wiped her hands on a tea towel from the bench, "Hang on, I'll find it. Do you think it's the same woman?"

"I don't know. It's not a common name, though."

Dee unlocked her phone on the bench and scrolled through the Police Service social media page looking for the missing person alert, then passed the phone to Rosie.

"Here it is."

Rosie took Dee's phone in her hands and stared down at an image she had taken of Hannah in the forest five months ago.

CHAPTER 6

When she finally left Dee's place, Rosie decided to skip the supermarket visit entirely and drove home in a daze, shocked and still shaking. She couldn't help thinking of Hannah and the day she shot her and Bryan's wedding. Rosie remembered it so well, it was her first shoot after Ben had died, heralding her emergence from the dark chrysalis of grief and back into the world. She and Lucy had been living with Kate then, having moved out of their home. Rosie couldn't afford storage, so she had sold off anything she couldn't fit into two rooms in Kate's house. Everything she sold felt like another blow on her already bruised heart; she had even sobbed when she sold the kitchen table.

"Do I have to lose *everything*?" She had cried on Dee's shoulder.

For five months, it had felt like she was walking through thick, sucking mud; every movement seeming to require more energy than it had before. She felt keenly aware of the weight of her own body, of her muscles straining to hold her upright. One day she had given up, slid to the floor and just lay there, which was where Kate had found her two hours later.

"What are you doing?"

"Lying here."

"Why?"

"Because," Rosie had slowly turned her head to the doorway. She stared at her mother, who was compulsively tugging at the sleeve of her shirt in a nervous manner. Usually, this would have made Rosie jump into action to prevent an upcoming anxiety attack, but at that moment, it just made her feel tired.

Kate had hesitated for a moment before tentatively sitting on the floor, wincing at the cold hardwood, "Because why, Rosie?"

"Because sitting up just feels like I'm committing too much to life at the moment, Mum, okay? Because I'm tired."

Kate was quiet for several minutes before she spoke, "Get up, Rosemary."

Rosie looked away.

"I mean it. Get up. You think Ben would want this? *He* would want you to get up. Lucy needs a mother."

Rosie snorted, Kate was the last person who should be lecturing on being a present parent. Kate sighed and pushed herself up, stalking out of the room. Rosie closed her eyes. *Good*, she had thought, *leave me alone*. She heard footsteps return, and a shadow moved across her closed eyes. Then suddenly, water hit her square in the face, cold and jarring, and she gasped, choking on it, scrambling into a sitting position.

"*What the fuck!*"

Kate stood there with an empty salad bowl, "Yes, exactly, Rosie, what the fuck?"

The word sounded strange out of Kate's mouth, and Rosie thought wildly, strangely excited, *she has never said that before*. And it suddenly occurred to Rosie that there were sides to her mother she may never have seen.

"You threw water on me!"

"Then get changed. You haven't showered in three days; those sweatpants have sauce on them, and you're a mess. Life goes on. You can't just sit here, in this house. You have to get out; you have to leave and go outside..."

They stared at each other. Kate's agoraphobia sitting between them like an unwelcome guest. *She is trying to save me*, Rosie realized. *She doesn't want me to become her*. It was barely an acknowledgement of Kate's mental instability, and yet it was the closest either of them had come to mentioning it out loud - an unspoken rule that it was a taboo subject, not to be talked about. It was that realisation - more than the water - that jarred Rosie back into the room, into life. They had sat there, mother and daughter both silent, until Lucy had wandered up the hallway and peered in.

"Mama? Why are you wet?"

Rosie had looked at her daughter, "Nanna was waking me up."

And she had gotten to her feet, held out her hands to Kate to help her up, and all three of them had walked out of the room, and back into life after Ben. That afternoon she opened her emails to a new shoot enquiry from the Avery's and booked them in. She sent messages to colleagues who had taken over her clients while she was away and thanked them, "I'm back in the saddle again," she had written.

. . .

The afternoon of the Avery shoot and Rosie's re-emergence to photography had been the end of Summer. The Avery's had a mini elopement, with just their parents and siblings, set in the state forest after Rosie had talked it up as quiet and beautiful. It had been the perfect reintroduction for her, a small intimate ceremony before Hannah and Bryan had left for the Whitsundays. Hannah was the youngest of the Avery children, a beloved daughter after three sons, who was clearly the apple of everyone's eye, including her brothers. Bryan was an only child to elderly parents who had had him later in life. Thinking of that afternoon felt like a stab to Rosie's heart. She was devastated to think about Hannah's parents and how they must be feeling. She couldn't imagine how frantic she would be if Lucy were missing. Losing Ben was awful, heart-breaking, but if she lost Lucy... And Bryan, my god, she had some idea of the pain he would be in worrying about his wife.

Rosie pulled into her driveway and realized she couldn't remember a single thing about the trip home, as though she had been driving on autopilot. *I'll go inside, upload the photos from yesterday's shoot and back them up. Check my emails, and then try to pull myself together before this afternoon's beach shoot. Focus,* she told herself.

The man from earlier was still on the street across from the house. He sat in the gutter clad in a dirty grey t-shirt and jeans with a rip in one knee. He seemed to be muttering to himself and was scratching at his arm in the repetitive fashion of a drug user. Rosie felt a panic rising in her, afraid for her safety, caught in the fear of Hannah being missing. It was a sudden feeling of the vulnerability of being female. It was something that usually happened as she pumped fuel into her car late at night, or realised she was alone in a forest or on a beach after a shoot - but never before in broad daylight, in her own driveway. She looked away and unlocked the front door, making sure the deadbolt caught as she shut it behind her.

"I have got to get out of this neighbourhood," she said for the second time that day.

Then again, better neighbourhoods hadn't helped Hannah. She threw her handbag down on the bench and opened her laptop on the kitchen table, and setting it to boot up, she went back to grab a can of cola from the fridge. She popped the tab, took a swallow, and began walking back to the laptop. Rethinking, she went back to the high cabinet over the microwave and pulled down a bottle of whiskey that was Ben's - *had been Ben's*, she reminded herself, *wasn't anymore* - and sloshed some into the cola can. *Screw it*, she thought, *after lunch is close enough to five o'clock.* She set the cards from yesterday to upload to the laptop and opened her emails while she waited.

One email was from James, saying she could come and pick up her order for January's clients, which buoyed her spirits a bit. It was always so lovely to pick up her framed prints from James. Seeing her work big and beautiful and knowing her clients were going to love it gave her a thrill. *James.* She smiled, thinking of Dee's suggestion of dating. She wasn't even sure James was single, to be honest. Violet's mother wasn't in the picture, but that didn't mean there wasn't a girlfriend somewhere. She felt strangely disappointed thinking of him having a girlfriend for some reason.

"You've lost it, Rosemary," she said aloud to herself.

The next email was from Grandma June, Rosie's father's mother, who had recently gotten both a computer and the internet and was delighted by it. June had asked Rosie to come over to help install it and immediately asked for assistance to create a 'Facepage'.

"Uhh... Facebook?" Rosie had asked.

"That's what I said," June had answered.

Surprisingly, Grandma June had quite a few of her friends also on there, and she had used it to organise a weekly craft gathering at her house for them all. Rosie read the email, *"Rosemary, would you come to dinner on Friday? I'm making beef roast, and I can't eat the whole damn thing. Talk soon. Grandma."*

She sent one back, agreeing to dinner.

The photos had finished uploading, but Rosie sat back and just looked at them, sipping her drink and enjoying the burning feeling at the back of her throat. *God, this is so surreal*, she thought, *I'm sitting in the kitchen drinking my dead husband's whiskey, feeling disappointed about the possible girlfriend of a guy I don't even want to date. Grandma June is planning a beef roast. And somewhere out there, Hannah Avery is missing.* It always amazed her, the way the world just kept turning, when for someone else it would never be the same again. *What had that news presenter said? Four women missing?* Rosie opened her web browser and typed 'missing girl Clayton Hills' into the search bar. She clicked the first link, a recent one about Hannah Avery's disappearance, and sipped at her drink. An hour later, she had trawled through all the kidnappings, and if she hadn't had a shoot to go to that afternoon, she would have skipped the mixer, pulled the whiskey down, and drank straight from the bottle.

Three of the missing women had disappeared after nights out, seemingly without a trace. Hannah's handbag was the only personal item recovered in any of them. Some reports were drawing parallels between the missing women and the body of Sarah Yarrow, who had been discovered in bushland in Willscray, some forty minutes from Olive Wood. Rosie had barely opened that article before abruptly closing the tab at the graphic account of Sarah Yarrow's murder. *That would not be Hannah*.

Rosie rubbed at her face as though she could erase the photos of missing women from her mind and got up to prepare for her beach shoot that afternoon. She wished, not for the first time, she had an assistant, someone to carry her bag and fix stray hair on her client's faces. But this time it was so she wouldn't have to go alone. Suddenly, she had a thought and smiling she went out to the backyard and stuck her head over the fence.

"Hey, Mr. Thompson? How do you and Tiny feel about a trip to the beach?"

CHAPTER 7

Rosie's afternoon beach shoot went off with relative ease; the children were all in primary school and easier to direct. Today she was back to pick up Lucy from Kate's with time to spare. At home, she ran Lucy a bath, waiting outside the door with her laptop editing while Lucy played in the tub; Rosie hadn't quite gotten over the habit of supervising bath time. Then, once Lucy was dressed in her nightgown, she left her to play with the dollhouse in her room while she went to the kitchen to begin dinner and empty Lucy's backpack. Cooking for one adult and one small child was a frustrating task. Lucy believed that fine cuisine was fish fingers and potato gems, and recently she had gone through a month-long phase where she wouldn't eat anything without a side serve of tomato sauce – including salad. Rosie settled on chicken legs - cheap - and pasta - oh, so cheap - and left the legs to cook in the oven and the pasta bubbling on the stove while she emptied Lucy's backpack.

. . .

Lucy's lunchbox was predictably still half full; she had scorned the yoghurt and the cheese and taken a tiny mouse bite out of an apple. Tucked in the pocket of the backpack was a white envelope with Rosie's name on it. *Ugh, fees*, Rosie thought, ripping open the top. It was not fees. The teacher, Mrs Bowen, wanted to chat with Rosie about Lucy. The note said Lucy had been caught trying to sneak one of the kindy dolls into her backpack. *"Lots of kids do try to take things home"*, the note read, *"but this has been ongoing with Lucy"*. Mrs Bowen wrote she had felt it was her duty to reach out and let Rosie know.

Rosie sighed and sat down heavily at the kitchen table. Lately, it felt like she was moving from crisis to crisis, too busy putting out the last fire to concentrate on prevention of the next. She would have to talk to Lucy about this, of course. Was it a big deal? Was it just a kid who liked a doll, or was it some sign of psychological trauma because Lucy had a dead dad and a mother who barely had it together? Rationally, Rosie thought that it was probably no big deal and Lucy just needed to be reminded that we don't take things that don't belong to us. Another part of Rosie felt like it was finally a concrete sign of her failure as a mother.

From the moment Lucy had been placed in her arms, a wrinkled, 6lb 11oz bundle, Rosie had known simultaneously that she would die to protect her child, and was also horribly unprepared for how not to make a mess of motherhood. None of the books really seemed to explain how to actually parent a child. They covered when to feed, how to dress, what to do if she was sick – but no one covered how much crying was too much, why as a toddler Lucy enjoyed watching the washing machine go around - or what to do if your kindergartener was revealing herself to be a kleptomaniac. Suddenly, Hannah Avery danced through Rosie's head and pulled the world back into perspective. Whatever her problems were with Lucy right now, at least both she and Lucy were here in the house, safe and unharmed. Impulsively Rosie got up and went up to Lucy's room, sitting beside her and drawing her into her lap. She buried her face in Lucy's hair and wished she could hit pause on her daughter, keeping her small and safe and in her lap forever.

"Why are we hugging?" Lucy asked.

Rosie laughed, "Can't we hug for no reason, sometimes?"

Lucy pondered, "Yes. Sometimes. But I can't reach my dollhouse from here."

"Oh. I'm very sorry," Rosie released Lucy who went to put tiny plastic plates down on the dinner table for a family of three-inch bears. Rosie sat with Lucy, taking up the role of the mother bear, and losing herself in something pure and good until dinner was ready.

The evening seemed to drag, Lucy picking over her chicken leg and pushing the pasta around. After dinner, the two of them sat side by side on the couch, Lucy watching TV as Rosie edited beside her, until finally - blissfully - it was bedtime. Lucy had asked to sleep in Rosie's bed, and Rosie had been too exhausted to argue, letting Lucy drift off while she read beside her, and then quietly carrying a sleep-heavy Lucy into her room down the hall once she had fallen asleep. Rosie stood on one of the little bear figures and swore softly, sliding Lucy into the bed and pulling up the covers. The transfer a success, she had gone back to her bed alone, intending to read some more, but sleep called to her almost as soon as she lay down.

Rosie was dreaming of closed doors and dark earth, disjointed, confusing. Faces slide across her subconscious, ethereal and insubstantial as mist. And then she was slipping through one of those doors, and into the pantry of the old house she and Kate lived in when she was small, before Kate's parents had died. She is very little - six? seven? - and she is hiding in the pantry beneath the bottom shelf. It smells dusty down there, like old dry dirt from the sack of potatoes beside her. Decaying cobwebs stick in the corners, and a lone daddy long legs crawls near Rosie's foot. Rosie is listening to Mama yelling — screaming — and something breaks against the wall... the sound of shattering glass, raining down on to the floorboards. Rosie has Pinkie wedged under one armpit, and in the other hand, a small Brownie compact camera she had been given by Grandma June that morning.

Grandma June had pulled the dark brown film from the canister and wound it through the spools in the open back of the Brownie, shutting it tight and turned a dial on the top of the camera to wind the film inside.

"You can catch any memories you like with this, Rosemary," she had said. "When you take a photo, it's like freezing time, like magic. There will never be another moment exactly like that one."

Rosie had taken a photo of Grandma June then, as she stood in front of Poppa's rose bushes, her hazel eyes that were exactly like Rosie's twinkling with a sparkle that Rosie had never seen in anyone else. Rosie fitted the viewfinder to her eye while June had sucked in her tummy and Rosie had pressed the button. Then June had shown Rosie how to wind the film on so the camera was ready to take the next photo.

More shouts from Mama in the next room pulls Rosie back out of her mind and into the pantry. There a man's voice, low and soothing, though Rosie could not make out the words. Mama's shouts turned to sobs - the raw, ugly kind that came from someplace deep within. Rosie crawls out and peers around the corner. Kate is on her knees in the living room, her face in her hands and her floral dress bunched around her thighs. All around her were roses, scattered in a way that Rosie thought would have looked beautiful - if not for the sobbing woman in the centre. The man squats on his haunches beside Mama and reaches to stroke her hair. Mama bats his hands away, her sobs momentarily becoming louder. The man waits another moment and then stands and begins to walk towards Rosie, who scuttles back into the pantry and under the shelf. She listens as his footsteps creak along the verandah floorboards, the door opening and shutting softly, like an apology. Rosie slips out and into the room with Mama and the roses; she goes to touch Kate but remembers the way she slapped at the man's hand and pulls back. Instead, she lifts the camera to her eye and takes a photo of the roses on the ground. Then Rosie runs to the verandah after the man and climbs on a chair near the window to look out. She lifts the Brownie up as he turns back towards her and raises his arm in a wave. Rosie clicks the shutter.

She awoke to darkness, and Lucy pressed beside her, her body warm and soft like the buns Dee would leave to rise on the bench. Rosie turned over and wrapped herself around her daughter, breathing in the scent of lavender shampoo and little girl, and oddly, underneath that, the faintest smell of freshly dug soil.

"Why do I have to have a shower in the morning if I already had a bath last night?" Lucy complained while Rosie turned the water on.

"You smell weird," Rosie said.

"I do not!" Lucy said indignantly.

"You do. You smell like you've been digging in the garden, it's weird."

Lucy stood there naked, her pyjamas in a pool by her feet and put her hands on her hips, "Well, if you didn't leave dirt in my room, I wouldn't smell weird."

Rosie looked at her, bewildered, "What are you on about? We're going to be late, Lucy. Hop in."

Lucy sighed and got under the water as Rosie turned to go grab fresh clothes from Lucy's room.

"And use the soap!" she called.

"I do!" Lucy yelled back.

Rosie walked into Lucy's room and pulled up in a stop as though she had been jerked back by a string. There *was* dirt in Lucy's room. Not a lot, just bits of it clumped here and there as though someone had walked through in dirty sneakers. Her eyes flew to the window, which was still shut, a piece of doweling wood stuck in the window track to prevent the window from being opened from the outside. *Lucy must have had dirt on her feet last night*, she thought. And then, on the heels of that thought, *but it wasn't here when I put her to bed.*

"It must have been," she said aloud.

She tiptoed into the room, an odd feeling settling inside her, as though there were trying not to disturb someone, and she knew it was stupid and made no sense, but she did it anyway. She quickly fetched Lucy's clothes from the drawers against the far wall and bee-lined back out. Rosie deposited the clothes in the bathroom for Lucy, who was now happily drawing in the steam on the glass with one small finger and went to grab the vacuum from the broom closet. By the time the room had been vacuumed, and Lucy's sheets stripped - there was dirt in them too which meant Lucy *must have* been the culprit of the mystery soil - Rosie had lost her uneasy feeling, and Lucy was dressed and ready for breakfast.

"Alright, peanut. Let's get some breakfast and get you to kinder."

Lucy raced down the hallway, waving her sheet in the air like a flag, Rosie following behind.

In Lucy's room, the lamp switched on and off three times before the bulb blew.

Dirt sprinkled to the floor from nowhere.

CHAPTER 8

James ran some water onto his hands and smoothed back his hair. He started to reach for the cologne before stopping himself. *Too much*, he thought, *just be yourself*. He was going to ask Rosie on a date. He had been psyching himself up for weeks now, wavering between just doing it and thinking he was an idiot to even contemplate it. How soon could someone ask out a widow and it not seem weird?

James had noticed her immediately on kindergarten orientation day; she had been hard to miss. Rosie had blown in, thirty minutes late, like a fiery hurricane, tripped over a paint easel and while trying to right it, knocked over an entire shelf of books. She had blushed a deep red that nearly matched her hair and apologised profusely to a room of gawking children, soccer mums and him - the only dad of the bunch. He couldn't keep his eyes off her. She walked around like she was permanently distracted, forgetting cultural day and hurrying back with vegemite sandwiches. She would come in for pick-ups on the days Lucy didn't go on the kinder bus with bits of grass in her hair, and one time showing up to drop off with her shirt misbuttoned, weirdly puckered under her breasts, so that he could see the creamy skin of her stomach in the gape of the fabric.

"She's off with the fairies," one of the other mothers had joked.

He had nodded in agreement and absolute fascination.

Violet and Lucy were like two peas in a pod from the first day and had wrangled their parents into a playdate that weekend. While he and Rosie had watched the girls, they began to talk, at first polite chit-chat about their businesses and how they might work together. They discussed raising children and the absurd things they say, laughing into their coffees. Then slowly, over the weeks, they had begun to develop a friendship. Her laugh made him feel like he had performed a trick; they were so hard-won that he found himself actively trying to elicit one from her. But the day he realised he liked her as more than a fellow parent was when he had taken Violet down to the beach one afternoon and saw her taking photographs.

Rosie was usually so distracted and clumsy that watching her shoot was like watching a different person. She was so focused that she didn't even notice he was there, as though nothing existed for her but what was down the lens of her camera. Rosie had moved and bent like a dancer as she shot and posed the family she was photographing. She laughed so freely that it made all the times he had worked for one seem small in comparison. The wind had pulled her hair from its braid, the shorts she wore showed off her legs, and he had to actively pull his eyes away from her and back into the world to focus on Violet. He hadn't felt this kind of magnetic pull since the early days with Amelia - and he still wasn't sure how much of the high with her had been *the high*.

So, today was the day. He was going to bite the bullet and do it. He reached for the cologne again. *A little effort can't hurt*, he thought.

"Violet!" He called, "Have you finished your breakfast?"

"Not the crusts!" She yelled back.

He walked into the kitchen where Violet was sitting at the table playing with her dolls, eight lines of toast crusts still on her plate.

"Crusts make your hair curly," he told her seriously.

"Like Lucy?" She asked, wide-eyed.

"Absolutely. She always eats her crusts."

Violet eyed him suspiciously but picked up one of them and delicately nibbled at it.

James was pouring a coffee when there was a knock at the door.

"I'll get it!" Violet shouted and abandoned the crusts.

James heard the front door open and a squeal from his daughter, "Uncle David!"

"Here is my favourite little dolly!" Boomed a voice and Violet came back into the room pulling along James's uncle, who was impeccably put together for first thing in the morning.

"I found Uncle David!" Violet exclaimed, turning to her uncle. "What did you bring me?"

"Violet!" James admonished. "You don't always get a present."

"Of course she does," David said.

He took a satchel off from his shoulder and pulled out a neatly wrapped gift from its depths before offering it to his great-niece. Violet squealed and began tearing into the paper.

"A bracelet," she gasped and ran to James to show him her treasure.

"You bought her a gold bracelet?" James asked his uncle.

"All women need jewellery. I learnt that long ago."

"Say thank you, Violet," James reminded her, "and then you need to go get dressed for kinder."

"Thank you!" She chimed and ran off to her room.

James poured his uncle a cup of coffee and sat down across from him at the table.

"So," he began. "Two visits in two weeks, not that I'm complaining, but Violet is going to be spoilt with gifts if this keeps up."

David laughed, "I've got business here for the next couple of weeks and figured I should make the most of being near family while I'm here."

David was the younger of the two St Clair brothers, only fifteen years older than James himself and looked younger than his forty-seven years. The two brothers couldn't have been more different, James's father Henry had looked like James, dark hair and eyes - and a stormy temper to match. David was fair, with clear blue eyes that never missed a thing, and a charm that meant he managed to get along with everyone. As the younger of the brothers he was given a trust fund, while Henry had inherited the bulk of the St Clair money, property, and investments. When Henry died three years ago from a sudden heart attack, all of that had all gone to James, who handed it to his solicitors to manage until Violet was older, and he could give it to her. In the meantime, he tried to raise her off his own back. He didn't spoil her. Violet saved her pocket money for toys she wanted outside of birthdays and Christmases, and a third of it went into her piggy bank for savings. When she filled it, they would head down to her bank, where she would solemnly hand over her little yellow banking book and her piggy bank to the teller. James's sister Brooke felt the same way. James had tried to offer her a share of his inheritance, but she had refused, "I don't want it any more than you do."

David however, took delight in spoiling Violet. With no wife or children of his own, he was incredibly generous to all his friends and family. Last week he had shown up with a tiny music box for Violet, pulling it from his pocket like a magician.

"Unfortunately, a cup of coffee is probably all I can offer you right now, I have to get Violet off to kindergarten short-ly," James said. "I could swing you a quick breakfast though, are you hungry?"

David waved his hand, "No, this is fine. I've got a meeting this morning with one of the realties. I just wanted to pop in and see you and the kid. Speaking of, I've had a workshop come up in one of the industrial estates, and it would be perfect for your business. How about coming down and having a look later?"

James sensed the conversation taking a turn he wasn't

interested in, "Thanks for the offer, but I'm really pretty happy right here. For one, I can work around Violet, and I don't have the funds in the business to be paying for a big workshop right now either. Maybe a few years down the track, but it just hasn't expanded to that stage yet."

David sipped his coffee and leaned back, "But you do *have* the money to expand. You inject a bit of personal money into your business, and you would see the return."

James rubbed a hand across his eyes, "I don't want to use St Clair money if I don't have to. The business is going fine on its own."

James loved David, growing up he had felt like more of a big brother than an uncle, but money was one thing they couldn't agree on. Since the day he and Amelia had decided to clean up their act he hadn't touched a cent of the family money except to buy this house, which he only did to give Violet a home she could grow up in. David had come with them to inspect the property.

"Why not pick one that needs less work?" He had asked.

James had stood in the large yard and looked at the house, in desperate need of repairs. It had beautiful bones, he could tell, and he could imagine he and Amelia painting and fixing it up themselves. He looked at Amelia's swelling stomach and knew this house was the right one. It was the only time he had touched the money in his account, deposited monthly from the time he turned eighteen and had access to his trust. He didn't want a child of his to grow up the way he had, a big cold house and a parent that worked away all the time. Here, he could cut frames in his workshop and watch Violet on her tyre swing. They had more than they could ever need right here with each other. David couldn't understand James's reasoning. He couldn't understand that part of the reason James loved the business was that he worked it himself, not just turn up once a week to see how his employees were doing.

Years ago, when Amelia was still pregnant, he had answered an advertisement for an assistant to a framer at a store called 'Picture Perfect'. He had entered a tiny showroom and been greeted by a short elderly man with smiling blue eyes, who introduced himself as Fred Goldman. Fred had taken a chance on James, who had never so much as picked up a hammer in his life. They had worked side by side for three years, Fred was kind, but a perfectionist and it turned out James liked being pushed to do something well.

"Good enough isn't good enough," Fred would say.

When Fred retired, James set up shop himself, asking Fred's blessing to name it 'Goldman Framing'.

"You're not going to name it James Frames?" Fred had joked, but the older man had been touched that James wanted to tip his hat to him.

For James, every frame was personal, as much a piece of art as the image it held. For David, it was money in the bank and nothing more. But the only real fight they had had was after Henry died and James had refused to move into the house James and Brooke had grown up in, built by James's grandfather, David and Henry's father, for his new wife when they first got married.

"Violet deserves more space," David had argued.

"Violet is three! She takes up two and a half feet of space!"

. . .

In the end, James had suggested selling the St Clair estate. The house held nothing but bitter memories for James - his father's belt, his mother sleeping off another hangover in the dark, bruises the colour of an angry sea decorating her arms, her neck. David had become furious at the suggestion of selling, pointing out that while the property may have been left to James, it belonged to David, Brooke, Violet, and Brooke's children too, selling it without considering the other family it might affect was selfish. James agreed David had a point; he hadn't even thought to ask Brooke, who hadn't gone back to the property since the day Henry had died, where she made a brief appearance at the wake before excusing herself. Clearly, the house meant something to David; he conceded that not everyone might have the same bad memories of the place he and Brooke held. James agreed to keep it in the family and have a caretaker come by once a week to maintain the property and log any issues, but he remained firm on not living there with Violet. When David came to the city, he would pick up the keys from the care-taker and stay there for the duration, and they steered clear of talk of the property now, but every now and then David would bring up James 'making the money work for him'.

Now, David took a final sip of his coffee and stood up, "I've got to run. If you change your mind about the workshop, let me know. I can hold it for a week for you, but then I will have to list it."

James collected both their cups and took them to the

sink, "Thanks for the offer, but I'm fine. Really. Go ahead and list it."

David clapped him warmly on the shoulder, "You're the boss. Sorry, to bring it up. Don't work too hard today. I'll say goodbye to the kid on my way out."

James smiled and nodded, "No problem."

CHAPTER 9

Rosie was driving Lucy to school when her phone rang. She quickly reminded Lucy to hush before answering - there was nothing like getting a business call and having a small child serenading a potential client with Old McDonald Had a Farm in the background. Lucy motioned zipping up her mouth, and Rosie smiled. She pressed the loudspeaker button to answer. *God help me when I have to return this car and go back to one that is so old it has a cassette player*, she thought, ruefully.

"Hello?"

"Hey Rosie, what are you up to?"

"Aunty Dee!" Lucy yelled from the backseat.

Rosie gave Lucy a mock frown in the rearview mirror, "What happened to being quiet when Mama is on the phone?"

Lucy shrugged.

"Oh, my. Is that a Lucy Locket I hear?"

"I'm going to kinder!" Lucy yelled in response.

"Awesome news, Luce! I hope you have fun. What about your Mama? Is she going to kinder too?"

Lucy laughed, "No! Kinder is just for kids!"

"I'm just going to be heading home to edit the last couple of sessions. You need something?"

"Do you think you and your super awesome rental car could swing by and drop some cakes into the coffee shop for me? My car won't start, and Mum already left for a yoga retreat, she isn't back until Monday. I can take a taxi in if you're too busy. The tow truck is arriving shortly to drag this piece of crap to the mechanic."

"No, that's fine, Dee. Don't take a taxi, save your money."

Even as she was saying it, Rosie was eyeing her petrol gauge and silently cursing the fact she would have to put more fuel in the tank. The last client was dragging their feet over the invoice; she would have to send a reminder email.

"Awesome, Rosie, you're a legend. I'll pay you in sugary treats and endless gratitude."

Rosie smiled, and Lucy clapped her hands in the backseat in anticipation of an upcoming sugar high.

"I'll be there in thirty minutes. Actually, I have to pick up some prints out that way, if you don't mind making a stop on the way back?"

"No problems at all, it's your car. I'll see you then."

"Wait!" Lucy called. "Aunty Dee, there is a girl living in my room!"

Rosie groaned, "Lucy, there isn't anyone in your room."

"Yes, there is!"

Rosie heard Dee laughing on the other end, "Don't worry, Luce, I have been saying for years there are fairies in my garden, and your Mama doesn't believe me either. She's too boring to see fun stuff."

"Don't encourage her," Rosie said. "I'll be by soon. Make mine a pink cupcake."

Rosie pulled up in front of the kindergarten and hurried Lucy from the car. She helped Lucy unpack her lunchbox and drink bottle from her backpack and kissed Lucy good-bye, watching as Lucy ran off to a small group of girls in the dress-up corner. Satisfied Lucy had settled in and wasn't going to miss her, Rosie turned to go. She was halfway out the door when she heard the teacher, Mrs Bowen, call out to her; Rosie groaned inwardly and turned around.

"Rosie," the teacher called. "I'm so glad to catch you. Did you happen to get the note I sent home?"

Rosie forced a smile, "Yes, sorry I was going to talk to you about it, but I was in a bit of a rush this morning. I really don't know what to say about it. I'm so sorry. Lucy has never done anything like this before."

The teacher looked embarrassed, "Ahh, see. The thing is... she has. I mentioned in the note that there had been a few times she has put items that don't belong to her in her bag... but this is actually the latest in half a dozen times I've seen Lucy *try* to take something. It's not a huge deal, lots of kids have favourite toys here, and they do occasionally go home 'by accident'. Usually, we go over the rules again, and they realise it's not okay. I have spoken to Lucy several times now. I just hoped if you had a chat to her, we could tackle it from both sides."

A half a dozen times? Rosie thought. She tried not to look as shocked as she felt.

"Oh. Right. Of course, I'll speak to her. I'm very sorry."

"I didn't want to say anything, but I wondered if it might be a bit of stress. Did Lucy have any counselling after her dad passed?"

Rosie felt her stomach drop. Was she supposed to have gotten Lucy counselling? She seemed to cope reasonably well with Ben's death - better than Rosie had in all honesty. She felt her mouth open, but nothing came out.

"Some kids," Mrs Bowen continued, "aren't obvious with their feelings. I just thought it might be worth checking with you."

"Of course. I didn't... ahh... get Lucy counselling. We didn't..." she trailed off.

"Okay. Well, I don't want to hold you up. I just thought I'd mention it."

Rosie sensed her chance to escape and rushed out the door, promising to talk to Lucy about it.

Should they have had counselling? Is that what good mums do when their spouses die? Lucy had cried when Ben died, of course, but aside from asking a few times when Daddy would be home, she seemed to accept Ben's passing as fact. For weeks when Lucy would draw her family, she would draw Rosie and Ben and herself until one day, Ben seemed to disappear from it as though he had never been there at all. Rosie sat in the car and rested her head against the steering wheel. Lucy was five. When would she finally feel like she had a handle on this parenting thing instead of feeling her way through? She loved Lucy more than anything, and yet she wasn't entirely sure she was maternally minded in the slightest. She didn't bake; she hated playing kid games; she didn't make sensory buckets full of different coloured rice for Lucy to filter through her chubby little fingers as a baby. She could barely sew a button on and detested every minute of being pregnant - and that had all been okay because she had Ben and they could work it out together.

There was a sudden knock on the window, and Rosie jumped. James smiled through the glass at her. Rosie wound down the window.

"James! Hi. Sorry, you probably thought I looked like I was having a nervous breakdown."

James laughed, "No way. Trust me, sometimes I get in the car and savour the silence for a second too."

Rosie tried to smile, and failed. She had never been very good at hiding her emotions.

James looked at her, quizzically, "Are you okay?"

"Not even in the slightest," Rosie said, half-jokingly.

James frowned, "Hey, if you need to chat-"

Rosie cut him off, "Oh, no, it's fine, really. I'm being melodramatic." She paused for a second before continuing, "Lucy has been stealing things from kindergarten? I just... god, I have no idea what I'm doing. Do you know what you're doing? You probably do. And Mrs Bowen said maybe Lucy needs counselling, but Lucy seemed *fine*... you know, except for her life of crime."

A smile curled on James's lips, "Her life of crime? Wow. I did not know your daughter was a hardened criminal. I'll be sure to watch my wallet."

Rosie laughed, despite herself, "Sorry for my meltdown. Did you need something or were you just saying hi?"

James cleared his throat, "Uhh, yeah. I was going to ask..."

Rosie raised her eyebrows expectantly.

"Sorry," James shook his head. "I lost my train of thought for a second. I was just seeing if you were still coming to pick up those prints today?"

"Sure. I'll be there about eleven if that's okay? My friend asked me to run her into town; her car is at the mechanic."

"Perfect. I'll see you then," he smiled at her and walked over to his car, throwing a wave over his shoulder before calling out. "Hey Rosie? Just so you know? Absolutely no one knows what they're doing."

"Good to know," Rosie said, smiling.

Rosie pulled up in front of Dee's house and went inside to help carry the boxes of baked goods down to the car. When they were all loaded on to the backseat - Rosie had to fight the urge to strap the boxes in - Dee handed Rosie a smaller box with a love heart scrawled on top. Rosie popped the lid to four pink iced cupcakes, two with an 'R' iced on top in white and two with an 'L'.

"Oh, Dee, they're beautiful. You know you didn't really have to pay me in baked goods, right?"

"I know. But Lucy would never forgive me if I promised and didn't deliver. Besides, it's nice to bake for family sometimes. Don't you enjoy taking photographs of Lucy more than clients?"

Rosie snorted. Lucy ran a mile at the mere sight of the camera, scarred from Rosie overshooting her when she was too young to object.

They set off on the road, Rosie driving as cautiously as a kid on their first driving lesson, hyper-aware of delicately iced cupcakes and buns in the back. Dee noticed and laughed at her, before launching into a long description of everything that had happened in her life in the short time since Rosie had last seen her. Rosie slowly picked her way through the traffic, which was unusually heavy for nine o'clock.

"When does Meg get back from her retreat?" Rosie asked.

"Two weeks time. Doesn't it sound blissful? They're not allowed any devices and even encouraged to talk as minimally as possible. Clean mountain air, clean food... ahh. I would love it."

"I wouldn't be able to stay still for that long," Rosie said.

Dee pointed ahead, "Take the next left. There isn't on-street parking, but you can pull around back, there is a delivery bay."

Rosie turned left and then up a driveway that wound behind the store.

"You need help unloading?" she asked Dee.

"Nope. Some of the kitchen staff come out and collect. You want to get a coffee or tea while we are here?"

Rosie looked at the time on her dashboard, "I could do a really quick cuppa, I have to collect those prints. Are you sure you're okay with stopping on the way back?"

"Absolutely!"

Dee knocked on the back door and directed some of the staff to the boxes in the back, Rosie passed over her keys so they could lock up when they were finished, and they went inside the little café. Rosie was immediately taken with the décor. The café had been furnished in an eclectic style, almost as though someone had driven around one weekend and picked up bits and pieces from garage sales. Overstuffed velvet couches sat side by side with old wooden chairs painted bright colours, surrounding mismatched coffee tables. The back of the store housed bookshelves filled with novels you could borrow or swap on a 'take one, leave one' basis. The walls were covered in artworks by local artists who sold on commission, and a display of old photographs of the city that people had donated to the store. A calico cat wound itself lazily around Rosie's legs and Dee stooped down to scratch it on the head.

They stepped up to places their order and Rosie came face to face with a flyer taped on the counter with Hannah Avery's face on it. *Missing*, it read, followed by a description of what Hannah had been wearing and where she was last seen. It was a photo Rosie hadn't seen before, a recent photo of Hannah at a party of some sort, her blonde hair had been curled and framed her face in soft waves. She wore a pale green cocktail dress; a delicate tree of life pendant was around her neck, and Rosie felt a strange shock seeing it – she had just recently looked at one similar for Dee's birthday. Hannah stared out at Rosie with an expression that looked as though she had been caught mid-laugh.

"God," Rosie sighed. "She looks so happy in this photo."

Dee squeezed Rosie's shoulder,.

"They have them all over the city," she said, nodding at the flyer. "Her brothers have been putting them up."

Rosie's heart ached at the memory of Hannah's brothers at the wedding, hugging their sister.

"Please find her safely," she said to the universe at large.

They ordered from the barista Dee had been flirting with who was, to Rosie's dismay, obscenely good looking. Dee asked for a pot of peppermint tea, and Rosie grudgingly agreed to chamomile since the only milk available for black tea was soy or almond, which she regarded with suspicion. They picked a couch tucked in the back near the books and Rosie began to flick through an old family photo album.

"Why is this here? Did someone leave it?"

Dee looked over, "What? Oh, no, the owner loves second-hand stuff. He is always going to second-hand stores, garage sales and estate sales. Sometimes he picks up really random stuff - he's found a bunch of family albums people have left or gotten rid of. Just really old albums or photos usually, their people are all gone, and there's no one to look after them anymore. They're fascinating."

"They are! This is amazing."

Dee sipped at her tea, "So, you got two girls living with you now?"

Rosie looked up, "What?"

Dee smirked, "Lucy's girl. The one in her room?"

Rosie groaned, "Oh, god. Don't get me started. She's been sleeping in my bed at night now. You don't understand how little sleep you get when you have a small child in your bed."

"You think she has an imaginary friend?"

"I don't think so. She doesn't seem to talk about her any

other time. Maybe she just wants an excuse to sleep in bed with me? I don't know."

"Maybe she really is seeing something," Dee mused.

Rosie cut eyes at her friend.

Dee shrugged, "What? Kids are more sensitive to things like that! Didn't you ever see anything like that when you were a kid?"

"No," Rosie said. "I didn't."

"Well, then I feel sorry for you. All emotionally stunted," Dee teased. "No imagination. It's sad."

The barista came over and placed a small plate of cookies in front of Dee, "I thought you might like these. They're gluten-free."

"Thanks," Dee said, holding a smile on her face until he left.

She turned to Rosie, "Seriously, I almost don't care what it says about me as a person because he is so pretty I can tolerate the boredom. I want to marry him and have his boring babies."

"Maybe he's just shy," Rosie offered, picking up a cookie.

"He's not," said Dee, biting into one, "He's just really dull. He has nothing to talk about but kale."

Rosie snorted and examined her cookie, which, to her surprise and relief, wasn't awful.

"Maybe you should have a cleansing?" Dee said.

"Pardon?"

"For your phantom girl. Like, burn some sage or something to cleanse the air of spirits. You know, in case Lucy *is* seeing something."

Rosie rolled her eyes, "Yeah, right. I'll get right on that."

Dee sighed, "Such a sceptic."

. . .

They sat in companionable silence for a few moments while Rosie continued to flip through the book of old photographs. One of the photos had taken her in; it was of an older style house, recently built at the time the picture had been taken. A man stood sombrely in long-sleeved shirt and trousers staring at the camera; beside him was a woman in a shapeless dress. She was smiling, almost like she had been caught in a laugh. *The house looks so familiar*, Rosie thought, but she couldn't place her finger on why. It was like waking from a dream and trying to hold it by the tail as it ran away in the light of dawn.

"Maybe you could talk to my mother about it," Dee said, suddenly.

"What?" Rosie reluctantly pulled her eyes away from the image.

"My mother. She's really good with those kinds of cleansing things. Even if it is just Lucy's imagination, it might help her to feel better if she thinks that it's been 'fixed' somehow, you know?"

"I don't know. I'll think about it. You know, today her teacher asked me if I had taken Lucy to counselling."

Dee remained silent.

"Do you think Lucy needs counselling?" Rosie asked tentatively.

Dee shrugged, "I don't know, Rosie. It's hard to say what kids do or don't need when things like this happen. There isn't a guide book and every kid is going to be different. But maybe, well... I guess it can't hurt, right?"

Rosie finished her cookie and reached for another as Dee delicately steered them towards less emotionally charged conversation. They finished their tea and Dee excused herself to use the bathroom before they left.

. . .

Rosie found herself staring down at the picture of the couple in front of the house again, drawn to it. She glanced around quickly and then, in a move that shocked her even as she was doing it, she slipped the image from its corners and took the photograph, slipping it into the pocket of her shirt. It sat there, hidden, warming a spot over her heart with a strange heat.

CHAPTER 10

A short while later, Rosie and Dee pulled into the suburb where James lived, fifteen minutes from the city. It was an older suburb that once had been considered on the outskirts, but as the city expanded, it became a sought-after place to live. Most of the houses were older style Queenslanders, carefully restored on large leafy blocks. James's house was one of the smaller ones on his street, a one story on short stumps with a deep wrap-around verandah. Unlike its neighbours, this house needed a fresh coat of paint and a new roof, but the windows were still the beautiful original coloured glass and inside the doorways were wide and the ceilings high. Rosie could see that with a little love and attention - and probably a decent amount of money - it could be a beautiful house. However, the real pride of the home was the workshop down the back of the block. James spent his days inside it where he created both frames and stretched canvases for photographers. He was still mostly a one-man operation, just hiring some help casually over wedding season and just before Christmas.

"Wow," said Dee as they pulled into the street. "These houses must cost a fortune. Look at the size of the blocks! Plus, you have the beach close by."

"Yeah, I don't think they're cheap."

"Clearly, the framing business must be lucrative."

"I'm not sure about that. He's always given me the impression his work was a labour of love, not money. Maybe the house was bought before then?"

"What did he do before framing?" Dee asked.

"I have no idea," Rosie said, "He has never mentioned it."

"Maybe he was a lawyer, who gave it up to work with his hands. God, that would be romantic."

Rosie laughed, "I don't think he was a lawyer." She couldn't picture James doing anything but framing.

They pulled up in front of James's house, and Rosie told Dee she would be right back. She found James in the workshop, sitting with a cup of coffee cooling in front of him. His jeans were stained with paints and varnishes, and his grey shirt had seen better days. His hair was dusted with fine sawdust, and a mask hung around his neck. He smiled when Rosie walked in.

"Hey! I nearly forgot you were coming. I'm not slacking off on the job or anything, just a quick coffee break."

James got up and walked towards the house, beckoning for Rosie to follow him. Inside, he led her to a sunroom off to one side where he had his office. A large portion of the room was taken up by an old kitchen table in the centre which was where James put the prints into the frames and packaged them up. A few canvases sat wrapped on the table. The wall beside his desk had even more cellophane-wrapped frames and canvases leaning against it. He sorted through them for a second and picked out the four that belonged to Rosie, placing them on the table for her to check over.

"They're perfect," she announced. "Like always."

"Awesome. I'm so glad. I'll just get you to sign for them to say they were all good."

Rosie took the paper and pen he held out and scrawled a signature on the bottom. She began picking up the frames to go when James cleared his throat.

"I was wondering if you might like to have coffee sometime?"

"Oh, yeah, sure. I'm sure Lucy would love to catch up with Violet; they really enjoy each other's company."

James let out a little laugh and looked down, "That's true. Except I was kind of thinking, we could go out... you know... without the kids."

Rosie stared at him blankly.

James chuckled, "Like a date. I'm actually trying to ask you on a date here. Which, to be honest, you aren't making very easy."

Rosie felt as though the floor had disappeared beneath her feet and like she couldn't trust her mouth to speak.

"Oh, god," she managed. "have you been speaking to my friend Dee?"

"You friend?"

"Sorry, that was a joke. A bad one, I'm afraid. She just said something the other day that... never mind. It doesn't matter."

James rushed to try to smooth the situation over, "Listen,

it's okay. Just have a think about it, maybe. Or we can forget I said anything."

"No, James. I'm sorry. It was just a surprise but... I'm not really sure I am ready to date..." Rosie trailed off.

"Sure, that's fine. We can forget it happened. We should still get the girls together for a play or something though. You're right, they'd like that."

"Absolutely," Rosie said, relieved she could agree to something.

A sharp knocking from the front of the house made Rosie jump, and her elbow caught a white ceramic pen holder which fell to the floor and shattered.

"Oh my god," Rosie said. "I'm so sorry!"

She put the frames on the table and began picking up pieces.

James bent down to help, "Don't worry about it. I always hated that holder anyway."

"I'll replace it."

"No, seriously, I hated it. Totally been thinking about smashing it myself, don't worry about it," he smiled at her.

Rosie sighed, "Do you have a dustpan and brush?"

"I'll grab one if you can get the door for me?"

"The door? Oh! The knocking! Of course."

Rosie moved towards the door and saw a smiling middle-aged man there.

"Hello, can I help you?" she asked.

"I'm just looking for James," the man said. "I'm Ricky, I'm here to pick up an order."

He stuck out his hand for Rosie to shake and held on to it for a moment too long, looking at her.

"Do I know you?" He asked.

Rosie smiled awkwardly and extracted her hand, "I... no. I don't think so."

Rosie stepped back to let Ricky pass and led him back to the office where James was sweeping up the last of the pen holder.

"Ahh, Ricky! How's it going? Just let me get rid of this and I'll be right with you," he disappeared out the door, and Rosie began collecting her frames.

"Fellow photographer?" Ricky asked, gesturing towards her frames.

"Yes," Rosie said. "Family, mostly. A few weddings but not since... not for a while."

"I do landscapes myself. But I think I recognize your work, you're good. I bet all the dads love having a pretty lady take their photos," Ricky reached out and touched her hand and Rosie fought the urge to shudder. She stepped back.

"Actually, I have my friend in the car, so I have to run. Will you tell James I said goodbye?"

"Sure, no worries, darlin'. I'll see you around."

She turned and hurried back to the car, placing the frames a little roughly into the backseat in an effort to make a fast getaway.

Dee looked at her strangely, "Dude. What is up with you?"

"I got asked on a date, and then I broke his pen holder."

"A date? By framer guy? Yes!"

"I said no."

"By breaking his pen holder? A little extreme, but that's okay."

Rosie looked at Dee in exasperation, "The pen holder was an accident! I jumped when Ricky knocked at the door?"

"Who the hell is Ricky?"

Rosie groaned, "Let's just go home."

Dee looked over at Rosie, "Hey? In all seriousness and just so you know? You are allowed to be happy. It doesn't mean you love Ben any less."

Rosie sighed and pulled out of the street.

"I know that," she said, tasting the bitterness of the lie in her teeth.

James threw the pieces of the holder into the bin and berated himself for being an idiot. He had lost his nerve this morning when he saw her at the car, she had seemed so overwhelmed, and he had thought he would wait until another day. Then seeing her in his office, the way the light caught her hair as she bent over the frames to inspect them, *man*, she was so beautiful. He just thought, *Why not? Go for it, St Clair. Shoot your shot.* So, he had, and it could not have gone worse. She had clearly no interest in him beyond a fellow school parent. Of course she wasn't ready to date! It was too soon. He would get rid of Ricky and apologise.

James came back into the office where Ricky had pulled out one of the chairs and was sitting down leaning on one of the wrapped canvases.

"Hey," he said to Ricky. "Sorry about that."

He took the canvases from under Ricky's elbow and cringed at the slight sag caused by Ricky's weight. That would have to be fixed. Leaning them carefully against the wall, he looked around the room.

Ricky laughed, "Your girlfriend had to go. Red sends her apologies."

James blushed, "She's not... our kids go to the same kindergarten."

Ricky leaned back in the chair, "Hmm. That piece of ass did not look like she has had a kid."

James frowned, "I am not really okay with you saying that, man."

Ricky held up his hands in mock surrender, "No harm meant."

"Right," James said coldly, crossing his arms. "What can I do for you, anyway?"

"Just here to pick up that order."

James turned and found two large landscape frames amongst the stack and put them on the table.

"Check them over and then sign here to say they're all good, please."

His words were clipped, and he found himself clenching his jaw, keen to get Ricky out of his hair as soon as possible. Ricky signed and picking up his pieces, turned to go.

"Maybe I'll go check out Red's website when I get back home. Since you're not interested," the corner of Ricky's mouth lifted in a smirk.

James felt his hands curl into fists and consciously relaxed them, taking a deep calming breath through his nose.

"Probably best if you don't."

Ricky laughed, "Later, St Clair."

James shut the door after him.

"Asshole," he muttered.

He should call Rosie and apologise for both him *and* Ricky, he thought.

James went over to his phone and went to unlock it as it rang, Brooke, his sister's face popping up on the lock screen.

"Hello?"

"Happy birthday!" She trilled.

"It's not my- oh, shit! Happy birthday, Brookie. God, I'm so sorry."

She laughed, "Wouldn't want to break tradition and have you remember."

James groaned, "I will make it up to you with cake this afternoon. I'll bring Violet after kinder."

"Perfect. Actually, the girls were wondering if Vi could have a sleepover? That's the real reason for my call, on top of guilting you for forgetting my birthday for the twenty-eighth year in a row."

James's nieces were four and three, and Violet loved her role as the eldest, bossing her cousins around. All three got along like a house on fire.

"Violet would love that," James said.

"Wonderful. I'll see you this afternoon. Chocolate cake, please." Brooke made a kiss noise and hung up the phone.

Cake, cake, cake, James thought, opening his phone and searching cake makers in Brisbane. His apology to Rosie would have to wait until later; he had to find his sister an apology cake first before he alienated all the women in his life. He clicked on the first link on the search page.

"Dee-licious," he read. "Well, that sounds promising."

James turned off his car and wandered up a rambling path to the door of a house. It didn't look like the house of a baker, but the sign out the front had said this was the right place.

"I suppose my house doesn't look like a business either," he said to himself.

Stepping over a cat sunning itself on the front porch, he knocked on the door. A small woman with a mass of blonde hair tied back in a braid opened it and smiled at him.

"Well, well, well," She said. "Look what the cat dragged in. You must be James St Clair."

She looked at him with amusement, as though they were in on a private joke.

James looked confused, "Uhh, yeah. I'm here to pick up the cake."

Dee laughed, "Absolutely, come on in."

She opened the door and led him into a sunny lounge room that was cluttered with plants, an odd assortment of furniture, and an extensive record collection taking up one wall.

"Wow," he said. "You like music, I take it."

"I do, but that collection belongs to my mother," she said. "Here, come through to the kitchen. I promise it's much improved on the rest of the house."

She took him through a small dining area into a refurbished kitchen. She was right, it was completely at odds to the rest of the house, the stainless steel gleamed at him, and in the oven, was a sheet of cookies. The room smelled like vanilla essence and chocolate and strangely, like comfort.

"I don't usually do requests this late, but firstly I felt bad for your sister for having such a forgetful brother, and secondly, I wanted to lay eyes on you in the flesh."

Dee opened the box on the bench and indicated for him to take a look. Inside sat a chocolate cake decorated with what appeared to be a complete bouquet of edible flowers.

"Wow," James said, appreciatively. "Thank you so much."

"Not a problem. It's what I do."

James stepped back, "What do you mean you wanted to lay eyes on me?"

Dee smiled, "I'm Rosie's best friend. I was in the car this morning when she picked up the prints."

Right, thought James, *this is the friend. Wow, of all the damn bakers in Brisbane.*

"Is this you kicking the tyres? Do you want to ask my intentions?" He said jokingly.

"I want to have a cup of tea with you."

"A cup of tea?"

"A cup of tea," Dee turned to put on the kettle. "Do you like lemon balm?"

"Uhh, no. Not really."

Dee turned to him, "Perfect."

CHAPTER 11

He stood behind some hipster asshole that was too busy flirting with the woman behind the counter to realise a line had formed behind him. The woman made polite chit-chat, diverting the hipster's attention with a practised skill all women seemed to possess. She had short dark hair, he would have preferred it long, but he didn't mind it too much. She was wearing a tight short-sleeved top, and her tattoos peeked out from under it when she stretched her arm out to reach for a cup lid. He didn't think she was wearing a bra. The hipster took his grande, no fat, sugar-free, triple strength, fucking nut-free, soy bullshit drink and left. He stepped up to the counter and ordered a coffee like a normal human. No Bra smiled at him and rung up the order. He paid in cash; her fingers grazed his as she dropped the change in his hand... her hands were too big, her nails were chewed.

He took his coffee and stepped outside and into the alley, a little way out of the foot traffic, sipping at it and checking his emails on his phone. The backdoor of the cafe swung open, and No Bra stepped out with a bag of trash and threw it in a skip bin before taking a cigarette out of her pocket and lighting up. She leaned back against the brick wall and took out her phone. He hadn't been able to see her legs behind the counter; they were long, muscular, her thighs looked soft as velvet. She looked up at him and took a drag of her cigarette, making eye contact. His pulse quickened.

"Having a break?" He asked.

She raised her eyebrows and looked back at her phone.

Definitely no bra. He could see her nipples through the fabric. She glanced up at him again and caught him staring.

"Are you fucking right?" She asked. She threw the cigarette butt on the ground and crushed it under her boot. "Fucking perve."

She wrenched the door open and disappeared inside.

His face flushed and he hurried to his car, slamming the door behind him. He ground his teeth and rubbed hard at his temples, a sweat breaking out on his forehead as the pressure rose inside him, and a buzzing filled his ears. He reached into his pocket and wrapped his fingers around the pendant inside, feeling the edges cut into his skin. He took a deep breath and tried to steady himself. This was fine. She was a skanky piece of shit anyway. He hated tattoos.

He drove out of the city and headed towards the highway, rolling the pendant around in his fingers like worry beads, keeping him calm and focused. It was like one of those things that kids play with to help their ADHD or whatever their snowflake parents claimed. It was a poor substitute for the ring, though. He liked to carry one his trinkets at all times, keep his girls close, so to speak. But the ring certainly got out more than the others, the fact he didn't have it was unsettling. He had retraced his footsteps the last day he remembered having it, and the last time he could remember it was at James's house. It was a simple gold circle, a small garnet inlaid in it. It was delicate and reminded him of her fingers, pale, slender and quick. During the day when he could feel the storm rising inside him, he would reach into his pocket and fondle that ring and remember her fingers, her hands, and the clouds would dissipate. The pendant was helping, but he needed the ring. Today he had hoped he might find the opportunity to look for it, but there hadn't been the chance.

He stepped out of the car and walked with purpose along a small track through the undergrowth. The bush was thick here, and the track was barely noticeable from where he had parked his car. He wouldn't usually be this reckless so soon after he had taken one, but in the absence of the ring, he needed to visit her. In his mind, he could already see her, the gratitude in her eyes when she saw him, the smile on her ruby lips. She needed him; he wanted her.

He pushed aside some of the low hanging brush and waded through grass that grew up to his knees. The closer he got to her, the faster he moved, a thrill rising within him even though he had only been with her days before. She was close now. He would be able to find his way to her even in the dark, she called to him. His hands relaxed. He was here.

He smiled, "Hello, love."

CHAPTER 12

After she dropped Dee back at home, Rosie went to the grocery store. Rosie was a list maker. At any given time, she had three lists on the go - her long-term list of things she hoped to get done that year, her list of things she needed to complete in the next week, and every morning she did a fresh list of tasks to get done that day. From the outside, it looks like organisation, but in truth, it was to attempt to make sense of the chaos inside her brain. Rosie was naturally forgetful and messy. Her room as a child had looked like it had been raided, a jumbled mess of books and photographs, magazines and CDs, clothes, and usually a good half a dozen empty mugs. Neatness did not come easy to her, but Ben had been the most organised person she had ever met. You could ask him for any of his possessions from the last ten years and he would not only more than likely still own it, but be able to fetch it within five minutes. For Ben's sake, she had become tidy, but it wasn't easy or natural.

. . .

Rosie would sometimes be taken with fits of creativity, and suddenly an idea for an image would come to her and not be ignored. Ben would come home and find the furniture pushed all to one side of the room, a newspaper jungle sticky-taped to the wall and a baby Lucy plonked inside a cardboard boat, a newspaper sailor hat on her head. Rosie's lists were a map for her to follow, a way to make sure that if she suddenly got side-tracked by a patch of golden light, she would still remember to buy the ingredients for dinner. Now, as a single mother, she felt like she simply ran from one task to another. Rosie didn't know how to rest, but once a week she did the grocery shopping, and she took her time. She would meander through the aisles, plucking items off the shelves and reading the back without seeing what they said. She would let her thoughts run away with her as her guard dropped down. It was peaceful, and she could pretend she was still achieving something, even if it took her three times as long because she used the grocery store as a strange kind of therapy.

Rosie put her handbag into the trolley and looked for a list she had placed in there earlier. She rifled through her bag, through lip balms and coins and a lollipop wrapped in tissue that Lucy had given her last week and she had forgotten to take out. Finally, she found the list and pulled it out, crumpled and covered in strange dust that Rosie had come to think of as 'handbag dirt'. She walked purposefully towards the bananas and began inspecting them for ripeness. She was still suffering from embarrassment over the situation at James's house earlier, and thinking of it now she began to blush. *And the pen holder! Oh, my god,* she groaned internally.

"So stupid," she muttered, and an old woman by the apples glanced over at her.

Rosie smiled at her, sheepishly.

"Talking to myself," she said by way of explanation.

The old woman narrowed her eyes and pushed her trolley away. Rosie sighed and headed towards the potatoes.

It wasn't that she didn't like James, he seemed like a nice, genuine guy, and... well, yes, he was attractive. She liked to watch his hands when he was showing her the frames; he would absently stroke the wood. His hands were large, calloused and generally, he had more than one nick on the knuckles, but when he touched the frames, he did so with a delicateness, as though he were caressing the cheek of a newborn. And today, when she had looked up after he had asked her out, his eyes had locked into hers with a connection that seemed... *like fusion*, Rosie thought. Yes, she liked him. But she had never truly considered dating him. She still felt married. That was the issue. It felt like it would be cheating on Ben to date.

She pushed the trolley down the cereal aisle and on impulse she put a little box of sugary cereal in the trolley as a treat for Lucy. She imagined what it would be like going on a date - kissing someone that wasn't Ben. Ben hadn't even been gone two years, wasn't that too soon? Was there an appropriate amount of time for a widow to wait before she started seeing someone else. *Widow*. It was such an old-fashioned word; she felt like she should be standing on a beach in the drizzling rain with a black shawl around her shoulders, staring out to sea, instead of standing in the supermarket clutching a bag of rice.

She said the word aloud to taste it, "Widow."

"Excuse me?"

Shit. It was that same old lady again.

"I wasn't talking to you," Rosie said.

"Well, you weren't talking to the rice," the old woman said huffily.

"I was talking to myself. I was just... never mind."

Rosie hurried into the next aisle and pinched the top of her nose where she could feel a headache beginning to form. She was losing it. Maybe she should move to the beach and away from everyone. She could lock herself inside her house like Kate. And she would do it too. She would do it if it wasn't for Lucy and needing to be present for her. Sometimes - and she could barely admit this to herself because to do so felt like a betrayal - she felt an almost resentment towards the fact that Lucy tethered her to the world so that she couldn't give in to the grief and go mad from it. Sometimes, she imagined the freedom of madness. It was like an ocean, and she could dive right in. Drown in it. What a relief to be somewhere else. She picked up a tin of corn kernels and studied the back of it. The problem was that the grief was so big and she had no way to release it that wouldn't destroy her. She had to hold it together and be functional and pay bills, and drive Lucy to kinder, and be *so sane* that she felt like she could feel the pressure rising inside her. She needed a black hole to scream into.

· · ·

When Rosie was little, her Poppa used to take her to the video store each weekend, and she would pick out a movie to take home and watch. It had been a little ritual of theirs, popcorn and a movie. He always sat through whatever she chose, although looking back, it seemed like he was more interested in watching Rosie's reactions than the movie. He would laugh with delight when she giggled at a comedy and chuckle and hug her when she cried during the sad scenes. Grandma June would poke her head in from time to time, replenishing the popcorn bowl before disappearing back to the garden. One time she had picked a collection of fairy tales that had been remade, and there was one where the princess had seven brothers. An evil witch had kidnapped the brothers and told the princess that the only way she could have them returned would be if she was silent for seven years; if the princess spoke one word, they would be gone forever. The princess never spoke and got married to a prince, but the witch tried to force her to talk by taking her newborn babies from their cribs. The princess knew what was happening but couldn't tell anyone, and when the third baby was stolen, her pain was so great that she went out into the moonlight, dug a hole in the earth and screamed down into it.

Rosie thought about that hole with a strange kind of envy. A deep black hole to scream into. Her grief felt like something dark and terrifying inside of her. When she waded into the depths of herself to look at it straight on, she was alarmed by the vastness of it; she felt as though if she really allowed herself to feel it, the grief would rip her apart and she would scatter like ashes on the wind.

She was terrified of it.

She needed it.

To let it go, to release it, felt like she would have nothing left. The grief was the last piece of Ben that remained to her. She would think about that hole the princess dug, and she could almost feel the dirt under her own fingernails, the cool touch of the soil, the sweat on her skin as she worked. She could almost feel the scream rip from her throat.

She placed a bag of sugar into the trolley. The old woman was back again, reaching for a kilo of flour.

"I wish I could dig a hole," Rosie said to her.

The old woman glared. Rosie pushed the trolley to the next aisle.

James sat awkwardly at Dee's kitchen table, with a delicate china cup of tea sitting in a saucer in front of him.

"Not that I'm opposed to a cup of tea, but Rosie did turn me down. I don't think we need to be having a conversation about this."

Across from him, Dee waved her hand like she was shooing flies, "She was just surprised. That's all she was reacting to."

James tried to pick up the teacup by the handle, but it felt like he was handling a child's toy. He gave up and ignored the handle, picking it up from the other side.

"She seemed pretty sure of herself. And I don't really want to push it, you know? I have never lost my spouse, and I have no idea how much that must have hurt."

"Yes. She did lose Ben, and it was awful and horrible, and the worst thing that could possibly happen. But... look. I love Rosie. She is my soul sister. But she is nursing her grief right now like she wants it to grow. I hate seeing that. Ben wouldn't want it, and Lucy doesn't need it."

James checked his watch, he would need to get Violet soon.

"I care about Rosie too," he said. "But I don't think I can make her date me. I think she would probably be pretty displeased if she thought we were even talking about this without her."

Dee laughed, "I *do* like you. I like that you thought about how that would make her feel. And yes, I know you can't make her. I just wanted to say, don't give up on her. You have given her the option, just give her some time to come around."

James stood up, "I'm sorry to run off, but I have to go get my daughter."

"No problems."

"How much do I owe you for the cake?" James asked, reaching for his wallet.

Dee shook her head, "I'm giving you this one on the house."

"I can't do that, Dee. I'm a business owner too, and I know you have costs to cover. I am happy to pay."

Dee turned him around and pushed him towards the door, "And I am happy to bake. Now off you go. I have cookies to ice for a delightfully boring barista I'm going to go on a date with tonight."

James stumbled out the door, "Well, thank you. Have fun on your date."

Dee winked at him, "Oh, honey. I intend to."

CHAPTER 13

Rosie pulled into June's driveway, coming to a stop beside the flame tree that shaded the front yard. All of Rosie's best childhood memories lived in this house. Lucy unbuckled her seat and escaped, running down the side of the house and into the backyard, her brown curls flying behind her. Rosie pulled out her handbag, locked the car and followed. Grandma June was in the garden, bent down beside one of the beds with Lucy wrapped around her like a spider monkey. She straightened up and held out her arm to Rosie.

"Hello, darling," she said as Rosie gave her a hug and dropped a kiss on her cheek.

June was a tiny woman, with bright blue eyes and a halo of white hair. She was the last of Rosie's grandparents, Poppa had died when Lucy had been three, and Kate's parents passed away when Rosie was only young. As a child, Rosie had spent most afternoons and weekends at June and Poppa's. Rosie had no discernible memories of her father,

96

Frank, from before he left, but Kate had maintained contact with Grandma June and Poppa. Frank lived only as still memories on June's walls – a smiling infant, a handsome high schooler, a framed portrait taken on Kate and Frank's wedding day. Rosie had stared at them for hours as a child, wondering about him and what about her hadn't been enough for him to stay. Poppa had filled the gap Frank had left, becoming the only father Rosie had ever known. She missed him like a piece of herself was gone.

"How have you girls been," June said, leading them towards the house.

Lucy began regaling them with a blow by blow description of her kinder day and describing Tiny's size to June by waving her arms in the air while standing on tiptoe.

"He sounds very ferocious," June commented.

"What's 'ferloshus'? Lucy asked, her eyes wide.

Rosie burst out laughing.

"Fearsome. Frightening," June explained.

"Oh, no!" Lucy shook her head. "Tiny is a scaredy pants. He is soft, not ferloshus."

"Never teach her the correct way to say that," Rosie whispered. "That's too cute to be said properly."

Rosie's phone rang; she didn't recognise the number.

"This could be a client, sorry. I will just be a minute," She threw them an apologetic look and stepped outside to answer.

"Would you like a hot chocolate, Lucy?" Grandma June asked.

Lucy enthusiastically agreed, begging for a marshmallow in it and June went to put on the kettle, pulling mugs from a cupboard and spooning chocolate powder into one for Lucy, before dropping teabags into mugs for Rosie and herself.

"You know who *is* frightening?" Lucy continued.

"Who is that?"

"The girl. There is one in my room. Sometimes she is nice, but sometimes she is scary."

June turned around, "What girl?"

"There is one in my room. She lives there now, I think. Mama says she isn't there, but she is."

"There is a girl in your room, and Mama can't see her?"

"No," Lucy said. "Only I can see her. Grandma?"

"Yes?"

"The kettle is done."

June turned to the kettle she had forgotten, which was whistling with an urgency. She pulled it off of the hot plate and began pouring water into the mugs.

"Lucy, you said sometimes the girl is nice, but sometimes she is scary?"

Lucy nodded, "Uh-huh. She said she can't go home."

"And she is a little girl? Like you?"

"No. She is big. Like Mama but not. Like less than Mama."

June sat the mug down in front of Lucy, "Younger than your Mum?"

She handed Lucy a marshmallow. Lucy dropped it in and watched as it began to melt.

"Lucy?" Grandma June prompted.

"Yes. Younger than Mama."

Rosie came back inside.

"So, that *was* a client. I have another shoot booked. It's last-minute though, they want it for tomorrow, their family has flown in and they decided to get some photos while they're here," She sat down at the table. "What did I miss?"

June forced a smile on to her face, "Nothing. We were just about to have tea."

James pulled into his sister's house, and let Violet out of her car seat. He could already hear his nieces inside making a racket. Violet carried her overnight bag, and James carried the cake for Brooke, Violet's pillow, and a second bag filled with toys that she insisted she needed. Audrey and Eloise met them at the door, and the three children began squealing excitedly. His nieces were both mini versions of their mother, Brooke was fair where James was dark.

Brooke stepped out of the kitchen where she had been preparing snacks for the girls, "Oh, good! Your timing is perfect. The girls were just trying to rope me into making cake, and I was insisting that you were bringing one."

She pulled Violet into a quick hug before the girls thundered down the hall to the playroom, and planted a kiss on James's cheek.

"Coffee?" She asked.

"Yes, please."

James followed Brooke back to the kitchen, where she began making coffees. She looked dejectedly at her tray of cut-up carrots, cheese, and crackers

"Of course, they won't eat any of these now. They'll be too busy playing."

She picked up a carrot stick and crunched it, and pushed the tray towards James, who obligingly began to eat the cheese. Brooke set mugs of coffee down in front of them both.

"So, what's new?"

"Nothing much. Same old, same old. Business is going well. David stopped by this morning, he gave Violet a bracelet."

"Gold?" Brooke asked with a laugh.

"Yes! Did he buy your girls one too?"

"You know it. He has no idea. The girls would be happier with a two-dollar beaded bracelet from the cheap shop."

"Exactly," James agreed. "But he means well. He just doesn't have anyone else to buy for. He probably needs a lady friend."

Brooke snorted, "I think he has plenty of 'lady friends', which is a term I think you should retire, by the way."

"No good?" he asked.

"Terrible."

"And," James began, "I asked a woman on a date and got an incredibly embarrassing rejection, followed by a weird interaction with her best friend - who is the woman who made your cake."

"So, you asked out the photographer finally?"

James's mouth fell open, "How did you know that was who it was?"

"Probably because you have been talking about her for months. It was pretty obvious."

James mentally scanned through his interactions with his sister over the last few months for signals he may have sent. He suspected it was just Brooke being Brooke, picking up things that no one else would ever notice. His sister was a master at seeing small details that everyone else missed, which meant she was probably right about David's 'lady friends' too.

"Well, that's even more embarrassing, since she seemed completely shocked by my proposal to go on a date."

Brooke sipped her drink, "You are just out of practice with flirting. You'll get there, stud. So, what was the weird interaction with the baker?"

James filled her in and a car pulled in the driveway.

"Daddy!" Audrey screamed and went barrelling for the door in time for Brooke's husband, Michael to swing her up into one arm, his other full of flowers.

He came in and placed the bouquet down in front of Brooke, "Happy birthday, good looking."

Brooke stood up and kissed Michael before turning to James.

"See? This is how you flirt."

The evening went along well. They ordered pizza and ate cake, then they set the kids up with a movie and popcorn before the adults retired out to the back deck. Michael handed James a beer, while Brooke sipped at a wine.

"God," Brooke said, putting her feet up on the outdoor ottoman. "All birthdays should be on a Friday. No one tells you that when you are an adult, you *can* set your own bedtime, but you still have to go to bed early because you have work the next day."

Michael groaned, "You play Bingo all day."

"I *lifestyle assist*. It's very important for the elderly to have social activities. Besides, Bingo can get wild; you have no idea."

"Yeah, well, we have been chasing down leads for this missing woman," Michael said. "And coming up with nothing, I might add."

. . .

Michael was a local police officer, and had been working overtime since the disappearance of Hannah Avery. He updated them on the hotline that had recently been set up.

"The problem is, we have to follow up all the leads, even the ones that are ridiculous. One woman suspected Hannah was the woman with the barking dog that walks to the park near her every day. The woman she is referring to is actually a man, by the way. We are no closer to finding her, and if I'm honest, it's not looking good for a safe recovery right now."

Brooke rubbed his arm, "That's awful. I'm so sorry. You win for the worst day."

Michael leaned over and kissed his wife on the forehead, "You just be careful at the moment. If this is the same guy responsible for Sarah Yarrow, then he is one really sick bastard. All women should be on alert until we catch this guy."

"You have no idea who it is?" James asked.

"Nope. We have some folks we looked into, but all of them came up clean. I hate to give this piece of garbage any credit, but he has left nothing. He has taken them from places where hundreds of people are every day, so any evidence we find nearby is basically worthless. There would be DNA and fingerprints of dozens of people. There never appears to be much of a struggle, so there is no blood... there was nothing on Sarah to identify her killer. Her clothes and jewellery were gone. Bryan Avery and Hannah's family are really on our ass about it at the moment. Which is totally understandable. If it were my kid, I would be busting down every door in the city."

James thought of Violet going missing and felt his stomach turn over. He pushed his beer away.

"You will find him," Brooke said, squeezing Michael's hand.

He nodded, "Not soon enough for Hannah, unfortunately. If it's the guy I think it is, when we *do* sit down her family, it will be to say we found a body."

June waved goodbye to Rosie and Lucy and stayed on the driveway until the car disappeared around the corner. She made her way back around to the backyard and stood staring at the stars for a few moments, breathing in the perfume of her night-scented jasmine. Out of the shadows, stepped a man. His hair was dishevelled, and his clothes were worn. He glanced around nervously before he crossed the lawn. Quietly, he walked up behind June and placed a hand on her shoulder.

June turned around, "You're out of time, I'm afraid."

"I only need a few more months."

June shook her head, "I can't give you that. Rosie needs to know now before anything else happens."

She led him towards the house and opened the door for him to enter, "It's been long enough, Frank. You're going to have to speak to your daughter."

In Rosie's dream, she is back in the old house she and Kate had lived in when she was Lucy's age. The dream comes to her in pieces, like a jigsaw puzzle. A large key slides into a lock. Makeup is scattered along an unfamiliar dresser. The smell of flowers and the way they lay upon the carpet. An old man. Rosie lies in a small bed with stuffed toys around her, and her mother lies beside her. No. Her father lies beside her. She tries to look up to see his face, the one she can't remember, but it slips away again. Then she is back in the pantry, hiding. Kate is yelling, a vase smashing. Frank... soothing her. Rosie stands up and crawls to the doorway, but it isn't Frank at all. It's James, he holds Kate by her arms, speaking softly.

Rosie awoke, Lucy beside her in bed again, her elbow jutting painfully into Rosie's ribs. What is the Freudian hell was going on with her? Rosie rarely dreamed, she hadn't for as long as she could remember. Her sleep was deep, uninterrupted; she had struggled to even wake for Lucy when she was a baby. Ben would go collect her from the crib more often than not, changing her and bringing Lucy to Rosie to feed. It seemed as though lately, her mind kept pulling her backwards.

Rosie leant over and checked the time on her phone. Four-thirty in the morning. Rosie groaned quietly. She had to drop Lucy to Kate this morning before the last-minute shoot she had booked in yesterday. She reluctantly slid carefully away from her sleeping daughter and slipped down to the kitchen to make tea. The morning was crisp, and the tiles in the kitchen had a chill to them, she could finally feel the cool change of autumn in the air that came so slowly to the river city. One year she wanted to take Lucy to the snow so they could have a 'real winter'. It had been a dream of Ben and hers to travel - something Rosie had never done because Kate had never left the house, let alone the state. They had been planning to go to Europe when she found out she was pregnant with Lucy and decided they were better off saving for a house deposit. There had been so much life they still had to live.

Rosie booted up the laptop while she waited for the kettle to boil. She made a tea in her favourite mug, retrieved a pass-able banana from the fruit bowl, and sat down at the table. Her social media feed was filled with photos and information about Hannah. None of Rosie's friends had known her personally, but there always seemed to be a mutual acquaintance between them. Rosie herself had stayed quiet about her own interaction with Hannah and Bryan; she knew first-hand how everyone reached out in a crisis. She imagined that every time Bryan opened a text, or message, it would be another blow to realise it contained no useful information. She clicked through to Bryan's profile; he hadn't shared anything himself but had been tagged in several posts by friends and family, news stories, heartfelt messages to Hannah that hoped she would be found safely.

On Rosie's newsfeed, someone had shared a police officer making a speech that urged women to be vigilant. In response, a women's group had demanded a grassroots change to the way men are raised, and more appropriate punishments for acts of violence against women. No one knew where Hannah was, though, no one had seen her since the moment she waved goodbye to her friends and walked away from them. The not knowing drove Rosie crazy. She had to know the why, the where, the how. When the police had come to her to tell her about Ben, she had kept asking why, as though she were a child. Why had it happened? How had her perfectly healthy husband, who was never distracted, who was attentive where she was absentminded - how had he crashed his car? What had happened? Why? And then the room had begun to tilt to one side as though it were a sinking ship. Her vision had tunnelled, and for one split second she thought - could have sworn - she saw Ben, standing there behind the officer - and that all of this was an awful joke. She opened her mouth to call to him, then the world had slipped into darkness, and when she came to, the police officer had been lightly tapping her cheek, and Rosie's life was changed.

. . .

Rosie drained her cup and rinsed it in the sink before going to wake Lucy and get them ready to leave. The sun would rise soon.

Rosie pulled back up to Kate's just after lunch. The shoot had been chaotic with so many family members, but she had managed to make it work. She grabbed her handbag and another small bag that held her memory cards, everything else in the car was insured, but she couldn't recapture those memories from today. They would travel with her until she had them uploaded and backed up.

She walked her way up the winding path, pushing past the large bush that had begun to overhang the walkway. She would need to organise a gardener to come out again. Kate had issues with making phone calls, and Rosie had to phone for anything that was required. Not for the first time, Rosie wondered why Kate couldn't manage the outside world. Clearly, there must have been a catalyst of some sort. At some point in the past, she must have been like everyone else, meeting up with friends, doing the groceries, going on vacation. There were photos of her mother in albums that showed her on the beach and at parties, and sometimes Rosie would look at them trying to fit who she knew her mother to be into these images. She had no one to ask, Kate's parents were long gone, she had no friends, Frank had left... there was no one but Kate herself - and Rosie had always known it wasn't a subject to bring up. She wore the burden of her mother's fragility, and she lived in fear that if she pushed her at all, she would be left with nothing. And she had already lost so much. Still, her recent dreams were in her mind, and she wondered if it had to do with Frank and the fight she seemed to remember them having; the flowers on the ground the day of Rosie's birthday.

Rosie let herself in the front door with her key and followed the sounds of Kate and Lucy in the kitchen, where she found them making cookies. Lucy stood on a kitchen chair, curled over the bowl as Kate mixed the ingredients. Their backs were to her, and the radio played easy listening music quietly. Neither of them noticed her arrival. Rosie watched them for a few moments with a smile. For all her faults, Kate loved Lucy. When Lucy was here, she had Kate's full attention, they baked, and read stories, and painted. Lucy took the years off of Kate's face, smoothing the lines caused by decades of worry, Lucy could coax laughter that was as sudden and pure as a sun shower. Rosie felt a sudden swelling of tenderness; she would call the gardener tomorrow.

"Hey," Rosie said. "What are you two up to?"

Kate and Lucy turned around.

"We are making the most delicious cookies in the world," Lucy said solemnly.

Kate nodded, "It's true."

Rosie put her bag on the table, "Well, then. I would definitely like to help."

Kate pointed to the pantry, "Make sure you put on an apron."

"I will."

"And wash your hands," Kate added.

"Yes, Mum," Rosie rolled her eyes.

"Now," Kate said, turning back to Lucy, "we add the secret ingredient."

Rosie fetched an apron and began tying it around her waist, "Is the secret ingredient love?"

Kate looked at her, quizzically.

"No, Rosemary," She pulled a jar from the shelf in front of her. "It's cinnamon."

"Right. Sorry."

"That's okay, Mama," Lucy said. "You're just learning."

An hour later, Lucy was hosting a tea party with some stuffed toys and homemade cookies, and Kate and Rosie were doing the dishes.

"I was thinking I would call the gardener tomorrow about the front gardens," Rosie said.

"That would be good, thank you," Kate replied, handing her a wet dish to dry. Rosie towelled it off and set it on the bench.

"Hey, do you remember that house we lived in before we moved here?" Rosie asked.

Kate placed another dish in the sink and began to wash it, "Oh, yes. Awful house. Absolutely no security. Although, I do think I still have that pot somewhere I took from the other side of the duplex. Cast iron. They last forever. Why do you ask?"

Rosie dried another dish, "I have just been having dreams about it lately."

"What sort of dreams?" Kate asked.

Rosie hesitated, "Just being a little girl in the house. You reading to me. I remember... a fight or something. Between you and Frank."

Rosie felt Kate stiffen, and her hands paused on the dishes for a second before resuming the washing, "Mmm. I thought you didn't remember Frank."

"I don't," Rosie said. "Or I didn't. I don't really know if it's just a dream. That's why I was asking. I was wondering if it actually happened or not."

Kate placed the last dish in the rack for Rosie to dry and pulled the plug. She dried her hands on a tea towel and began to take off her apron.

"So," Rosie prompted, "did it happen, or..."

"Yes. We had a fight."

"Right... Did he... hurt you? Is that why he left?"

Kate hung the apron on a hook in the pantry and turned around. Rosie noticed Kate's hands were tugging at her clothing, a sign of an anxiety attack, and she wanted to reel back in her questions. But, at the same time, she had to know *the why*.

"Mum? Did he hurt you?"

"I don't know why he left, Rosemary. He had been on night shifts, and that had been hard, but finally he began days, and everything was going fine. It seemed like things were just going well, you were turning into this wonderful little human, and we had been talking about moving somewhere nicer, so you would be close to a good school for when you started. Then he came home one afternoon... different. Wild. It was like he had been drinking, which he did sometimes, but not like that. He stayed out all night. Then all the next day. He missed your birthday party at his own mother's house. That afternoon he came in out of nowhere, and told me he had to go. No explanation, no warning. He didn't even pack his things. He just... left. I was beside myself, asking why, pleading for him to explain himself. I was angry and upset, and I threw the vase. So, yes. It was real. And yes. He hurt me. Just not how you think."

CHAPTER 15

The next night, after Rosie had finished doing the dishes and Lucy was curled up beside her on the couch dozing, Rosie slipped the photograph she had taken from the café out of a drawer in her room where she had placed it. She sat down on the couch and looked at it.

Since the moment she had taken it, she had felt its presence subconsciously, like a constant drone of thought in the back of her mind. It felt like when she had an appointment later in the day that she could not miss and her mind kept quietly sending out messages. Or like when she found out she was pregnant with Lucy after taking a home pregnancy test. She had been unable to part with the one tangible thing that connected herself to the baby, carrying it in the pocket of her dressing gown all morning, her hand reaching down to trace its outlines. This photograph felt like a secret, like a treasure, like a word dancing on the tip of her tongue but just out of reach.

· · ·

When she had first seen the image, she had attributed her fascination to the expression of the woman, but now Rosie realized this was not the case. The woman was naturally engaging, but for Rosie, it was the man in the image that drew her. And the house. The house in the background. For some reason, it made Rosie think of her father, a man she had virtually no memories of at all. Lucy let out a soft snore and Rosie put the photo down, and picked up her daughter, carrying her up the hall and into her room. She felt the crunch of dirt under her feet, looking down she saw there was more soil on Lucy's carpet and... pine needles?

"What the hell?" she muttered. She slid Lucy beneath the covers and pulled them up to her chin, sweeping her daughter's hair back from her forehead. Rosie took a moment to soak in Lucy's sweetness. She grabbed Lucy's sneakers on the way out and inspected their soles in the light of the hall. No dirt. Maybe it was coming home inside the shoes? Lucy was forever bringing home half the kinder's sandpit inside her shoes. Rosie put them in the laundry for washing in case.

With Lucy safely in bed, Rosie went into her room and into the walk-in robe, feeling around in the top of the cupboard for a box she kept up there. Her hands groped blindly under winter jumpers and sweatshirts until she felt it's outline, she pulled it down and sat on the floor and lifted the lid off the box. Inside were trinkets from her childhood that she had carried from house to house after she left home. There was a tiny signet ring given to her by Grandma June and Poppa on her sixth birthday, a little Troll doll with yellow hair, birthday cards, her first love letter received in the fifth grade from Peter Brown. Under it all, in a yellowing envelope were the images from the first roll of film she ever shot. She had never opened it. Kate and her father had fought, she remembered, Kate on the floor with flowers strewn around her, the way they looked wrong and beautiful at the same time. Then, later, she had been picked up by Kate's parents and taken back to the farm Kate grew up on. Kate had stayed behind. Rosie had stayed with them for a long time. She would follow her Oma out to feed the poddy calves in the morning and play in the cool grove where the macadamia trees grew, the feeling of their smooth shells in her hands. Opa's smell was of soil and old spice, his hands roughened by work. Rosie remembered the sight of his back in the soft flannel shirts as he rode his tractor across the paddock. At some point, Kate had come back. They had stayed on for another month or so, and then Kate had bought the house she lived in now; a gift from her parents. It was the last gift they would give her before they died, Oma after six months of horror at the hands of aggressive breast cancer, and Opa followed her three months later after he lay down in bed one afternoon and never woke up.

Before the afternoon when she had been picked up by Oma and Opa, Rosie had no memories at all. Ben had been shocked when Rosie told him that.

"You can't remember anything before five or six?" he had asked, incredulously.

"No," Rosie had answered, "Nothing at all."

The photos had been developed at some point during her stay with Oma and Opa but for whatever reason, Rosie had never wanted to open them. Now, after her dream and the strange feeling she got about that old photo, today she felt compelled to look, driven by the spectre of a memory that kept slipping out of her grasp.

She slid the images from the envelope and began to look through them. Grandma June standing in her yard, sucking in her stomach. The next one was a tyre swing that once hung from a tree in Grandma June and Poppa's front yard. She had forgotten the tyre swing. Her five-year-old feet in the clover. An old ginger tomcat staring at her from under a bush. It was like a time capsule from the day she received the camera. She knew she should be more interested in the images that captivated the mind of her young self, but she rushed through to the last three images on the camera, roses on the ground, blurry – the camera struggled with the low light in the house. Here... an overexposed silhouette of her father, his arm raised as though he was waving. Rosie felt numb; for years she had avoided that image, frightened to see the face of the man she couldn't remember. She was sure when she saw his face as she had seen it the last time, she would feel a flood of recognition – and now she held nothing but a shadow, the frame of a man who could be anyone at all. She dropped the photos into her lap and closed her eyes.

'Stupid,' she berated herself. 'Stupid sentimental bullshit.'

She went to stuff the photos back into the envelope when

the last image from the roll slid out and on to the carpet and Rosie gasped. She'd forgotten she had taken it, driving down the driveway that afternoon, Opa had stopped to open the gate, and she had twisted around in the backseat and shot a photo of the house through the window. She pulled the stolen photo from her pocket and placed it side by side, her hands shaking. The house was the same house, that much was certain. But what chilled Rosie was the man. In the stolen photo he was much younger, but still, it was definitely him. In her photo he was older, his face more wrinkled, a hat on his head, standing in front of the stairs, looking out to the yard. Something was off about it; she leant down closer and then reached behind her for her phone, turning on the torch and shining it on the photo.

"Holy fucking shit," she breathed.

She could see the stairs right through him.

The next day, Dee and Rosie were sitting at Rosie's kitchen table with the two photographs in front of them.

"Maybe it's one of those things where there are two images in one?" Dee suggested, peering closer at the photo.

"A double exposure?" Rosie asked.

"Yeah, that."

"It's not a double exposure."

Dee picked up the photo and squinted at it, "How do you know? You can barely even remember taking the photo."

Rosie took the image back and pointed at the translucent figure, "Because this man is dead. He was dead before we moved into the house. It was being rented out after his death, that's *why* we were living in it. I called Kate this morning to ask. I'm a fairly good photographer, but even I can't take photos of the spirit realm."

Dee looked up, startled, "You told Kate about this photo?"

"Shit, no. I just asked about the old house we lived in, said I'd seen the other photo in the café and it looked familiar. Kate would have a stroke if I'd told her the truth."

Dee smiled, "Okay, well I thought I'd check since you did call me to come have a look at your ghost photo so strange things happen all the time apparently."

Rosie picked up the photo she took from the café and examined the two images side by side again. She felt like she was losing her mind. On Friday she was scoffing at Dee's suggestion that Lucy's invisible friend could be real and by Monday she was calling her over to examine a photo of a ghost man. What exactly did this mean? Was the man there in the house, watching them, did he come to farewell them?

Dee stood up and took her and Rosie's teacups over to the sink and began rinsing them, "Well, it's pretty cool that you have a ghost photo. You may have to start believing in my garden fairies now. And in Lucy's mystery girl for that matter."

"You read my mind. I was just thinking about Lucy's friend," Rosie shuddered. "It's a bit creepy though, don't you think? I hate the thought of that."

Dee began rummaging through Rosie's fridge, pulled out a withered apple from the crisper and gave Rosie a disapproving look, "Well, I guess there is no reason to think that Lucy's girl would be harmful. Apparently, you grew up with a ghost man, and you're just fine except for the fact that your pathologically shy and eat like shit. You have four blocks of chocolate in here by the way, do you realise that?"

"I need all that chocolate. Seriously though, I barely remember anything from that house. Maybe I didn't see anything; maybe it is something to do with the camera. Like... you might not be able to see them, but you can take a photo of them?"

"Maybe that's your answer to Lucy then. You could take a photo of Lucy's room, tell Lucy if there is anyone in there then it will show up, and then when she sees nothing she might feel better. But do have Mum come over and do a cleansing. It can't hurt, and houses definitely hold energy of previous people who've been in the house."

Rosie rolled her eyes and relented, "Fine. Meg can come and smoke the house out or whatever when she comes home from the retreat."

Dee clapped her hands to her chest, her eyes sparkling with mock emotion, "Aww, I'm so proud of you, my little non-believer. Look at you, opening your mind to the possibilities!"

Dee found a passably fresh orange in the fridge and began to peel it, dropping skin into the bin under the sink as she went. She popped a piece of orange in her mouth and chewed thoughtfully for a moment.

"So," she said. "Should we... take a photo now?"

"What? Of what? Oh! Of Lucy's room?"

"Yeah. Why not? You have the camera right there on the table. We can take a quick photo, check it out for any semi-transparent girls... and then we know."

Rosie reached over and got her camera out of the bag and opened the side to slip a memory card into it.

"I feel like an idiot," she said as she slipped the strap over her head.

Dee and Rosie crept up the hallway, and at the same time they stopped and looked at each other, realizing what they were doing, and collapsed into giggles.

"I just came up here before to go to the toilet and walked normally and now I'm basically tiptoeing," Dee said, breathless with laughter.

"I live here. I walk up here all the time," Rosie said, wiping her eyes. "Oh god, okay. Let's just do this."

They started up the hallway again and despite their best efforts to 'act normal' they both ended up walking as quietly as possible up to Lucy's room, the mood sobering. Rosie flicked the camera on and adjusted the settings quickly with a practised hand. She raised the camera to her eye and snapped two photos, then lowered it and turned the screen to face up. Dee leaned over her shoulder and Rosie hit the viewing button so she could see the images she just took.

Dee let out her breath in a gush, the movement stirring Rosie's hair, "Well, now you know. Nothing there. Just Lucy's perfectly ordinary room."

"Yes," Rosie sighed in relief. "I didn't really expect there to be anything."

Dee started back down the hallway, "Is it weird that I'm kind of disappointed?"

"Sorry," Rosie said, "I'll try to be more entertaining."

A half an hour later, Rosie was walking Dee out to her car

when Dee turned to her and said, "Hey, I was thinking, have you given any more thought to the James thing?"

"Dating him? Ahh, no. Mostly because I already thought about it and said no."

Dee rolled her eyes, "You thought about it for all of three seconds. And, hey! I went on a date with boring barista which went so well that I'm going to let him bore me again tonight. Have you even seen James since Friday?"

Rosie flushed, "I missed him at kinder drop off this morning."

In actuality, she had left the house early for the first time in her entire mothering career in order to drop Lucy off as the doors opened to avoid James. *Also, had he been wearing cologne the other day? He smelled great. No. Different*, she corrected her brain.

Dee narrowed her eyes and gave Rosie a look like she wasn't buying it. Mr. Thompson's front door banged, and Rosie and Dee turned to look as Tiny bounded across the lawn.

"My God," Dee said. "I just love horses."

She went over to the fence and patted Tiny who was half hanging over.

"Tiny!" Mr. Thompson yelled. "Get off the lady."

Dee laughed, "Oh trust me, any day I get to pat a dog is a good day."

Mr. Thompson hobbled over to the fence, "Rosie, you think you could do me a favour and feed this boofhead for me for a week or so? My daughter is going out west to visit her cousin and doesn't trust me not to set the house on fire without her to check in on me, so apparently, I'm going on a road trip."

Rosie nodded, "Oh, of course. We would love to mind Tiny."

Mr. Thompson reached out and patted her hand, "Thank you, love. I'll leave his food on the back patio in the cupboard. Can't stick it out or the great pig would eat it in an afternoon and starve to death over the next few days."

"You have a safe trip," Rosie said.

She turned to Dee, "Well, it looks like I already have a date for the next few days."

CHAPTER 16

That afternoon, on the way to Kate's, the news on the radio had said Bryan Avery had released a statement asking for Hannah's safe return and any information that may lead to her whereabouts. They cut to a sound bite, and suddenly Bryan's voice had filled the car. Rosie pulled over, her hands shaking and leaned her head against the steering wheel.

"Hannah is loved; her family is missing her. I am missing her. She wouldn't leave on her own. We just want her back safely. If anyone has any information, please, please... we just.. .even if it's something small, that you think might not matter. Please just call the police and let them know."

Rosie thought of how many times she had left clubs and bars when she was younger, walking off into the night, always with that slight unease that something might happen. The click of her heels on the pavement, the emptiness of a car park. It made the hair on the back of her neck stand up, even now. A feeling of rolling the dice, hoping tonight you would get home safely. She thought of all the tricks girls had passed to each other, leave your hair loose so you couldn't be grabbed by it, thread your keys through your fingers, call your friends. Hannah would have known those things too. That was what was making her blood run cold. You can do everything right, and still... How many times had she made the same walk Hannah made? How many times had Dee? How many times would Lucy? Hannah Avery was all of them.

When Rosie arrived at Kate's, Lucy had been thrilled to learn they would have Tiny as a guest for the next few days.

Kate had screwed up her nose, "Do you think that's wise? You said he is a very big dog and he might end up hurting Lucy."

Rosie had assured Kate that Tiny was well socialised and that she would keep an eye on the pair of them.

"Call me tomorrow," Kate had begged. "Just let me know the night went okay. If you need to, Lucy can stay here while the dog is there."

"Thanks for the offer, Mum. I'm sure we will be fine. I'll speak to you tomorrow, okay?"

Truthfully, Rosie felt relieved to have Tiny in the house as a security guard. She wasn't sure he would do much but lick an intruder, but his size was a deterrent enough.

Rosie and Lucy drove home to Olive Wood and fed Tiny at Mr. Thompson's before bringing him back to the house.

"Can Tiny have a bath with me?" Lucy asked.

Rosie stifled a laugh, "Uhh... no. I don't think he would like that."

Lucy settled for Tiny sitting outside the bathroom with Rosie. Lucy serenaded them both with songs she had learned that day at kinder, then Rosie helped her out and into her pyjamas. Rosie left the pair to go play in Lucy's room while she went to the kitchen, deciding to order pizza for dinner. As she walked down the hall, she overheard Lucy begin to introduce Tiny to her dolls and her beloved Sheet. "Come in, Tiny. Come on. You can meet my doll, Lillian."

What a day, Rosie thought. She remembered when she and Dee had crept up the hall to ghost hunt, and smiled to herself. She couldn't remember the last time she had felt so silly, and she wondered if there wasn't some truth to what Dee had said the week before about Rosie needing something fun in her life. She pulled a voucher for pizza off the fridge and put her handbag on to the bench, digging for her phone.

An icy scream from the other end of the house made Rosie stop in her tracks, the pizza voucher fluttered to the floor, forgotten. Tiny began barking furiously. Rosie had heard a lot of screams from Lucy in the last five years - excitement, anger, the time she got stung by a bee and Ben had sat holding an ice pack to Lucy's foot for two hours. This one was different. Pain and terror. Rosie's heart picked up as she bolted down the hall to Lucy's room. At the doorway, Tiny was pulling Lucy by the back of her shirt out of the door. Rosie gasped, thinking for one horrifying moment that he had hurt Lucy. Then the smell of smoke hit her nostrils, and she looked up to see a small fire on the rug in Lucy's room, half of Lucy's sheet burning brightly. Rosie felt frozen for a second, as though her brain couldn't process what it was seeing.

"My sheet!" Lucy shouted, struggling to get away from Tiny, reaching with her small hands towards the room. Tiny held tightly, pulling her further down the hall. Rosie jolted into action, and ran into the room, her feet falling on dirt and pine needles and began to stomp out the fire with her shoe. The fire went out quickly enough; it hadn't had the chance to take hold of the surrounding items. Still, half the sheet was burnt, pieces of it flaking away to ash, the rug below was scorched and the fibres melted into a congealed mass. Down the hall, the fire alarm began to go off, with a shrill shrieking. Rosie went down and stood on tiptoe to press the button to silence it.

Lucy and Tiny were sitting in the middle of the lounge, where Tiny had dragged her, Lucy crying pitifully into Tiny's fur. Rosie burst into tears and fell to her knees, pulling Lucy into her lap.

"Baby, what happened? Are you okay?"

"Is Sheet gone?" Lucy asked.

"We can fix it. Some is gone, but it will just be a little smaller."

Rosie pulled Lucy back from her and began looking her over. Bits of Lucy's hair were singed at the bottom, she held out Lucy's arms and Lucy yelped, pulling away from her. Lucy's right forearm was deep red and blistered in spots, and Rosie gasped at the sight of it. She stood quickly, swinging

Lucy into her arms and shuffling her on to her hip to carry her to the kitchen sink.

"We have to run that under cold water, Luce."

She propped Lucy on the bench and turned on the tap, holding Lucy's arm beneath the stream, as Tiny butted his head against Rosie and whined. Rosie reached out with her other hand to pat him in gratitude.

"Thank you, Tiny. You're a good boy."

Lucy was sniffling steadily; her face screwed up in pain.

"Lucy, how did the fire start?"

"The girl did it. The one in my room."

"Lucy, there is no girl. She's not real. Did you start the fire?"

Lucy shook her head, "It *was* the girl. She was mad and then the fire started and I tried to save my sheet, but Tiny took me out. Is it going to be okay? Can I have it?"

Lucy popped the thumb of her other hand in her mouth, something she hadn't done since she was a toddler. Rosie sighed and closed her eyes for a second, to steady herself. Under the water, Lucy's arm was an angry red, the blistering made Rosie's knees feel weak, and her stomach rolled with nausea. They needed to go to the hospital. Keeping one hand on Lucy, she reached behind her on the counter and fumbled for her handbag and phone. She dialled for 000 and waited for the operator.

James stared at his phone. Violet was reading quietly in her room, and he could hear her sounding out words she was unfamiliar with. He had been hoping to catch Rosie at kinder drop off this morning and apologise if he had made her uncomfortable on Friday, but Violet had misplaced her shoes, and by the time they got to kindergarten Lucy was already playing in the dress-up corner, and Rosie was long gone. He just didn't want things to be awkward between them, they still had to work together, and Violet and Lucy were such good friends. It would be a shame if they didn't see each other outside of kinder anymore because he and Rosie were avoiding each other. Additionally, he had to admit he just wanted to hear her voice, and this also made him hesitant. He had been thinking all weekend about how hard it must be for Rosie to trust in relationships again; he had only just started to wonder if his own heart was ready for one. He picked up his coffee and sipped it. No matter what, he should just smooth things over. Decided, he picked up his phone and dialled Rosie's number from his contacts.

"Hello?"

James took a deep breath, "Hi, Rosie. It's James. I just wanted to touch base with you and apologise if I made things awkward or-"

"James, I'm sorry to cut you off. It's fine, honestly. I'm just at the hospital at the moment, though. I really have to go. Can I call you tomorrow or something?"

Rosie sounded distracted and upset, her words tumbling out in a rush. And now he could hear the sounds in the background of hospital chatter, an intercom paging someone to the emergency room.

"Are you okay?" He asked. "Are you sick? Is Lucy okay?"

On the other end of the phone, Rosie drew a shuddering breath, and he could hear her begin to cry. Panic flooded him.

"Rosie?"

"There was a fire, not a bad one, but Lucy burnt her arm.

We came in the ambulance, and she is going to be okay, but we have to go to the GP for dressing changes. I have to go through. I need to call a cab to take us... I don't know? Maybe my grandma's. I tried to call my friend, but she isn't answering, and my mother... she doesn't drive. I just can't think at the moment."

"Rosie, I will pick you and Lucy up. What hospital are you at?"

Rosie sniffed, "No, it's okay. I can't ask you to do that. It's late, and Violet would already be in bed."

James peeked around the corner at Violet who had put down her book and was curled up on her side, looking at the moving stars that drifted across her ceiling from her night light.

"Actually," James lied, "she's staying at my sister's tonight. So, it's fine. I would like to do this for you. It sounds like you've had a rough night."

"I just..." Rosie sighed, "I should be able to manage this on my own. I'm just tapped out."

"Then let me tap in," James said.

Twenty minutes later, James pulled up outside the hospital in the pick-up zone. He had dropped Violet to Brooke's house on his way, his sister meeting him at the car in her night-gown and taking a sleeping Violet from his arms.

"She's going to be fine, I've set up the trundle bed in Audrey's room."

"Thank you for this, Brooke."

She waved the thanks away with her hand, "Is the little girl going to be okay? How did the fire start?"

James had shrugged, "I didn't even ask, to be honest. I

think she will be okay, but Rosie sounded exhausted and stressed. I just wanted to help."

Brooke had kissed him on the cheek, "You're a good man."

Now, James saw Rosie exiting the glass doors of the emergency room; Lucy cradled in her arms, her little bandaged arm tucked protectively against her chest. He jumped out of the car and hurried over to her, easing Lucy from Rosie who, to his surprise, uttered no protest and offered her up gratefully before shaking out her shoulders and wincing a little.

"Thank you," she said.

"It's fine," he assured her and began placing Lucy into Violet's car seat, being careful of her injured arm. He closed the door softly and turned to Rosie.

"Are you okay? You didn't get burned?"

Rosie shook her head, "The fire started in Lucy's room. It wasn't big, but her sheet was on fire - the little one, she carries with her? She tried to save it and hurt herself. Luckily, Tiny was there, and he pulled her away."

James opened the passenger door for Rosie, "Tiny?"

"My neighbour's dog. We are minding him for a while. I have had to leave him back at his house for the night. I don't want to take Lucy back to our house tonight. In case the fire was electrical or something. So, I couldn't leave Tiny there either for the same reason."

James climbed into his seat beside Rosie. She smelled of smoke; he noticed her shoes were marked with soot.

"You don't know how it started?"

"No idea. Lucy said it was the imaginary friend that lives in her room, which is obviously untrue. I can't figure out how Lucy could have done it herself, though. I only own a BBQ lighter that is in the top shelf of the kitchen cabinets. It must have been an electrical thing, right? We have had a lot of bulbs burn out in that room in the last week or so. It's an old house."

James put on his indicator and pulled out of the hospital driveway, "That does sound a bit suspicious. It would be worth calling your real estate tomorrow. I think you're right not to stay there tonight though. Where is your grandmother's house?"

Rosie gave him directions, and they drove in silence for a few minutes.

James cleared his throat, "Rosie, I know this isn't a good time, but I just want to apologise for what happened the other day. I don't want things to be weird between us. I do like you, but if you're not ready, or don't want to, obviously I'm not going to say anything about it again. I hope we can still be friendly for the girls."

"Of course we can. It was nothing against you. It's just been a strange time for me lately. I've had a lot on my mind... you know that missing woman? Hannah? She was a client of mine. And Lucy! I just don't know what is going on with her. The stealing, and then the fire, and this imaginary friend who she seems scared of and won't stop talking about. And of course, there is Ben, and missing him, and I'm still trying to figure out where I fit in this world without him. The timing was just not great."

"I understand," James said. "Well not really, because I haven't lived it. But I get it. God, Hannah Avery was your client? Jesus, Rosie, that's awful. My brother in law has been working the case."

"I don't suppose he is close to finding her?" Rosie asked.

"No. I'm sorry."

Rosie sighed, "Make a left up here, near that white fence."

James flicked on his indicator, and Rosie directed him to her grandmother's house; he guided the car up the driveway under a sprawling flame tree and shut off the engine.

"Let me help you get Lucy out. I can carry her up for you."

Rosie shook her head, "It's fine, thank you, though. And thank you for picking us up. You didn't have to, but I'm glad you did."

Rosie lifted Lucy out of the car seat and shifted the weight of her bag on her shoulder to balance the load. She waved a goodbye with her fingertips, and walked up the path to the stairs. James waited by the car until he saw a light go on and the door open, making sure she got safely inside.

CHAPTER 17

Rosie opened her eyes to daylight filtering through the blinds in her old room at June's house. She had spent so many nights here growing up that June had converted her sewing room into a bedroom for Rosie. Last night, June had answered the door quickly, almost as though she had expected Rosie to arrive at any moment. Rosie had put Lucy into one of the twin beds in the room and collapsed herself, stripping off her jeans and sleeping in her shirt. She rubbed at her face and sat up. Lucy wasn't in the room, she must have slipped out earlier. Rosie got out of bed and pulled on her jeans from the chair she left them on the night before, wrinkling her nose at the smell of smoke that was still on them. She caught sight of her watch and gasped. It was a quarter to ten already - she couldn't remember the last time she had slept so late. Rosie grabbed her handbag and rummaged for the dressings the hospital had given her the night before but found them gone; it looked like June had also crept into the room while she was out cold.

· · ·

Padding down the hall, she heard voices in the kitchen and came out to Lucy perched on the kitchen bench and June finishing up a dressing change on Lucy's arm.

"How is it?" Rosie asked, kissing June on the cheek, and then reaching out her arms to help Lucy down from the counter.

"It looks sore," June admitted, "It is quite blistered, but Lucy was a trouper and didn't complain at all."

"I was brave," Lucy agreed.

Rosie put the kettle on and began to make a cup of tea, "I'm sorry I slept so late."

"You must have needed it," Lucy said, wisely and Rosie laughed knowing that Lucy must be mimicking something June had said while she was sleeping.

"I must have."

Rosie took a seat at the kitchen table and began finger combing Lucy's hair, trying to tame it into a ponytail.

"I was thinking we would go home this morning and take a shower and make sure Tiny is okay. Then maybe we could come and stay here for a couple of nights while the real estate sends an electrician out to check the house and make sure there are no more fires. Does that sound okay?"

Lucy nodded, "Except I will stay here, I don't want to go back. Can you bring Tiny here? And Sheet?"

Rosie felt her heart break thinking about Lucy's beloved sheet in flames the night beforehand. Of course Lucy wouldn't want to go home right now. Her poor little girl.

"If it's okay with Grandma June, you can stay here. I will go home and get some things and Tiny?" She looked to June for confirmation, and June nodded. She wrapped her arms around Lucy, "Then it's settled. I'll grab Tiny and your sheet and then come back. It will be like a sleepover. You and me and Tiny and Grandma June."

"And Grandpa," Lucy said.

Rosie frowned, "Grandpa Bill? Daddy's father? Peanut, he lives far away, remember? Down in Melbourne. That's way too far to come for a sleepover."

Lucy turned around, the ponytail Rosie was tying pulling sideways on Lucy's head, "Not Grandpa Bill. Grandpa Frank."

Rosie felt her heart thump out of time in her chest. She looked to June who stood frozen holding a mug of tea out to Rosie. She had never discussed Frank with Lucy; she didn't even know his name and Lucy had never asked. She waited for June to say something about discussing the photos on the wall, something innocent and easy to explain, but instead June stared at her like a deer caught in headlights, her mouth opening and closing with nothing coming out. *Something strange is happening here*, Rosie thought, *this feels like I've walked into something halfway and everyone knows what is happening but me.*

"What's my line?" She said, only registering that the words had left her mouth as she spoke them.

Even Lucy seemed to pick up on the strange tension in the air, looking back and forth between June and Rosie.

"Rosie," June began, and then the back door opened, and a man walked though it, carrying a loaf of bread. He stopped dead as he saw Rosie, the bread swaying in his hand which had begun to shake.

Rosie pushed her chair back and stood abruptly, scraping it loudly along the floor.

"Oh my god."

"Rosemary," he said.

She held her hands in front of her body and stepped in front of Lucy as though to shield her, "You? You were outside my house!"

She recognised him immediately as the man that had been lurking in the street the week beforehand, the one she assumed was on drugs. *My god, had he been following her?*

"I just wanted to see you," he said. "To make sure you were okay."

"Are you kidding me? You don't stand outside someone's house to see if they're okay. You knock on the door. You pick up a phone. And why? No. Don't answer. I truly don't care."

June put her hand on Rosie's arm, "Let's just all calm down. Have your cup of tea. Frank grabbed some bread - Lucy wanted French toast, I'll make some, and we can talk about it."

"Lucy wanted... what? French toast?" A sudden realisation dawned on Rosie, "He's been here all morning, with Lucy. Hasn't he?"

"He's Grandpa Frank, Mama," Lucy said. "He's your Daddy."

Rosie put her face in her hands and took a deep breath.

She opened her eyes and looked around the room, "Okay. Okay. Here is the thing. I don't *know* you. I'm sorry. You are just a random guy that showed up outside my house and then appeared in my grandmother's kitchen. I am sorry if that's hurtful, but I don't want to have tea and goddamn French toast with you. I don't want you to check on me to see if I'm okay. You had twenty-five years to do that. You don't get to spend the morning with my daughter without my knowledge or permission. You aren't my father. I know what a father is because Lucy had the best father. Lucy and I are going now. Have a good morning. Thank you for letting us stay the night, Grandma June."

Rosie took Lucy's hand and walked out the front door.

"Mama, how will we get home?" Lucy asked.

"I'll call Dee," Rosie said, fumbling for her phone.

"But where will we stay? What about Tiny?"

Rosie sighed and knelt down in front of Lucy, "Honey, I will figure it out, okay? Everything will be okay. Just... I have to go now, alright? I just need to be... away."

Slowly, Lucy nodded. Rosie pulled her daughter into a quick hug and pressed Dee's name in her contacts.

"Dee, I need you to come and grab me. Also, can I keep that really big dog at your house for a while?"

Fifteen minutes later, Dee pulled up in her battered sedan. Rosie ushered Lucy into the backseat, and into the car seat Dee kept for times when she babysat Lucy or one of her many nieces and nephews. Dee gasped when she saw Lucy's arm, and plied them with questions about what had happened as they drove back to Rosie's so she could collect her car and Tiny. Rosie filled her in about the fire, and James taking them to June's house. And then about Frank's unexpected arrival this morning. Dee fussed over Lucy, pulling over the car at one point so she could hop in the backseat and cuddle Lucy and assure her that she was the bravest little girl Dee had ever known. As they neared Rosie's house, Lucy fell asleep, and Dee finally was able to get the full story out of Rosie about Frank, both of them trying to avoid the topic as much as possible while Lucy was listening.

.   .   .

"He just, what? Showed back up?" Dee asked incredulous.

Rosie nodded, "Just waltzed on in with supplies like he had been having breakfast every morning. Which, *god*, maybe he has. I don't know how often he kept in contact with June. I've never asked, and she has never mentioned. For all I know, he stops by all the time."

"And where did he say he has been? Why did he leave? Did he explain it?" Dee asked.

"No idea. I didn't ask. I left."

Dee was silent for a few moments, "You didn't hang around for an explanation? I mean, he kind of owes you one, after all these years."

Something in the way she asked the question made Rosie's anger flare.

"Of course I didn't ask! What explanation could he possibly give me? Parents don't leave their kids without a word, and never send so much as a birthday card, and then get to just turn back up!"

"Still," Dee said, "He *is* your dad. If you don't listen to his reasons, then you will never be able to get closure on this."

Rosie snorted, "He is *not* my dad. Biology doesn't make you a dad. Ben was a dad. Poppa? He was a dad to me. A dad shows up. I don't even know this man. I don't need closure. I was doing just fine until he blew into town and started chatting with my daughter. June should have known better."

Dee pulled into Rosie's street and came to a stop alongside the front of the house. She turned to Rosie, "You know, in all the time I've known you, you have never even brought him up. Not like how I do with my dad, who also wasn't around, but I just mention little things sometimes, you know? I might say that he used to cook the best spaghetti sauce, or my brother has his dimples. For you, it was like Frank never existed. It just seems like... you were hurting about it. Which is why I never pushed the matter."

"I'm not hurting about it."

"I think you are."

"Well, I'm not!"

"Rosie. Usually, when people are hurting, they either talk about something all the time or never at all. Your complete denial of his existence says to me that there is a hell of a lot of baggage you need to work through. All I'm saying is, talk to him. Let him explain, and then forgive him or tell him to piss off. Have a reaction."

Rosie felt heat rise to her cheeks and angry tears filling her eyes, "You know what? Of absolutely everyone, I really thought you would have my back on this!"

Dee reached out for her, "I do. I absolutely have your back-"

Rosie opened the door and climbed out, tripping over her feet, "Just don't. Thank you for the ride. Lucy and I will be fine."

Dee climbed out of the car, "Don't be like this. You can't stay here until the place is cleared by an electrician."

"We will stay with Kate!" Rosie pulled Lucy out of the seat, juggling her in one arm with her handbag in the other. Lucy began to stir and open her eyes sleepily. Rosie stormed towards the house, and Lucy began to stiffen in her arms.

"No, Mama! I don't want to go in!"

"It's okay, Lucy, we are just getting some clothes."

"No! No!" Lucy struggled and began to kick her legs to get down.

"For god's sake," Rosie burst out.

Dee called after her, "Just let her stay with me and we can go back to my house after you get some clothes."

"We are fine!" Rosie shouted. "Just go!"

Lucy began to scream and shout, and then bit Rosie's arm. Rosie let out a yelp, and promptly put Lucy down on the ground, not altogether gently. Lucy, shocked, stopped wailing and looked at Rosie wide-eyed.

"*For fuck's sake!*" Rosie shouted at the sky.

She looked over at Dee, who was raising one eyebrow at her. They stared at each other for a moment before they both burst out laughing.

"You're a goddamn wreck, Parker," Dee gasped, slapping her leg.

Rosie sat down on the driveway beside Lucy, laughing until tears ran out of her eyes. Dee came over and sat beside them, and the both cackled while Lucy looked from one to the other as though they had both gone mad. Finally, they caught their breath, and Dee pulled Rosie's arm towards her to examine the bite mark. Two red half crescents of teeth marks had begun to welt on Rosie's skin.

"My goodness, Lucy! You really bit your Mama hard! What on earth came over you?"

Lucy offered no explanation and Rosie took a long breath.

"Okay. Lucy. You stay out here with Dee while I go and get some clothes. We will talk about the biting later. Then, we will collect Tiny and go to Dee's place."

"I want to go with Aunty Dee now," Lucy said.

Dee looked at Rosie, "We are going to the same place

anyway? She can come with me, and then you can take your time with collecting stuff and getting Tiny."

Rosie agreed, and Dee bundled Lucy back into her car and drove off. Rosie waved goodbye and sighed, the hysteria of earlier fading.

Fumbling in her bag for the keys, she unlocked the door and stepped inside. The acrid smell of smoke hit Rosie's nostrils, making her cover her cough once, loudly. The house seems strangely quiet, and she had an unsettled feeling inside her, as though she shouldn't be here, as though it was no longer her house. She shook her head to herself, trying to push away the whispers of her instincts saying she should leave immediately. Shutting the door behind her, she made her way quickly up the hall to her room and began shoving clothes into an overnight bag. She worked quickly, gathering jeans and t-shirts, her toothbrush from the en-suite, her camera gear. As she pulled out her tripod, she noticed the old Polaroid camera, sitting on her desk and took that too, grabbing a foil-wrapped cartridge of film from the desk drawer in her room. She carried all these things to the door of the house and deposited them beside it and made her way back up to Lucy's room.

Here, the smell was stronger; Lucy's sheet was abandoned on the centre of the rug, the scorched fibres melted into each other. She walked purposefully into the room, pulling open Lucy's drawers and ripping clothes out of them, not noticing what she grabbed as the whispers of unease from before began to shout. Something wasn't right. She grabbed the burnt sheet and Lucy's toothbrush and shampoo from the bathroom and carried an armload of things back to the front of the house. She was shaking as she ripped open the film cartridge and put it into the back of the Polaroid camera. She didn't stop to tell herself she was being stupid; she didn't try to talk herself of it. Rosie walked back up the hall, stopped at the door of Lucy's room, and raised the Polaroid to her eye. She snapped a photo and waited as the camera whirred and the photo popped out the bottom. Then without waiting for it to develop, she dropped the photo into her shirt pocket, turned on her heel and walked swiftly back to the kitchen, gathered her things and left the house.

CHAPTER 18

Outside the house, Rosie popped the boot of the rental car and put her bags inside. Then she headed to Mr. Thompson's to let herself in the back gate; Tiny was dancing in excitement at the sight of her. Rosie's phone rang as she ruffled Tiny's fur, and tried to connect his leash to his collar. She answered the call to find out that her car had been fixed and was ready to be picked up. The accident seemed so long ago now, so much had happened since then. She did some mental work in her head, she still had to call the real estate about a possible electrical issue, and drop Tiny to Dee's. Then she needed to reschedule shoots for the next couple of days, call Lucy's kinder to tell them she would be away for a few awhile, and call her doctor to bring Lucy in for review. And now she needed to figure out how to squeeze in dropping the car back to the rental place - and somehow get from there to her car at the mechanics. She groaned and turned to Tiny.

"You made a good choice living life as a dog; being a human is a lot of work."

Tiny licked her hand. Rosie sat down on one of the outdoor chairs and started making phone calls, beginning with the real estate and Lucy's kinder and ending with the doctor. She shot two quick emails to her clients to let them know here had been a family emergency, and she would be in touch to reschedule in the next few days. Then she dialled James.

Forty minutes later, Rosie saw James pulling up outside the car rentals.

"Thank you for picking me up," she said as she slid into the passenger seat.

"Are you kidding? I love an excuse to take a long lunch."

Rosie smiled, "I just need to get to the mechanics on South Road in Clayton Hills, do you know the one? Dee has Lucy at the moment, and she was a bit upset this morning, I didn't want to drag her out again if I could help it."

James pulled out into the flow of traffic, "Absolutely understandable. She had a rough night. You didn't end up staying at your Grandma's?"

"What?"

"You stayed at your Grandma's last night, didn't you? You didn't leave Lucy with her?"

Rosie sighed, "Oh, yeah. We did. It's just... my dad showed up this morning. So, we didn't stay."

James nodded but didn't say anything for ten minutes, deciding whether he should press the matter further or let it go.

He coasted to a stop at the traffic lights, putting on his indicator, and took a breath before saying, "So, you don't get along with your dad, huh?"

Rosie laughed, "I don't even know my dad. I haven't seen him in twenty-five years."

"Wow," James said, in disbelief, "He just showed up? Did your Grandma know he was coming?"

They arrived out front of the mechanic, and James put the car in park. He turned to Rosie, who found she was having trouble not crying, as though all the emotions of the last twenty-four hours were catching up with her. Rosie buried her face in her hands, her hair falling forward and shielding her. She doubled over in the seat and sobbed, James quietly rubbing her back and saying nothing.

Finally, she sniffed and sat back. James reached across and popped the glove compartment and handed her a box of travel tissues.

"Thank you," she said, blowing her nose, "God, I'm such a wreck. I'm so sorry, I'm not usually like this but it just feels like things *keep happening*. You know? It's like, you're barely past the last crisis, and bam! There is another one."

"I can completely understand how it would be a shock to you," James said. "Seeing your dad after all this time? And you just had an awful fright with Lucy last night. Cut yourself some slack, Rosie, anyone would be upset right now."

"Oh, god, Lucy. She was so upset this morning she wouldn't even go in the house, she *bit* me when I tried to carry her inside. And Frank! Shocked is an understatement. I just don't understand why he would turn up now, after so many years. It seems like such a cop-out, just showing up when he feels like he wants to. That's not how parenting works. You don't just leave because it's hard and then turn up because it suits you. Even Kate, my mum, who - believe me - is not a well person, showed up. She was there every day, even though I could see it was hard for her. Christ, I cannot believe I've found a less present parent than Kate." Rosie laughed bitterly.

James sat silently for a moment, "I don't even know what I would do if Violet's mum turned up one day. Sometimes, I think that would be great for Violet, to have a Mum? But sometimes, I think it's easier without her. Amelia was not a stable parent. And when she left? Man, I could have killed her. Walking out on this little girl, and Violet was just the sweetest, easiest baby in the world. I just think, maybe Amelia just didn't deserve her, if she could leave her so easily."

"And leave you?" Rosie asked.

"Me too, I guess."

"How old was Violet when she left?"

"Barely eight months old. It was drugs." he said by way of an explanation.

Impulsively, he pulled out his wallet and reached behind the cards, pulling out a creased, worn photo. He looked at it for a moment and handed it to Rosie. Rosie took the image in her hands and looked at it. It was a snapshot. In it there was a chubby baby, Violet, with her big brown eyes like James's, and she was being held by a beautiful woman with long straight dark hair and incredible deep green eyes, framed by thick lashes. Amelia, Rosie assumed. She looked vaguely familiar, and Rosie tried to place where she knew her from. She felt a strange stab at seeing the photograph, the way the edges had softened by James's fingers. He has spent hours looking at this image, she knew. She handed it back.

"I don't know why I keep it," James said. "It's just I can't bring myself to get rid of it. It's the only one I have of her. She hated having her photo taken after she had Violet. She was self-conscious about her looks after she had a baby, I guess. Violet never asks about her. Does Lucy ask about her dad?"

"Not anymore. She used to talk about Ben, but she doesn't now. She hasn't for months. I'm half terrified she is forgetting him, and the other half of me thinks that it's a kindness. I would hate her to grieve forever."

James nodded, "That makes sense. I think you can have room for both those feelings in your life."

Rosie sat there for a moment, staring out the window, "What do you think would make you leave your wife and child?"

James let out a low whistle, "Gosh. There are so many reasons people just walk out, Rosie. Me? Well, maybe I would have left Amelia if she kept running off and doing drugs and we couldn't get her straight. I just don't know that I would have been able to trust her with Violet, and I would have worried she might put her in danger. Violet, though? Nothing could make me leave her, unless I guess, if I thought *I* was a danger to her. Sometimes I wonder if that was what made Amelia go, too. I know she loved Violet. When the anger runs out of me, and I stop thinking 'how could she', then I think, well, maybe she knew she couldn't be a good mum to Violet just then. Maybe she left her to save her."

Rosie thought about that for a moment; she couldn't imagine leaving Lucy, not for anything in the world.

James cleared his throat, "Rosie, we could spend all day

wondering why your dad left, but if you really want to know you could just ask him."

Dee had said that, Rosie thought, *right before I snapped at her*. She and Dee had never fought before. Not even in high school when girls could be so mean to each other. They had always had each other's back.

"I *could* ask him," she conceded.

"Hey," James said. "I'm not saying you don't have the right to be angry. I would be angry. I'm just wondering what I would want Violet to do if Amelia showed up in twenty years time. And I think for all her flaws, I would want her to hear Amelia out. If for nothing else, for closure for Violet. She would deserve that. You deserve that."

"I'll think about it," Rosie agreed. She opened the door and thanked him for the ride, "And for letting me cry in your car."

"Anytime," James said. "I do framing *and* car counselling, actually. I'm going to have business cards made up."

Impulsively, Rosie leaned over and kissed him on the cheek; she inhaled the smell of him, wood shavings and aftershave.

Smiling, she stepped out of the car and waved goodbye before walking into the mechanics.

James watched her go, her red hair catching the sunlight as she moved. He looked down at the photograph of Amelia still in his hand from when Rosie handed it back to him.

"What do you reckon?" he asked the photograph.

But her already knew what Amelia would have said; he could almost hear her tinkling laugh in his mind, "Oh, you are so gone for her, Jimmy."

Amelia was the only person in his life that had ever called him that because she knew he hated it and she loved riling him up. That's what Amelia would have said. She would have been right.

CHAPTER 19

Rosie pulled back up at Dee's place after stopping back at Mr. Thompson's for her bags and Tiny. She let the large dog into Dee's backyard, and he immediately began sniffing around happily, startling the fat ginger cat sleeping on the porch - who dashed inside the house through the cat flap. She pushed the front door inwards and called out to Dee to let her know she had arrived. Lucy was sitting on the couch with a plate of cut-up apple, watching cartoons. She looked over at Rosie, her eyes filled with sadness and guilt.

Dee came up beside Rosie and whispered, "She has been very upset about biting you."

Rosie sighed and dropped the bags on the ground. She went and sat beside Lucy and pulled the little girl into her lap.

"It's okay, peanut. It's been a really hard couple of days, hey?"

Lucy nodded and began to cry softly.

"How is your arm, baby? Is it sore?"

Lucy nodded again. Rosie lay down on the couch and

curled around Lucy, stroking her hair and singing to her softly until the crying stopped, and Lucy's breathing slowed to a steady rhythm. She lifted her head and peeked at Lucy's face; she was sound asleep.

Rosie untangled herself from her sleeping daughter and slipped out, meeting Dee in the kitchen. She handed Rosie a freshly made cup of tea.

"Thank you," Rosie said, gratefully.

"I was making myself one anyway," Dee replied.

"I didn't mean for the cup of tea. Well, yes, for the cup of tea, but for other things too. Everything, I guess."

Dee gave her a quick one-armed hug and pulled out a chair for Rosie before taking a seat herself.

"I'm sorry I upset you," Dee said. "I know it must have seemed like such a shock to you, seeing him after all this time. I should have just listened to you and let you feel your feelings. I do think you should give him a chance to explain himself, though. If only so you can put this to bed. If he is garbage, then he's garbage. I'm your friend, and if you say we hate him, then we do."

Rosie smiled, "You were right."

"I usually am."

Rosie snorted, "Don't be annoying about it. I just wasn't ready to hear it right then. James said basically the same thing, actually."

Dee raised an eyebrow and delicately sipped her tea, "You spoke to James about it? In the short time between when we had our very first fight and now, you had time to go and talk to your boyfriend?"

"Well, he is just so *dreamy*."

Dee burst out laughing and spilt tea over the tablecloth. Rosie got up and grabbed paper towels and threw them to her.

"If you're done ruining your mum's linens," Rosie said. "Yes, I spoke to James, he dropped me off to pick up my car from the mechanic."

Rosie filled Dee in on the conversation, and about how James had spoken to her about Violet's mum and her leaving.

"I just can't imagine leaving Lucy, ever. I can't relate to why you would do that, and it feels like there can't be a good enough reason, you know? James showed me a photo of Amelia. She was gorgeous. Like, actually model gorgeous. She looked so familiar, and I can't think why? Maybe she was at a wedding I have shot or something?"

"Maybe. So, are you going to go and talk to Frank?"

"I'll think about it. I want to get Lucy settled back at home first and make sure she is okay. Frank can wait."

"That's fair," Dee stood up, "Come on. We are going to do a proper hug. It's the only way to end a fight. We talked it out; we drank tea, now we hug and let it go. It's how my mum settled all the fights between my siblings and me."

Rosie laughed and pushed back the chair and let Dee pull her into an embrace.

"Ouch!" She said.

Dee pulled back, "What? Did I squeeze you too hard?"

"No, something in my pocket stabbed my boob," She reached into her shirt pocket and pulled out the Polaroid she had taken earlier.

"What the hell is that?" Dee asked, peering at it.

"A photo I took of Lucy's room."

The pair looked at it; the whole photo was blown out to a bright white.

"Is it supposed to look like that?" Dee asked.

"No, maybe it was dodgy film."

"What were you trying to take a photo of?"

Rosie blushed, "Lucy's room. I've gone off the deep end. I just wondered if maybe it was film, we tried the other day with digital, but the photo of the old man was a film photo. I know it's stupid."

Dee smiled, "It's not stupid. I mean, I *am* incredibly surprised you entertained that idea. Maybe I can get you to believe in fairies after all."

"I half wanted there to be something. Just to have an explanation for Lucy, because if it isn't something, then it means she is... I don't know. Just not the same happy little girl she used to be. I feel like I'm doing a really awful job of being her mum. The stealing, and the imaginary friends, and being scared to sleep in her room. This fire? If it isn't electrical, then did Lucy start it?"

"With what?" Dee asked.

"Christ, I don't know. Maybe she stole matches or a lighter from somewhere. The point is, I don't know - and shouldn't a mother know these things?"

"You're not a bad mother, Rosie," Dee took Rosie's hands in hers, "I mean that. I would definitely tell you if you were dropping the ball here. Let's order pizza, okay? It's been a really weird couple of days. We can worry about your failings as a mother tomorrow."

Rosie laughed despite herself, "Pizza sounds good."

Brooke flicked on the news on the television in the kitchen while she crumbed chicken schnitzels for dinner. Michael came in, smelling like body wash from his shower, and wearing boxer shorts and a t-shirt.

"You've dressed up for dinner, I see," Brooke commented.

"Nothing but then best for you, baby," Michael glanced over at the television, "Now, why would you want to watch the news? There is never anything good on it. It's depressing."

Brooke placed a crumbed chicken breast on the oven tray, "Not true. Just yesterday there were dogs that visited sick kids in the hospital. It was very heart-warming."

Michael opened the fridge and grabbed a beer, "Sure. Of course, you could argue it was depressing because of the sick kids."

Brooke stopped midway through dunking a chicken breast in egg and looked stricken, clearly not having thought of that side of it before.

Suddenly, Hannah Avery's face popped up on the screen, "News emerged tonight that the missing twenty-six-year-old, Hannah Avery, may have been with another man the night of her disappearance, lending weight to the theory she may have been having an affair-"

"What the hell," Michael said, putting down his beer and reaching for the remote to turn it up.

"Hannah was having an affair?" Brooke asked.

Michael shushed her and then immediately cast her an apologetic look, but she shook her head to say it was okay.

The news was showing an image taken from a mobile phone,

in the foreground was a smiling trio of friends posing, behind them and off to the right was a woman that fit the description of Hannah Avery and what she was wearing that night. She had her shoes off and was carrying them, and appeared to be leaning on a man dressed in slacks and a long-sleeved button-up shirt.

"That could be anyone," Michael said to convince himself. The image was poorly lit, the couple in the background difficult to make out.

"Why would they be reporting this? Do the police know about this photo?" Brooke asked

Michael shook his head, "You know as much as I do about this image."

He placed his beer on the counter and looked at Brooke.

"You have to go, don't you?" She asked.

He nodded, "I'm sorry."

"It's okay. Go. I'll put dinner in the fridge for you."

He kissed her cheek and left the room to get dressed again.

Brooke turned back to the image that was flashing on screen again; something about the photo gave her a strange feeling as though she had seen this scene before. It was familiar somehow. She squinted at the television, trying to pull the couple into focus, but it was useless. She listened to Michael saying goodbye to the girls up the hall and went back to crumbing the chicken.

Dee turned to Rosie, "What do you make of that? You think Hannah Avery was having an affair?"

Rosie shook her head, "I don't know. I don't think

anyone can assume from a photo that may or may not be Hannah that she was having an affair. Either way, does it matter? She is still missing. It's still out of character for her to have not been in contact with anyone. Even if she was seeing that guy, so what? Maybe he has something to do with the disappearance."

Dee sighed and grabbed another slice of pizza, "You're absolutely right. People will be jerks about it though."

The television cut to reporters standing outside of Hannah and Bryan's house.

"Jesus Christ," Rosie swore, "Can you imagine having your wife missing and everyone camping out the front of your house on the worst time of your life?"

Bryan came out of the house with one of Hannah's brothers. Rosie barely recognised Bryan; he looked like he had aged ten years. He appeared to have carefully chosen a button-up shirt and combed his hair, but he hadn't shaved in a few days, and his eyes were bloodshot, and there was a look in them that Rosie had never seen before, a wildness.

Hannah's brother stayed close to Bryan as he stood before the cameras, his hand on Bryan's shoulder. Bryan cleared his throat and began to speak, "My name is Bryan Avery, Hannah is my wife," his voice cracked, but he took a breath and carried on, "Hannah's family and I wanted to respond to statements being made that Hannah was having an affair at the, uhh, the time of her disappearance." He glanced down, and Rosie realised he was reading from palm cards. Hannah's brother stared defiantly at the cameras, squeezing Bryan's shoulder in solidarity.

"We wish to make it clear that we do not have any reason

to believe that Hannah was unfaithful," Bryan continued, "Hannah and I are very happy and very much in love. We all miss her very much, and we just want her to come home safely. She is the best person, the very best, you wouldn't meet a more kind-hearted person than Hannah."

Bryan began to cry.

Rosie glanced at Dee who had covered her mouth, her own eyes welling.

Hannah's brother turned Bryan towards him and allowed his brother in law to cry on his shoulder for a moment while reporters peppered them with questions.

Bryan wiped his eyes and looked back to them, "We just want to ask that if anyone did see Hannah that night, either with this man, or anyone else, or alone, please come forward. If you recognise this man, please call the police or the hotline and let them know. We will be holding a candlelight vigil tomorrow night at seven at John Scott Park - to light the way for Hannah to come home."

Bryan and Hannah's brother turned and walked back to the house.

Dee switched off the television.

"Well, that was just awful," she said.

Rosie nodded. She looked up the hallway to where Lucy was sleeping. She wondered how she would ever let Lucy out of her sight in a world where women could just vanish without a trace. Occasionally, when things like this happened, she would wonder if she made a dreadful mistake having children. To love someone so fiercely, and know that they would have to navigate a world with so many shadows in it. She said this to Dee, who reached over with one arm and hugged her.

"There are good things too, Rosie. Look over there for instance," and Dee pointed to the corner of the lounge room where Tiny was curled up on an old quilt, the fat ginger cat sleeping with her back against his stomach. "You always have to look for the good things."

Rosie phone dinged with a text message. James. *I hope your car is running well and Lucy is on the mend. If you ever need me for anything, just shout out.*

Good things.

CHAPTER 20

The next morning Rosie and Dee met over tea in the kitchen. Dee had been up early baking, the kitchen smelled of vanilla and home.

"Good morning," Dee said, perkily.

Rosie grunted a response and slumped in the chair.

"Gosh, you are *not* a morning person. How do you manage sunrise shoots?"

"I fake it," Rosie answered.

Lucy came down into the kitchen clutching the salvaged sheet that Rosie had mended last night, carefully cutting away the burned bits and hemming it on Dee's sewing machine, before giving it a wash and throwing it in the tumble dryer. She had sniffed it cautiously afterwards, but the only smell had been Dee's orange fabric softener she made herself from citrus peels and vinegar.

"Good morning, Lucy Locket!" Dee exclaimed.

Lucy gave her a half-hearted wave. Dee set down fresh croissants and blueberry muffins in front of them and made Lucy a hot chocolate. Rosie discussed Lucy's doctor appointment that morning for a review of the burns and a dressing change.

"The real estate sent me a text this morning to say the electrician has cleared the wiring in the house," Rosie said, "Looks like we can go home tonight."

"No!" Lucy cried.

Dee patted her arm, "It's okay, Lucy."

"I won't go!" Lucy jumped up from the table and ran up the hall, slamming the door to the spare room that she and Rosie had slept in the night before.

Rosie started to get up from the table, but Dee put her hand out, "Just leave her for a bit, Rosie. She's had a big few days. I think she's really scared. Maybe you should stay here for a while."

Rosie sat back down, "I was thinking last night, maybe I should call around for child psychologists. I think it's time."

"That might not be the worst idea. You might even consider talking to one yourself."

"You think I need a shrink?"

"I think everyone needs someone to talk to."

"I have you to talk to," Rosie argued.

Dee let out a sharp burst of laughter, "I am barely qualified to handle my own problems, let alone yours. Seriously though, stay here a few days. Give Lucy a chance to settle after the fire. Speaking of which, have you called Kate?"

Rosie gasped, "I forgot! She will be expecting Lucy to turn up on the kinder bus this afternoon. I'll call this morning. We will stay another night then see what happens. Thank you."

Dee shrugged, "It's fine. The house is too quiet without Meg and her Gregorian chanting anyway."

Rosie got up from the table and rinsed her cup in the

sink, "I'm going to go get dressed and get Lucy ready for that doctors appointment. I'll speak to the doctor about referrals for a child psychologist then too."

Dee waved her away, "Go, get ready. I'll be here all day, slaving away in the kitchen, making delicious miracles. Let me know if you need anything."

Rosie started to leave the room and stopped, "Hey, I was thinking. I think I'm going to go to the vigil tonight for Hannah. Do you want to come with me?"

"Of course," Dee said. "What will we do with Lucy? You don't want to bring her?"

Rosie shook her head, "No, definitely not. I will ask Kate to mind Lucy when I call her. Thank you for coming. I just want to show my support for Bryan and Hannah's family."

Making her way down the hall, Rosie rapped gently on the door to the spare room and opened it. Lucy was lying on the bed with her sheet, staring grumpily out the window.

Rosie came and sat beside her, stroking Lucy's hair and noticing the little details like the dimples on the backs of Lucy's knuckles, and the way she was twisting one of her curls around her fingers; she was still just a little girl. Lucy was still holding her sore arm protectively against her chest. Rosie's heart ached for her daughter.

"I don't like how much we have been fighting lately, Lucy," Rosie said.

Lucy cut her a look filled with anger and defiance. Rosie sighed. What was she going to do? What could she even say? She spent every day with stranger's children photographing them, making them smile and laugh, and yet she couldn't manage to get her own daughter to talk to her.

"Lucy, what can I do? What do you want me to say to make this better? You have to help me here."

Lucy sat up abruptly, "You never believe me!"

"I never believe you?"

Lucy shook her head, angrily, "You never do! I *told* you there was a girl in my room and I *told* you she did the fire! I told you I didn't want to stay in my room and I didn't want to go home! Aunt Dee and Grandma June believe me, so why can't you?"

Lucy's stared at Rosie, challenging her to come up with an answer. Rosie looked helplessly at her daughter, it was such a small thing she was asking, to be believed, but what did that mean? That they never go home? *She spoke to June about this,* she wondered, *When? The morning Frank was there?*

She felt disconnected from Lucy just then, wondering if Frank knew about Lucy's imaginary girl - had he said he believed her? Had he comforted her? She shook her head as though she were trying to erase Frank from her mind.

"I'm sorry, peanut. I just... I can't see her. So, it doesn't feel real to me. I can see the girl is real for you. Can you... tell me about her, maybe?"

Lucy looked at her warily. *She is not buying this for a second,* Rosie thought, but then to her surprise, Lucy nodded.

"She came the day we had the accident. She can't go home. She is nice sometimes, but sometimes she is not friendly. Like... she doesn't make any sense."

Hearing Lucy talk gave Rosie a strange feeling, like she was trying to recall something she was meant to know, it reminded her of the feeling she got when she looked at the photo from the cafe.

"Okay," she said, "And the girl started the fire? How did she do that? Did she have matches, maybe? Or a lighter?"

"No. I don't know how. It was just like one minute she was standing there, and the next she just did the fire. Tiny didn't like her. He wouldn't come in my room, only when the fire was happening."

Rosie took a deep breath, "Alright."

"Do you believe me?"

Rosie wasn't sure what she believed, but she knew there was only one way to answer this question, "Yes. I believe you."

***

The doctor's visit went off without a hitch. Lucy was brave during the dressing change, and the doctor gave her a finger puppet afterwards. Rosie tentatively asked for a referral to a child psychologist stating she had concerns that Lucy might be having some trouble since Ben had died, and came away with a list of places to call. Lucy has asked to go to the park, and Rosie looked dubiously at Lucy's bandaged arm but agreed to the trip, life hadn't been much fun for either of them lately.

Rosie drove them to the big playground by the beach that was mostly empty on a Tuesday in the middle of the day and watched Lucy play while she made phone calls to the people on the list. She gathered information on pricing and waiting lists. Some of them had no openings for weeks, and all of them were more than Rosie could afford, she jotted figures down on a notepad from her bag, and tried to calculate how she might make up the costs somehow. She quickly discounted seeing a therapist herself; there was no way she could afford double therapy bills. She looked at the ibis walking past her.

"Can't even afford to lose your mind these days," she told it.

An old man walking his dog gave her a funny look.

"Christ," she muttered, gathering her things. "Lucy! It's time to go!"

They were making their way back to the car when Rosie's phone rang. It was June. Rosie looked at it for a moment and put it back in her bag without answering. She wasn't ready to deal with whatever was going on between her grandmother and Frank yet. She helped Lucy into the car and buckled her in, her mind turning over the events of the last few days. She had never not answered a call from her grandmother, and she felt a stab of guilt in her heart as well as a softening of the anger she had felt. That had always been how it was for her; June used to say when she was little, "Quick to temper, but quick to forgive."

She sighed as she pulled out of the car park and drove towards Kate's house.

As they pulled up out front, Lucy ran ahead and knocked on the door, hopping from foot to foot.

"C'mon Nanna," she called. "I have to pee!"

Rosie followed up the path, hearing the locks click back and Kate's sharp intake of breath at Lucy's bandaged arm, before Lucy pushed past her and into the house.

"It was the dog!" Kate said, looking accusingly at Rosie.

"No, Mum. It wasn't the dog."

"I called you yesterday because you never called me to tell me how it went. You didn't answer because the dog hurt her!"

Rosie held up her hand, "Can I at least come inside before you start in on me?"

Kate pursed her lips, swung the door open and stepped back. Rosie made her way to the kitchen and put on the kettle. Tea was soothing and routine, on top of everything else, she couldn't deal with Kate having a meltdown right now.

"Well?" Kate demanded, "What happened to her? I hope you remember that I told you not to have that dog there."

"Mum, God! It wasn't the damn dog!" Rosie rubbed her temples, "It's a burn, okay? She got burned."

Kate looked momentarily stunned, "A burn?"

"Yes. There was a fire - a *very, very* small fire - but Lucy got burned. She's going to be fine, though. She's okay."

Kate sat heavily in one of the kitchen chairs while Rosie made a cup of tea and pressed it into her mother's hands. Lucy came into the kitchen, stole a few cookies from the jar Kate kept on the bench and scampered back to the playroom.

"But how did Lucy get burned? I don't understand."

Rosie filled Kate in and made a big deal of Tiny's heroic efforts, which earned her a dubious look from her mother.

"And Mum? Look, don't freak out, okay? But Frank? He's back."

Rosie anxiously studied her mother's face as though at

any moment she might spontaneously combust. Kate's face remained impassive. The seconds ticked on, and Rosie became alarmed, *god, she has gone and stroked out or something.*

"Mum?"

"What?"

"Are you... okay? I know it's a big shock. It was for me too, I barely even-"

"Is he okay?"

"I... have no idea. I didn't ask. I'm not sure I care, to be honest with you."

Kate nodded slowly and stood up, taking her cup to the sink and rinsing it carefully before turning, "So, do you need me to mind Lucy or were you just having a visit?"

Rosie was taken aback, she had expected at best Kate would be hysterical, and at worst she may take to her room and not leave it for several days. She had debated the entire trip over whether to tell Kate at all, but she knew if Lucy mentioned anything that it would seem as though Rosie had deliberately kept a secret from Kate. And she wouldn't ask Lucy to lie or keep secrets to protect Kate. Rosie had done enough of that in her own childhood. This calm face, what did it mean?

"I was going to ask if you would have Lucy for the night. There is a vigil for Hannah Avery, the missing woman, Dee and I would like to go."

"Well, of course I can have Lucy. But *not* the dog."

"No, Mum. Not the dog. Mum? Are you okay about Frank, though? It's okay if you aren't."

Kate shrugged.

"I couldn't control him leaving, and I can't control him coming back. I can only control this house and what's in it. And that is what I do. I know I wasn't a perfect mother,

Rosemary. It bothered me too. This place," Kate swept her arms out wide, "was both a sanctuary and a cage for me. I know you took on too much. I did my best. I hope when you sit down with him, he can see I raised a strong and wonderful woman, though. Despite everything. Tell him, I didn't need him after all."

Rosie nodded, choked with emotions from all the words her mother had never said before, things she had waited her whole life to have acknowledged.

"I will. I'll tell him."

CHAPTER 21

"Ugh," Dee said, "I wish we went the other way. Turn around and go up Sawyer Road."

"Why?" Rosie asked, "This way is quicker."

"That path on Dean Street, it gives me the creeps."

Rosie burst out laughing, "A *path*?"

She glanced over at Dee, who had pulled her legs up against her chest and was staring with narrowed eyes out the window.

"It's true! It completely freaks me out. I never drive up Dean Street."

"I genuinely don't even know what path you're talking about. You're going to have to point it out to me."

Dee groaned and slumped down in her chair, "Fine. Take me past the place of bad vibes."

Rosie smiled to herself and continued on.

A few minutes later, Dee sat upright, "Okay... there! See it?"

Rosie looked at an innocuous-looking path between a house and some bushland, "That's the path of your nightmares? *That* one? With the wisteria growing along the fence line? With the fluffy white dog in the yard next door?"

Dee nodded emphatically, "Isn't it awful?"

"No."

Dee sighed, "You have no intuition."

They made idle chit-chat as they drove towards John Scott Park, Dee telling Rosie about her day, and Rosie filling Dee in on Kate's reaction to both Lucy's arm and the revelation that Frank was back.

"And she just... took it like a normal, well-adjusted person. She took it better than I did actually," Rosie admitted. She still wasn't sure what to make of Kate's ambivalent attitude towards Frank's return. It made her feel somehow ashamed, as though she had overreacted. She said as much to Dee, who shook her head.

"Not at all. All feelings are valid. You can't help what you feel. We can only try to moderate our reactions to them."

As they neared the park where the vigil was to be held their mood sobered, and they both became quiet. Rosie felt an unsettled feeling inside her, as though ants were crawling under her skin. Cars lined the streets along the main road and spilt into side streets; it looked like something you would expect to see at a night time market. It became apparent they were not going to find a car park nearby.

"So many people," Dee whispered.

Throngs of people walked towards the park, filling the sidewalks. Some carried balloons, others held cardboard signs, many of them held flowers. Rosie pulled up a side street and drove slowly down it, looking for an opening where her car could fit when an old man flagged her down, and Rosie wound down her window.

"Are you going to the vigil?" He called out to her.

"We are," Rosie called back.

He pointed to his front lawn where several cars were already parked, "You can park on my driveway, love. Save you walking for miles."

Rosie thanked him and swung up on to his driveway, parking the car.

"Thank you," she said, when she got out. "My name is Rosie, this is my friend, Dee."

He nodded to them, "I'm Harry. That's my wife Edith up there on the verandah." He pointed up to the second story where a small woman with white hair sat in a wheelchair, she waved down to them, and Rosie raised her hand and waved back.

"We would come down ourselves," Harry said, "but Edith's chair doesn't manage well on grass. Do you know the missing girl?"

Rosie paused, then nodded, "Yes. Yes, I know Hannah."

He reached out and put a warm, dry hand on her shoulder, "I hope they find her, love. I really do."

Rosie felt her eyes well up, "Me too."

Rosie and Dee found space towards the middle of the gathering crowd. Off to the side news crews filmed, and a tent had been erected from which coffee and tea were being served. Rosie offered to go and get both her and Dee a cup, handing Dee her bag for safekeeping. Music had begun to play and some people had started to sing.

Rosie hadn't seen Bryan or Hannah's family anywhere as yet. The tea was free, but a donation box sat on the table, and Rosie fished in her pocket for a $5 note, hastily shoving it through the slot in the top. She turned around and came face to face with Bryan. His face stared at her blankly for a moment before lighting in recognition.

"Rosie," he said, "thank you for coming."

"I... Bryan, of course. Of course I would come." She trailed off, unsure what to say next.

'I'm sorry' felt too much like she was giving up hope of Hannah's return, and yet there didn't seem to be a proper phrase to say right now that didn't sound clichéd or awful.

"You don't know what to say," Bryan stated.

A passing woman jostled into Rosie's arm, causing the tea to spill from the cup and over her fingers.

"Ouch!"

Bryan took one of the cups from her and moved her to the side, out of the crowd and behind the tent.

"Thank you," Rosie said, "and no, I have no idea what to say. I'm so sorry, Bryan. I want to give you something, anything to make this better, but I know the only one that can do that is Hannah. I cannot tell you how much I hope she is found."

Bryan nodded and stared off towards the gumtrees in the park, their ghostly white trunks seeming to give off their own light.

"I hate everything right now. Everyone is trying to help; I know that. I'm just so angry all the time."

He shot a look at her, guarded, slightly ashamed.

"It's normal," Rosie said. "It's okay if you're angry."

He absentmindedly sipped at the tea he had been

holding for her and then realised what he was doing, "Shit. Sorry."

Rosie smiled, "Don't worry about it. Hey, I'm sure you have a lot of friends and family around you, but if you do need someone to talk to, I'm here."

Bryan nodded, patted Rosie awkwardly on the shoulder and disappeared back between the tents.

Rosie took a deep breath to steady herself and went back to get a second cup of tea.

She made her way back to Dee's side and handed her a cup, "Here, take this one. The other one is cold."

"Why is one cold?" Dee asked.

Rosie shook her head, "I'll tell you later."

Dee shrugged and sipped at her tea, "While you were gone the police have made a statement, basically the same thing on the news, hotline number, what she was wearing etcetera. Hannah's mother is about to come up."

The vigil continued, various family members and friends talking, and music in parts. Another song began playing, the same one that played as Hannah walked down the aisle to at Bryan and her wedding.

Dee leaned over, "I know we are coming here to be support-ive, but this is about the worst thing I've ever been to in my life - *ever*. It feels like a funeral mixed with a fair - and I love you, but I absolutely have to get out of here."

Rosie nodded; she had been feeling similarly but felt too uncomfortable to express it. They picked their way out of the crowd, apologising in whispers until they were walking back through the park, the sounds of music fading in the background.

Just then Dee stopped, patting her pocket.

"Damn it. I think my keys have fallen out," She looked back towards the crowd in dismay.

"We'll go back," Rosie said. "They're likely on the ground where we were sitting."

"I guess we will have to," Dee agreed.

They had only taken a few steps before Rosie's phone rang, "For God's sake!" She snapped as she looked at the caller ID.

"June?" Dee asked.

Rosie nodded and cast an apologetic look at her friend.

"Answer it. I'll run back for the keys."

Rosie nodded and answered the phone as Dee hurried back.

"Hello, Grandma," she said expectantly.

Dee raced as quickly as she could through the crowd of people, while still trying to be respectful of the mood of the moment. She reached the spot where she and Rosie had been sitting and scanned the ground for any sign of her keys, but she couldn't see them anywhere.

She looked over to the people standing nearby, "I'm sorry, have you seen any keys on the ground?"

They shook their head, and she continued to retrace her steps since she had entered the crowd, asking people if they had seen them every few metres.

"Have you tried over by the police tent, love?" one man asked. "Someone might have handed them in."

Dee thanked him and wound her way over to the tents to the side of the gathering.

She strode up to the tent and pulled up suddenly, "Oh! It's you."

James smiled, "Yes. And it's you."

Dee looked confused, "Are you with the police?"

A tiny fair-haired woman beside him broke into a sweet grin.

"He's with me, actually. I'm with the police. Well, just one of them. My husband Michael is an officer, so I came to help run the tent. I just enlisted James to keep me company," She held out a hand. "I'm Brooke, James is my brother."

Dee took her hand and shook it.

"Dee," she said by way of an introduction. "I'm a friend of a friend."

"How can we help you, Dee?" James said.

"I don't suppose anyone has handed in some keys?" She asked, hopefully.

Brooke shook her head, "No, sorry. Do you remember where you had them last?"

Dee held up her hands, "Not really. I know I had them when I came, but after that? Not until I checked on the way out with Rosie."

Both James and Brooke sat up a little straighter.

"Rosie is here?" James asked.

Dee pointed out where she had left Rosie, and both Brooke and James offered to help Dee retrace her steps, leaving the running of the tent with a couple of other volunteers. They moved through the crowd and weaved their way back to where Rosie and Dee had been.

"We were here by this tree, but I've looked around and can't find them anywhere."

Brooke looked several meters to the right, "Are you sure it was this tree and not that one."

"No, it was this one," Dee said, although she felt doubt creeping in even as she said it.

The trio walked over to the other tree, and James swooped down and picked the keys up off the ground, "Ah-ha!"

A few people nearby gave him disapproving looks, and he apologised and handed them over to Dee.

"Thank you so much," she said gratefully. "I feel like such an idiot. Of course this is the tree."

"It's fine," Brooke assured her. "Kinda like leaving your car in a carpark and not remembering which level you were parked on, hey? We will walk you back to Rosie."

James cut a look at his sister that Dee didn't need interpretation to understand. It was clear that Brooke knew about his interest in Rosie and wanted to lay eyes on her herself.

"We will," James said, pointedly, "but only because it's probably not a good idea for anyone to be walking through the park themselves at the moment."

Dee suddenly felt stricken; she hadn't even contemplated the potential danger of leaving Rosie on her own in a darkened park far from the crowd, she subconsciously quickened her step, hurrying back to where she had left her friend.

Rosie had gotten off the phone to June after agreeing to come by tomorrow to talk things out. June had seemed unlike herself on the phone, her voice vibrating with a strange energy that Rosie hadn't heard before, almost like she was both relieved and concerned at the same time. She hung up the phone and slipped it back into her pocket, staring back at the crowd, scanning for Dee. The wind had begun to kick up a bit, and she could see the tops of the tents shifting in the breeze. Rosie's hair blew in front of her face, and she pushed it back, using the hair tie on her wrist to pull it up into a haphazard bun when she felt a hand grab down on her wrist. Her heart instantly leapt into her throat, and she gasped, wrenching herself away and wheeling around.

"Christ! You scared me!" Her voice catching.

Ricky smiled, "Sorry, darlin'. Saw you standing here and couldn't resist. You come for the vigil of that girl?"

Rosie nodded warily, "Yes. I'm just waiting for my friend; she'll be back in a moment."

She realised she was slowly putting space between herself and Ricky and that he was matching her movements, edging her closer to a scrubby bush like area.

"It's strange to see you here," he said. "I've been thinking about your pretty red hair for days."

Rosie shuddered involuntarily, a few more steps and she would be in the scrub. She forced herself to stand her ground, hoping he would leave her be. Her flight response was screaming at her, but she found herself frozen to the spot. He continued moving in. So, it would be fight then.

Rosie went to push past him, and he grabbed her roughly by the arm, he was stronger than he looked for such a weedy build. She tried to pull her arm free, but his grip tightened, and he pulled her against him, whispering words in her ear, which were no longer subjective, but vile and direct. She felt a hardness against the back of her thigh and tasted bile that had risen in her throat. She raised one boot and came down hard on his foot and then, out of nowhere, someone called out clearly in the night.

"Everything okay here?"

Rosie was no longer alone when they reached her, she appeared to be speaking to two men, and while Dee couldn't hear what they were saying, Rosie's body posture was tense, her arms crossed across her body. The two men were close to each other. One had a dark ponytail and was dressed casually in jeans and a t-shirt and wearing a smirk on his face - the other was clean-cut, pressed business pants and a button-up shirt, he appeared to be positioning himself between the other man and Rosie.

"Huh," James said, surprised.

"What?" Dee asked.

"That's our uncle," Brooke said.

"David!" James called out and raised an arm in a wave while squinting. "Is that? Oh, shit!"

James broke into a jog, and the two women looked at each other and followed suit.

"St Clair," the ponytailed man called. "I was just keeping Red company for you."

James came to a stop and was silent for a moment, his eyes scanning Rosie's face, her crossed arms and the red mark on her wrist that was deepening into a bruise by the second. Dee saw it at the same time and gasped.

James spun around to face Ricky, his fists clenching and

unclenching as though he was contemplating something, he looked at his sister for a moment.

"James," she said warningly.

James shook his head infinitesimally, then shrugged and landed a right hook hard against Ricky's jaw.

The women gasped collectively, and David let out a small snort. Ricky fell to the ground and lay there for a few minutes, before scuttling up to his feet and walking off, calling threats and obscenities back to the group.

"You're an idiot," Brooke said to James, but without any anger. She then turned to Rosie and went immediately into mother mode, cooing over her wrist and wrapping her arm around her shoulder.

"I'm okay, I'm okay," Rosie assured them. "This man helped me. I'm sorry. I don't know your name."

Introductions were made as Dee filled Rosie in on finding Brooke and James, and then James introducing David to Rosie.

"Thank you so much," Rosie said to him, gratefully.

"It's no problem, I was coming down to the vigil, but I guess I got here a bit late. Probably lucky I did," he shrugged.

Rosie looked ruefully at James, "Is your hand okay?"

"It'll do," he said as Brooke grabbed his hand and inspected it.

"You're still going to need ice," she said disapprovingly.

Brooke asked where Rosie and Dee had parked and suggested David walk them back while she takes James back to the tent to put some ice on his hand.

"I can put ice on my own damn hand," he argued. "I'll walk them back."

"Will you stop being such a frigging hero?"

"Will you stop being such a nag?"

David interjected, "I will walk them back. You two go have your argument somewhere else."

James cast a last look at Rosie, opened his mouth as though to say something and then closed it again before nodding.

"We are quite a bit of a walk away," Dee said, apologetically as they turned to go.

"It's no problem," David assured them and turned to lead the women back towards the road.

Brooke took her brother by the elbow and guided him back to the crowd.

"Honestly. You are an idiot for hitting him, and I'm not going to say it was the right thing to do... but I'm also not sad you did it. Okay?"

James grinned, "Okay."

Brooke looked over her shoulder to where David was walking the two women across the grass. Rosie stumbled slightly on the uneven ground, and David caught her by the elbow, placing his other arm around her to steady her. Brooke stopped up short.

"What?" James asked, looking back.

Brooke shook her head, "Nothing. I just had a weird sense of déjà vu. I don't know."

She took a breath and turned back around, "Okay, Rocky. Let's get you some ice."

CHAPTER 22

Later that night, Dee sat beside Rosie, wrapping a strip of fabric that held beaten herbs inside around Rosie's wrist.

"Ouch! What is that anyway?"

"A poultice of Yarrow and comfrey. It's good for bruises and cuts. You'll be fine."

Rosie looked dubiously at her wrapped up wrist, but she realised it *was* feeling cool and soothed, and she sighed in acceptance and sank back into the couch.

Dee had quizzed Rosie on the way home about what had happened with Ricky and begged Rosie to go to the police station to make a statement, but Rosie just wanted to go home and take a shower.

"Maybe in the morning," she said to Dee to make her stop talking about it, "Please. Can we talk about something else? Anything else?"

Too much had happened in recent days and her head was spinning trying to make sense of it all. She realised Dee had stopped talking and was looking at her expectantly.

"What?"

"I said, did you at least sort things out with June?"

Rosie closed her eyes and groaned. The phone call with her grandmother had been one more strange occurrence in a string of them lately. She went over the phone call with Dee.

June had been relieved when she answered, asking how Lucy was and whether she was okay, and Rosie had assured her she was fine and had been to the doctors and was healing well. Her tone had been clipped, and she had a vague sense of embarrassment hearing her own voice but had been unable to conceal it.

"Have you been back to the house?" June had asked.

"No. We stayed the night at Dee's. It's been cleared by an electrician though, so, we will go back at some-"

"Don't!" June cut in.

"Why?" Rosie asked.

"Please, just come and talk to us first. It is important."

Rosie had grit her teeth and taken a deep breath.

She had asked, "When you say '*we*', are you meaning you and Frank?"

"Yes."

"Can this not wait? Lucy and I have had a really rough couple of weeks. I... look, I've thought about talking to him and I probably will, but we just need some time and space so I can settle Lucy back at home."

"You cannot go home, Rosemary. I forbid it. I would give you space if I could, but it isn't an option. Please, trust me on this. Come and talk to us."

"Forbid it?" Dee asked.

"Those were her words. Like I was twelve years old or something. Anyway, I said I would come, and she seemed satisfied with that. We left the phone call on good terms though, I thought."

"Hmm," Dee said. "Well, that was weird. Still not the weirdest thing that happened to you tonight, but definitely weird."

Rosie nodded and felt tension run out of her body, leaving her exhausted and her eyelids heavy. Dee helped her up and walked her up to the room, tucking her into bed like a mother would a child, before walking towards the door.

"Dee?" Rosie asked, "Would you... mind keeping on the hall light? Sorry. I know it's stupid, it's just-"

"It's not stupid. Of course, I'll leave it on."

Rosie smiled at her and shut her eyes, praying for a dreamless sleep.

Next morning, Rosie had called Kate to ask her to mind Lucy a little longer, and then spent the drive over to June's, imagining various scenes in her head. Frank would be contrite, and she would shout at him. Frank would be a jerk, and she would shout at him. Frank would tell her how he had been overseas for the last quarter of a century - and she would shout at him. In all honesty, she had no idea what he would be like, because she was telling the truth to James when she had said that she didn't know her father. She had no clue what he would say or how he would act.

Her stomach was in knots by the time she pulled into June's street and parked the car on the driveway. She rubbed her wrist, absently. This morning Dee had removed the poultice, and the bruising hadn't been nearly as bad as Rosie had been expecting the night before. You could barely see anything at all. Still, the bones felt tender. Dee had wanted to wrap it with fresh herbs, but Rosie had refused, she wasn't going to see her grandmother wearing crushed plants on her wrist. She glanced at her appearance in the rearview mirror.

"Just be calm," she told herself. "Be a rock in a stream."

Rosie walked up to the front door and knocked, feeling oddly self-conscious. June had answered, smelling of lavender and the tangy, fresh smell of tomato leaves. Rosie glanced to the basket in her grandmother's hands, clearly the source of the smell, filled with sprigs of lavender and sun-ripened tomatoes.

"I've just come in from the garden," she said, "Come in. I'll make tea."

Rosie nodded and stepped inside, placing her bag and cardigan on the couch.

As she entered the kitchen, her father looked up at her from his seat at the table, and Rosie took a moment to really examine him. He had her eyes. Or rather, she supposed, she had his eyes. He didn't smile at her or try to get up and hug her, and she realised she had been afraid that he would be overly familiar with her. He was dressed in an old flannel shirt of her grandfathers but still wore the pants she had seen him in last. He appeared to have showered recently, and his hair was still damp and cut bluntly, it looked as though he had cut it himself without a mirror, which, she supposed, was possible. The anger she felt ebbed and flowed like waves; one minute she felt nothing towards him, the next she was furious he had the audacity to show up at all. Rosie took a seat at the table to the side of him, scooting the chair closer to June to put some distance between herself and Frank.

"I shouldn't have stormed out the other day" Rosie began, "It has been really hard for Lucy and me lately. There are a lot of things that have happened that I won't get into now. But, I guess I was on edge and snappy, and I do apologise. Lucy is not herself lately, and I guess that's making me act not like myself either. Lucy told me she told you about her imaginary friend. It's lots of things like that. I am looking into a child psychologist for her."

She directed her words to her grandmother, still finding it difficult to look at Frank, who was jittery and shaking his leg up and down rapidly in a way that was making Rosie anxious and also getting on her nerves.

"Rosie, I don't think there is anything wrong with Lucy," said Grandma June.

"Well, I wouldn't have thought so either, but she isn't acting like herself. I think losing Ben has affected her more than I realised. It can be hard for little girls to lose their fathers."

Be a rock in a stream, she chanted in her head, but Frank kept tapping his leg in a way that Rosie feel like she was going to scream.

"So, what are you here for anyway? Why come back now?"

The tapping stopped. *Thank god*, Rosie thought. She looked at him expectantly, *here we go. What does this man want, the one I have never known, who has suddenly arrived at what would appear to be the most challenging moment in my life? What could he possibly want now?*

"It's a long story," Frank said.

Rosie sat for a moment, waiting for him to continue, but he just began tapping his leg again. *Be a rock in a stream?*

Rosie snorted, "Seriously? Well, why don't we start with something easier then? Why did you leave? Kate said you didn't even tell her why, you just left her - and me, actually."

"Rosemary," June said, covering her granddaughter's hand with her own. "We both want to tell you what happened. But you are going to need to listen, *really* listen and promise not to storm out of here."

Rosie opened her mouth to say something hurtful but shut it again. She had decided to come here to put this behind her, and that meant she would have try to bite her tongue.

It was only now that she realised how foolish she was to think she could be unemotional about this. Yes, she *did* want there to be an explanation, she wanted him to say something had taken him away and kept him from coming back, and that it wasn't just that she and Kate had meant so little to him that he had chosen this. Sitting here with him hurt a part of her that was still little and wondering why he wasn't coming home. It brought back old memories of Father's Day stalls at school and watching the other kids buy things plastered with the word 'Dad' while she looked for something she could give her grandfather. It reminded her that when she got married, she had no parents there because Kate wouldn't leave the house and Frank had never come *back* to the house. There were wounds that she never realised she had until the moment she saw him in June's house and realised who he was. God, *yes*, she wanted there to be an explanation - she just couldn't think of one that would be valid. Nothing would keep her from Lucy. Nothing would have kept Ben from Lucy. She looked at Frank, the tapping leg and shaky hands, there was a nick on his chin from shaving. A handkerchief peeked out of the breast pocket of his shirt, a small spot of dried blood on it from where he had dabbed at the nick after he cut himself. Small things. Small, human things that steadied her.

"Go ahead," Rosie said, "I'm listening."

Frank wrapped his hands around the mug of tea in front of him and nodded, opening his mouth and hesitating a moment before finally speaking, "I left because I saved you. Or I thought I was saving you. I just wasn't sure," Frank didn't look at her as he spoke, staring out the open window to the backyard where birds were eating seed from the feeder under the tree. Frank suddenly sat bolt upright as though he had seen something outside. Rosie followed his gaze, but there was nothing but the birds and the empty white garden bench that sat in the shade of the flame tree.

He squeezed his eyes tightly shut and squeezed the bridge of his nose.

"Mum," he begged.

June reached out and grabbed hold of Frank's hand, "Hey, hey! Feel my hand; feel it. Now squeeze my hand back... that's it. Open your eyes, Francis. Look at me."

Frank slowly opened his eyes and June held his gaze with a direct, calm stare.

"That's it," she said. "Deep breaths. Now, let it just fade

away to static. It's just background noise... Are you doing okay, now?"

Frank nodded, his eyes looking tired and pained.

What the hell was that, Rosie thought, *June just talked him down like a hostage negotiator.* Frank was not a well man, Rosie realised, whether it was drugs or mental illness or a mixture of both, he was very unstable. Rosie thought about what James had said about leaving if he thought he would put Violet in danger and wondered if Frank left because of something he couldn't control. Unstable from mental illness, maybe that's what he meant, he was trying to save her from having to look after him the way June just had.

Frank slumped back into his chair and June reached out and tenderly brushed his hair back off his forehead, as though her son were a little boy and not a grown man in his mid-fifties. Rosie looked down, strangely embarrassed by such an intimate display of motherly affection. She had never stopped to realise that while she had lost her father for twenty-five years, June had lost her son.

She cleared her throat, "So... you thought you were saving me?"

Frank nodded, "It's also why I came back. Lucy isn't seeing things that aren't there, Rosie. She's seeing things that are there. Things that you can't see because of what I did to you. But I swear to you, I thought it was the right thing, and I had no idea what would happen."

"What are you talking about? What did you... do to me?"

June stood up and went to the sink, "Rosie, right now as I look out this window, I see the garden. I see birds at the feeder and I see the garden chair underneath the flame tree.

If you came and stood beside me, you would see the same thing. The difference is, I can also see your grandfather sitting on that chair, he's having a cup of tea in his favourite mug, which right now is in *my* hands. In a few minutes, he will be gone."

Rosie drew a breath, "You can see his ghost?"

June turned around, "Not exactly. Your grandfather is gone to wherever our souls go when we pass from this world. What I'm seeing is just an imprint, a footprint of sorts. Rogue energy left behind that attaches to people, places or things. An imprint can be left where energy is strong, something someone does all the time, or sometimes a place of intense emotion - hospitals are something to avoid, births and deaths can leave a lot of imprints. Your grandfather sat on that chair every afternoon just past lunch. It is a place where the energy is strong, but it isn't 'him'. If I walk out there now, I can't talk to him; I cannot touch him. If I call his name, he won't look up. And in a few moments, he will be gone until this time tomorrow."

Rosie wanted to stand up and walk out. She wanted to think this was all crazy. For weeks, she had been trying to piece together what had been happening to Lucy, and no matter which way she put the puzzle together, there was always a part that didn't fit. *You never believe me*, Lucy had shouted at her. Now her grandmother was asking for the same thing. To be believed. Imprints?

She glanced at Frank to see if he was buying this story, and he met her eyes and nodded. Slowly, Rosie rose from her chair and walked to the window, her heart beat a little faster, wondering if she was about to see her grandfather again, wanting to believe he was there, desperately wishing for faith. But the chair was empty. She let out a breath she didn't know she was holding, disappointment filling her heart.

"Is he gone?" She asked.

"Not yet," June said. "You just can't see him. I'm sorry, honey."

"Say I believe you - that you are really seeing an imprint or something, but I can't see it. Are you saying it's... like a gift?"

Frank snorted, and June shot him a look. June took Rosie's hands.

"Yes," she said, holding her gaze with an intensity. "This is a gift. And one that should have been yours. But you have been shielded - and badly too," she added, throwing another look Frank's way.

"Why? No. Wait. Answer that later. Is this what Lucy is seeing? An imprint of someone? Is she able to do... what you do?"

June's mouth tightened, "Let's start at the beginning."

June had poured the tea and taken them out to the garden where they sat around the chairs. Rosie had an odd urge to cackle wildly; she was sitting in her grandmother's rose garden with her estranged father while they discussed ghosts. *Maybe we* are *all mad here*, she thought briefly. Frank looked around nervously before he sat and placed his mug shakily in front of him. When they were all settled, and Frank had begun to relax a little into the chair, June began to talk.

. . .

"When I was a little girl, for as long as I can remember, my mother would tell me stories of the Others. She would take me into the garden, or she would tell me while she sewed or baked. She would talk about it the same way all mothers tell stories to their children of fairies and goblins. She was Irish, my mother, with hair like yours Rosie, and she came over here shortly after she and my father had gotten married.

In her tales, she would talk of her adventures with the Others in Ireland and how she would help them. She spoke of people coming to her for comfort after a loved one had passed away and how she would reach out to the Others for help. She told me it was a gift that all the women in her family had; her mother and her grandmother, and her mother before her. Mother to daughter, it was passed down. She spoke of it so often that when I was a bit older and I began to see things, I wasn't afraid. It always happens around five or six years old. Little glimpses at first - for me, it began with seeing my cat who had died a few weeks before. I would see her walking into the kitchen where she would beg my mother for a saucer of milk. The first time I saw her, I ran after her, wanting to scoop her in my arms, before I remembered she was dead. I told my mother, of course, who explained about imprints.

Two weeks later, we went to the dam to swim with some friends. My mother packed a basket for a picnic, and her friends came with their children; we had a lovely day. It was hot, and all the children were wild. I had little friend about my age called Betty, and she and I were splashing each other on the shoreline - when Betty's mother began to scream. I've never heard a sound like that in my life, and it makes your blood run cold to think of it. Her mother began to run for the dam, and when we looked to see what had happened, there was Betty's little brother, Ian, floating face down in the water. He was only a baby, really, two or three years old. Some of the women pulled him out and began to try to get the water out of his lungs, but his lips were blue, his eyes staring blankly at the summer sky.

That's when I saw him standing there, near the dam's edge. Small and dry and serene looking. I remember tugging at my mother's skirt and pointing to Ian, perfectly fine, right there. I was confused by what I was seeing, wondering if the drowned child was somehow another child that looked like Ian, but my mother shook her head at me - and I could tell from the look in her eyes that I shouldn't say a thing. My mother pulled myself and Betty into her arms - Betty was wailing by now - and she held us both, stroking our hair and whispering comforts to us. My mother had whispered to me to watch Betty for a moment, and I had sat there holding Betty's hand, while my mother walked down to Ian by the side of the dam. She squatted by the water, wetting her handkerchief, and I could see her mouth moving as though she was talking. Then she stood, and as she did, Ian disappeared.

That night my mother explained that her stories of the Others were about spirits. She said that I would see them more and more as I got older – until, by the time I was a grown woman, I would see them all the time - but I mustn't be afraid. She explained that while the cat I had seen had been an imprint and wasn't really there, that Ian's spirit had been that of a newly departed soul, who sometimes stay for minutes, hours, or even days afterwards, until they move on. She told me that most times, they just want to know that their family will be okay, that they don't have to be afraid. I asked her what she had told Ian, and she had said she offered him comfort to move on - and he had of course, I saw him leave with my own eyes.

I told my mother that I was wondering why no one else had seen Ian - if it was a gift, then couldn't we have given it to Ian's mother or Betty who would have liked to see him one more time? My mother told me it wasn't possible. Everyone is born with a shield, like a veil attached to their soul, that protects them from the Others, the spirits - and only a few were born unshielded. It's not a gift you are given; it is one you are born with, or *not*, as the case may be. I saw that this was true because when I looked at my mother, I saw her clearly, but my father and my friends had a... a shimmer, to them. Like when you look at the road on a hot day. It wavered all around them, barely there, but noticeable."

June stopped speaking, and Rosie felt as though she had been pulled out of a trance, lulled by her grandmother's voice.

"So, this shimmer? You see it around me? But not Frank? Not around Lucy?"

"Not around Frank and not around Lucy, no," June said,

"and *your* shield, Rosemary, is full of holes as though it's been torn and ripped."

"Holes?"

June nodded, "It doesn't 'fit' properly because you were never meant to have it. It's not your shield - it's your father's."

CHAPTER 23

Twenty-Five years earlier.

Frank drives up the bumpy road to the old house as the sun was setting, looking forward to some dinner and a beer after a long day in the sun. He sent up a prayer that the work from this job would last awhile. Kate had been doing okay recently, but her nerves were getting to her working part-time as a receptionist, and he was hoping if he worked hard, he might get a full-time contract - then Kate could stop working and focus more on Rosie. He smiles, thinking of his daughter, his wild little firecracker. It was her birthday soon; he had his eye on one of the dolls she had been asking for. He pats his pocket where the yellow envelope inside contained his weekly pay. Pulling the car up on the grass in front of the house, he pulls his small esky out behind him and shuts the door, whistling as he walks up the steps. Rosie flies to him almost before he gets through the door and wraps her little arms around his legs.

"Daddy!" She cries.

"Hello there, carrot top," he swings her up into his arms and carries her towards the kitchen. "How is your Mama doing?"

"She was worrying," Rosie whispers.

"She'll be okay now," he whispers back, kissing her forehead and putting her back on the ground.

In the kitchen, Kate stands in front of the oven, having just pulled a casserole dish out of the oven. His stomach rumbles loudly at the smell. Kate was pulling at her fingers, and he could tell by the redness near her eyes that she had been crying.

"Hey there, good looking. The food smells great. How was work today?" He hates to ask since she had obviously been upset - but he knows if he didn't she would accuse him of not caring enough. He pulls her into his arms and Kate leans into him, clinging like he is a life raft, which is exactly what he was much of the time.

"I'm okay now," she mumbles into his shirt. "But if you don't mind dishing dinner for yourself and Lucy? I would really just like a bath."

"Of course. Go relax."

He gently steers her towards the doorway and washes his hands at the sink, using the nail brush to get out the days grime from under his fingernails. Rosie opens the cupboard and pulls out two bowls, putting them on the bench, before pulling over a small stool. She peers into the dish.

"It looks gross," she says, wrinkling her nose.

"Shh, your Mama worked hard cooking this for us," he admonishes her. "And besides, I think it smells great."

He takes the bowls and jerks his head towards the dining table, indicating for Rosie to follow him. They eat companionably, Rosie tells him the dish doesn't taste that bad, after all. She tells him about her day at his mother's house.

"And Grandma June let Poppa put a swing in the tree and now I can swing whenever I want to!"

She asks about his day, and he tells her about the house they were building.

After dinner, he goes to check on Kate - already in bed and sound asleep. He sighs, another bad day. They were becoming more frequent. He wonders if he should get her to see someone... but the problem seemed so big he can't quite wrap his head around where to start. He runs Rosie a bath, and they sing songs. He dries her off and helps her into her nightgown.

"Will you read me a story, Daddy?" Rosie asks. "Mama sometimes reads me a story."

He looks down at his dust-covered clothes, "I don't think I'm clean enough to lie down in bed with you, Rosie. Daddy is still dirty from work. Can we do a story tomorrow?"

If he was being honest, he also really just wanted to sit down with that beer and tune out to some television. Rosie looks at him with hurt eyes, and her bottom lip begins to tremble; he feels a piece of his heart break.

He sighs, "One small story. Daddy will sit on the floor."

Rosie runs to pick one of her books, before climbing into her bed and snuggling beneath the covers, carefully piling a host of stuffed toys around her. Frank lowers himself to the ground beside his daughter's bed.

"Do you really need all of these?" He asks, picking up a giraffe and waggling its head at her. She nods solemnly, and he tucks it back in beside her. They read for a few moments before Rosie interrupts him.

"Daddy?"

"Yes?"

"Can I tell you a secret?"

Something about the way she said it made his skin prickle. She didn't sound like a little girl with a birthday wish, or who broke something she shouldn't. She sounded like she was terrified. He looks at his small daughter in her sea of stuffed animals, and every fear he ever had for her flew through his head like birds taking flight.

Swallowing them back, he nods.

"Daddy, there is a man. He comes at night time. Can you stay here, please?" She begs. "Just until I fall asleep? Please, Daddy?"

An hour later, Rosie and Frank lie side by side in her bed, he didn't care about his dirty clothes anymore, and he didn't want a beer or to watch tv. He had never been more awake in his life. Rosie's curls felt soft on his arm, and she was breathing steadily beside him. He would kill him. He would beat this man with his own hands. Suddenly, Rosie stiffens beside him. Frank looks towards the door and back at his daughter.

"That's him," she whispers. "That's the man."

Frank looks at the empty doorway, "Honey, no one is there."

"Right there," She points out of the room, before tucking her head into his shoulder and closing her eyes tightly.

And right then Frank realises what his daughter is seeing.

"I don't remember any of this," Rosie said. "I don't remember seeing a man."

"You were so frightened, Rosie. I just wanted it to stop for you," Frank said, and for the first time, Rosie felt like she could completely relate to what he would have been feeling.

"So, what did you do?" She asked.

"I came to your grandma first," he said.

"And I told him you would learn to manage it, to not be frightened," June interjected. "I wanted to talk to you about what was happening."

"And *I* thought it would be better if you didn't have to deal with it at all," Frank shot a look at June that let Rosie know that this particular battle between them was far from over.

"I wanted her to take it away from you," he continued, "but the problem wasn't that you had something you shouldn't, it was that you didn't have something you should."

Grandma June let out an angry breath of air.

Rosie nodded, slowly, "So you... what? Gave me your shield?"

"In a manner of speaking, yes. It isn't perfect, it's not meant for you, so there was a risk sometimes bits may 'slip' through, you might see something out of the corner of your eye - or it may work fine. We just don't really know."

Rosie remembered the woman in the car the day of the accident, there and then gone. A blur really, a flash... but trying to remember it was like trying to find a word right on the tip of your tongue, it was just out of reach.

"I saw something. The day Lucy and I had the accident. It was a woman; she was there for a second, and then - there was nothing."

June nodded, "A shield slip. When you are stressed or frightened, you catch a glimpse through the veil."

Rosie turned to Frank, "So, you took this shield off and then you could see spirits?"

Frank stumbles out of the cottage blindly, his ears ringing. His head thumping, he makes his way to his car and looks at the small glass jar in his hand, this was it? The shield shimmered inside, and he could see it now - a haze - like steam - with iridescent thread like mother of pearl. Inside the jar, it spun and danced. It was beautiful. He, on the other hand, felt... wrong. Violated and dirty and as though everything inside him had tilted slightly to one side. And he had spent every last cent of his pay. He feels a stab of guilt knowing he has nothing to give Rosie for her birthday, but if he could give her this... surely it was worth more than a doll? He starts the car and begins driving home. Halfway home, the problems begin. A man on the side of the road, jogging along, then suddenly he is cartwheeled through the air. A girl playing jump rope in the dark. A dog runs in front of his car and disappears. Everywhere he looks, there is someone. Here and then gone.

"When someone who was shielded becomes unshielded it's not a kindness, Rosie," June said. "Imagine you are driving to work, the same as usual but there are people all over the road, on the paths, more people than you have ever seen. Some are real, some are not, and you don't know which is which. They're there - and they disappear. You see a child choke to death in front of you, and no one notices but you, because *that* child choked fifteen years ago, but you are seeing it now. It is a terrible assault on the senses."

"That would be awful," Rosie agreed. She imagined all the imprints that must be left behind and tried to fathom walking amongst them, "So, how do you manage it?"

"Firstly," June said, "for those of us born this way, it happens piece by piece, not all at once. You end up treating it like background noise, and over time you can manage to pick up the differences in the vibrations put out by a living being in front of you and an Other. It becomes easier to focus and filter it all. Still, there are places I would never go because the haunting would be too much. Places of sorrow and grief where the energy would cling to it with such an intensity that even after nearly eighty years on this earth, I wouldn't be able to block myself off. I think I'd go mad."

Frank pushes open the door and runs into Kate, who was hovering behind it.

"Where have you been?" She wails.

He pushes past her and runs for the sink where he vomits until he feels weak.

"Frank?" Kate says. "Are you sick?"

"Where is Rosie?" He asks. He runs a hand over his face, trying to stop the pounding in his head.

Kate looks at him strangely, "She's asleep, it's after eleven-"

He walks past her and to the door of Rosie's room, looking at his sleeping daughter, her red hair spread over her pillow, a teddy tucked up under her arm.

He reaches into his pocket and removes the jar, unscrewing the lid. He begins to say the incantation the shaman had told him. The shield rises from the open jar, and Frank pushes it towards his sleeping daughter, repeating the words.

"Frank?" Kate whispers from the doorway. "What are you doing? What's going on?"

Ignoring her he presses the shield down on to Rosie's chest, where he feels it latch on, like a hook into a fish, and there it spreads out across her sleeping form, shimmering and sliding. There are holes in it, he sees. But it would be better than nothing.

He stands and turns, heading towards the door, walking past a stunned Kate. As he opens the front door, she comes to life.

"Wait! Where are you going? Frank, you're scaring me!"

"I'll be back," he says, shutting the door behind him.

Rosie thought she already knew the answer to the question, but she asked anyway, "You said, those that are born unshielded learn how to block it out? So, what if you are born with one and become unshielded?"

June and Frank remained silent.

Frank finds the way to his mother's house and opens the door with shaking hands. In the kitchen, June sits in her nightgown, a cup of tea beside her, a crossword puzzle half done. She glances up at him and does a double-take.

"Oh Frank," she says, sadly. "What have you done?"

CHAPTER 24

Rosie rubbed her face; this was all too much. The old man in Frank's story, was this the man in her photograph? Had she truly taken a photo of a spirit?

"If I hadn't become shielded back then, what would have happened? Would the imprint of the old man have hurt me?"

June shook her head, "No, not at all. Imprints aren't sentient or corporeal; they don't interact with us at all. It's just energy."

"But some can, right? Some of the Others? Like the boy from your story that drowned - you said your mother spoke to him."

June agreed, "Yes. There are three types of Others. The imprint - which attaches to people, places or things, residual energy that remain long after a person has passed on. These are who you would encounter most often. Then there are the newly dead, people who have recently died and have yet to move on. You can talk to them if you're unshielded, and you can touch them, and they can touch you."

"Which is awful, by the way," Frank added.

"It's different, not awful," June argued.

Rosie thought about when Ben died and how much she would have given to be able to say goodbye, to have been able to talk to him or have him touch her. She remembered the moment when she thought she had seen Ben there in the room after she was told the news. The shock of it, the strangeness. *Another shield slip*, she supposed. He *had* been there. She cannot imagine how awful that would have been for him, to see her find that out.

"You said there were three types of Others? What is the third?"

June took a deep breath, "The third kind are tethered spirits. Spirits that didn't move on, or spirits that can't. Imagine for a moment that someone cannot bring themselves to leave their wife, they stay a week, two weeks, following her around. She is shielded, she can't see him. He cannot touch her or speak to anyone. He stays so long that he cannot move on because he cannot let go. He becomes tethered. No one is supposed to straddle two worlds, it... has an effect on the psyche. The energy of the spirit grows, and it might move objects or create disturbances. Electricity is often the easiest to manipulate, the energy of it seems to be similar to the energy of an Other. They become a Haunting."

She felt a dawning of realisation. June and Frank suspected that Lucy's girl was a tethered spirit. The blown lightbulbs, the fire. Rosie felt a moment of sheer horror and terror. All that time, Lucy had been frightened. Tiny wouldn't go in the room. Even the dog believed Lucy - and Rosie hadn't. Her poor little girl.

"Another tethering can happen," June continued, "where the spirit's passing was brought on by violence."

"You mean someone killed them?"

"Yes."

"Are you saying my house is haunted? How do we make it stop?"

June explained that she and Frank had talked about this for days, and didn't believe the house itself to be haunted, Rosie had lived there too long without any disturbance.

"It's more likely that you have brought something into the house that the spirit is tethered to."

Rosie mentally scanned her mind thinking of anything new she had brought into the house. *Of course, it wouldn't be new*, she thought, *it would be something old, but recently brought in.* Something that belonged to someone else. But they hadn't brought anything new or 'new to them' into the house. Everything they owned they had owned for months on end.

She shook her head, "There isn't anything."

"Are you sure," June asked. "It could seem like nothing. A button from a shirt. A book. A trinket."

"Nothing," Rosie was adamant.

"What about Lucy?" Frank asked.

"Just things she made at kinder. Paintings and things like that. Nothing that seems haunted."

"There has to be something," Frank said, almost to himself.

Rosie shook her head, "Look, say we do find something. What do we do? Can I just... throw it out?"

Both Frank and June grimaced.

"What?" Rosie asked.

"It's still a person, Rosie," June said. "Someone who was loved. You can remove the tether from your presence, but the Other will still be tethered to this world. The only true way to get rid of it is to give the spirit peace."

Rosie felt momentarily aghast. Of course. Of course you couldn't just throw it out like trash. What was energy? Was it the soul of a person or a part of it? What made them truly them? Was part of her grandfather always drinking tea on the bench outside? Was the old man from the house in her photograph still walking those halls? She stood up abruptly, pushing the chair backwards with a loud screech.

"I have to go," she said.

"Rosie," Frank began.

She held up her hand, "No. No, I'm not mad. I'm not... I just, I need to think."

Grandma June stood, "You can't go back to the house, not with Lucy."

Rosie walked backwards.

"I won't. I just need to go and process this, okay? Just give me..." she trailed off, walking towards the house and collecting her things before getting in her car and driving away.

She drove aimlessly for over an hour before the needle on her fuel gauge forced her to stop and fill the tank. She should think they were all mad and yet she didn't. It was that final puzzle piece that had slipped into place. She thought about driving out back to Dee's house, but she couldn't face the questions right now. She thought about going back to Kate's, but she couldn't stand the thought of her gaze either. Or Lucy. God. Lucy. All those nights she had climbed into Rosie's bed and Rosie had thought it was normal kid stuff... but Lucy had been frightened. She had wanted Rosie to shield her, like Frank had shielded Rosie. Is that possible? *Could* she actually shield Lucy? Frank had done it for her. *And gone mad for it*, she reminded herself. As difficult as her childhood had been with Kate, what if Rosie reacted the same way to unshielding as Frank had? Lucy would have no one. *But I was never meant to have it,* she reminded herself, *it might be different.* Or it might not. There was no way to tell but to do it. She paid for the fuel and walked back her car in a daze. It took her a moment to realise someone was calling her name.

James walked over to her car, "Rosie? Are you okay? You look like you've seen a ghost."

Rosie looked at him for a moment and burst into laughter.

"Oh, god! If only! Oh James, that's actually hilarious!"

James laughed uneasily, "I have no idea what's going on."

Rosie wiped her eyes, "No, I know. Sorry. Are you busy right now?"

James looked over at his Ute that held cans of stain for frames he was behind on.

"No. I'm not busy at all. You want to go for a drive?"

Ten minutes later, Rosie was in the passenger seat of James's truck. He had asked her how she was feeling after last night. To her surprise, she found she had managed to forget what had happened between her and Ricky for a couple of hours while at June's house. James told her that his brother in law was checking into Ricky after what had happened.

"It was half the reason for the police presence last night, you know? Michael said, sometimes attackers like to... you know... go to things like that. It turns out Ricky is a bit of a garbage person, and I'm sorry I seemed to be the vector for him meeting you. I feel awful about that, Rosie. I really am sorry."

"It's not your fault," she assured him. She shuddered, "They think the person who took Hannah might have been there last night?"

James shrugged, "It's possible. You might want to think about making a complaint against Ricky. It's unlikely you're the first woman he has done this to."

Rosie was silent. Finally, she spoke, "The thing is, James, I should make a complaint and I probably will, and I will be believed because your uncle happened to be there. And maybe something might have happened if he hadn't been, or maybe Ricky would have backed off and let me go. That sort of thing? The aggression and then the backing off? It happens all the time. You have no idea how many drunken uncles I've had to fend off at weddings, scooting past them as I exit the bathroom while they lean in close so their body is against mine. Or when I was younger, and Dee and I would go to clubs, or when I was in school and at parties. And it was never their fault some-how. It was always mine for being friendly, or wearing a short skirt, or dancing with someone - as though that were a green light. Look at Hannah. She is married; I was there at her wedding. She is a good person. She and Bryan are in love. Then there is this photo - which might not even be her - but even if it is, it's just one split second. It's blown up into her being unfaithful. It's like the public only wants to see Hannah - or all women, in two ways. Either as demure virgins... or too easy, too loose, too loud. What category you fall into determines how much sympathy you receive and how much you are believed. So, I will go make the complaint, but I just don't know how much faith I have in the system, as a woman who has lived it my whole life."

James drove silently for a while, "I'm sorry, Rosie."

She shrugged, "We're all sorry."

"Do you want to go back to your car?"

Rosie shook her head, "No. I'm not angry - or not with you in any case. Where are we going, anyway?"

"I have no idea. I'm just driving. We could go get a late lunch?"

"Ugh. No people. I really can't do people right now. Where is Violet?" She asked suddenly.

"With Brooke. She has two daughters, and the three of them are thick as thieves. They're probably turning Brookie's house into a princess palace as we speak."

Rosie smiled, "I wish Lucy had cousins."

James looked over at her, "You don't have siblings?"

Rosie shook her head, "Both Ben and I were only children. We wanted to have more kids. One more at least, maybe two. The timing just didn't seem right, and then, of course, I lost Ben. So, looks like Luce will be an only child too."

Rosie suddenly realised that any more children she had would run the risk of sharing Lucy's... 'gift'. What had June said, the girls were all unshielded? She thought about knowingly bringing a child into the world that could be hurt by things Rosie couldn't see and shuddered. No. Lucy would definitely be an only child.

"How about you? Is it just you and Brooke?"

James nodded, "Just us. Perfect pigeon pair." He snorted.

"Your parents must love having three little grand-daughters."

"My parents are dead."

"Oh, god. I'm so sorry."

James shook it off, "Don't be. It wasn't like we were close. They were both alcoholics. My father died in his office of a heart attack which is probably the place he would have liked to go. Mum died in the hospital. Cirrhosis. That was about ten years ago now."

They were driving down a road Rosie realised she knew, "I shoot up here," she said suddenly, "Just up in the state forest."

James smiled, "Yeah, I know. I recognised it from the prints. But, we aren't going that far up."

He turned up a road that ran beside the forest. The pines shaded the road, to the left was a large field, well-tended, the grass was recently slashed.

Rosie sat up straighter, "Where are we going?"

"There is a place I know. It's good for thinking. I thought it might help bring you some peace."

They drove in silence for another five minutes before turning up a gravel driveway, through large gates and into well-tended grounds. A large house sat at the end.

"Umm, are we allowed to be here?" Rosie asked anxiously.

James laughed, "Yes. We aren't going up to that house, don't worry."

He drove down a little road to the right of the house and

back towards a small cabin that sat far at the rear. The cabin was in stark contrast to the rest of the property, which seemed precise and sterile. It was made of dark wood with a slate tile roof, a large deck out the back of it filled with an eclectic assortment of lawn furniture that looked like it had been collected on hard rubbish day.

"This is my cabin," James announced, pulling the car to a stop.

"This is yours?"

"Eh. The whole place is technically mine. David stays up at the house when he is in town, but it looks like he isn't in at the moment. The garage door is stuck, so he has been parking his car in front. I don't go up there - at all, actually. The cabin I come to sometimes when I want some time to myself to think."

Rosie's mind was reeling, "Oh. Oh! You're *that* St. Clair. The real estate St. Clairs."

"Not me. I'm just a framer. But yeah, my family were in real estate and a whole bunch of other crap that I couldn't care less about, if I'm being honest."

They walked up to the cabin and James unlocked the door, revealing a cosy living room inside, with a small kitchen. The whole place was technically one large room, carefully divided by furniture and a screen that Rosie could see hid a queen-sized bed. James went over to a small fridge and pulled out two cold beers, handing Rosie one, and sat on a stool near the kitchen bench watching her take in her surroundings. Rosie felt almost embarrassed to be here, every inch of it felt so personal, that she felt as though she was looking inside James to who he was at his core. Like the deck, the cabin had been furnished with odds and ends, an old couch covered in worn green canvas sat beside a battered white wooden kitchen chair. Well used handmade quilts covered the seat of another sofa. Rosie wandered over to a guitar and ran her hand over the strings.

"Ahh, my failed excursion into music," James laughed.

"You can't play?" She asked.

He hung his head in mock shame, "Not at all, I'm afraid."

"Why do you keep it?"

"I don't know. I guess I keep hoping it will click one day."

Rosie nodded and sipped her beer, walking over to a wall with photos on it. She recognised James and Violet of course, and in another Violet was with Brooke, and two little girls she assumed were Brooke's daughters. In some images, James was much younger than he was now, shirtless and with several other young men she didn't recognise, at a beach. The sun was in his eyes, and he had raised an arm to shield it from his face which was split in a large grin. His skin was golden brown, his body had beautiful lines to it that she knew came from a naturally active lifestyle instead of anything he had deliberately set out to cultivate. She would love to photograph him. She realised she had been staring at the image for far too long and blushed, turning back to him where he was smiling at her with amusement.

"You want to go sit on the deck?" He asked.

She nodded. James held out his hand to her, and she looked at it for a moment and then into his face, which was open, unassuming, kind. She took a deep breath and placed her hand in his.

CHAPTER 25

David walked back to his car from the warehouse he had been walking a potential commercial tenant through. It was the same one he thought would have been perfect for James. His business was nearly finished here now, and he was supposed to fly to Melbourne next week. A few more days to see his niece and nephew, and then he would be off. In all honesty, he could possibly leave tonight if he wanted to and he should, he had stayed here too long already and was making mistakes. Going to the vigil had been stupid - he didn't even know himself why he had gone. It was as though a strange compulsion that had driven him there. He had intended to stay back, view it from a distance and had been standing there in the shadows when he had seen that woman, Rosie, with that asshole. Before he even realised what he was doing, he had intervened. He climbed into his car now and slipped his hand into his pocket, running his fingers back and forth over a pendant like a talisman. Which, he supposed, is exactly what it was. He pulled out his phone and put Rosie's name into the search engine. It pulled up multiple images, but none were of her. Eventually, he found his way to the 'About' page of her website. There she was. Her red hair was lit by the sun; her skin was so pale it was almost iridescent, like opal. Damn, if James didn't have exquisite taste in women. Still, the way Brooke had been looking at him lately, it was as though she was seeing beneath the surface, and it made him feel exposed and uncomfortable. If she said something to that asshole cop husband of hers... well, he didn't need that. Still... Rosie Parker did have beautiful hands.

He sat back in his seat and closed his eyes. He hadn't been careful that night, walking through the city after a meeting on his way to where he had parked his car, up an alley at the back of a building he had been looking at as a potential investment. He had seen her up ahead of him; her hair had caught the streetlight, turning it a vibrant gold, cascading down her back in bouncing waves.

"Damn it," she had said.

She turned around holding one heel in her hand, and when he looked down, he realised she was wearing only one shoe, her other foot, long and elegant - was bare, like Cinderella. She looked embarrassed, her cheeks flushed a soft pink.

She shrugged at him and said, "Broken heel," by way of an explanation.

"Uh oh," he had joked and smiled at her, walking past her a few meters before his phone rang and he stopped to answer it.

. . .

He had a brief conversation with one of his employees and was preparing to walk on when he realised there was conversation behind him. He turned around to see a group of five men, drunk and loud, had stopped a short way from his Cinderella whose face was pinched as she pulled out her phone. The men were whistling, one of them being pushed forward by his friends, who were clearly egging him on to approach her. They were all wearing those ridiculous skinny jeans, their shirts too tight. He hated men like that; they probably had a favourite fucking protein powder. They acted like they were untouchable, but he probably made more a week then the five of them did together in a year. He could own them if he wanted to. The male being pushed forward suddenly broke from the pack and began sauntering towards her. This asshole definitely had a coffee order that ran for a paragraph. The beautiful blush was gone from her face, which had turned pale.

It was none of his business, of course, and he might have walked away... but as he reached into his pocket to feel for the ring, he had come up empty, and that had left him feeling lonely and hollow. The buzzing was back, an uncomfortable panic that rose within him. The men would be a problem, but he had learned that witnesses were sloppy, forgetful. Tomorrow they wouldn't remember him - or her. So, he had gone back.

"Where are you off to?" He had asked.

She looked at him gratefully, glancing quickly over her shoulder to the men, who had settled down in his presence.

"The station, I guess. My phone died. I was trying to order a ride."

She leant against the brick wall of the building, one hand playing with the pendant at her neck. Silver, a tree surrounded by a circle. His hand twitched.

"I'm going there myself," he began, a simple lie, his car *was* in the same direction. "I can walk you if you like?"

He held his breath; this one answer would decide everything. She had hesitated. He had expected she would, she didn't know him, women were naturally skittish, he had discovered. Then one more look back at the drunks behind her made up her mind, she nodded.

She had slipped off her other shoe. As she bent over, he tried to catch a hint of the top of her breasts beneath her blouse, but her shirt was buttoned a bit too high for his tastes. Women who acted as though their bodies were some kind of fucking prize tended to be uptight and boring. She carried her shoes looped over her fingers; her ankle had been sore from when the heel broke, and she held out one perfectly shaped leg to show him where it was indeed swelling. He had clucked paternally at it, and she had allowed him to put his arm around her to let her lean on him as they walked towards the station. Her skin felt like satin. It seemed like she was deliberately leaning into him, prattling on about her friends and her work as though he gave a goddamn shit. She stumbled a little, and he caught her, her breast pressing against his arm - she was definitely doing this deliberately.

They had been near the alley when he looked around. This was another coin toss moment; if anyone was nearby, he would walk her to the station and wish her a goodnight.

The streets were empty, and he almost wished they hadn't been, he liked her by now. Her laugh was like chimes. He wondered what noises she would make in bed. He always loved women too much - but they were fickle, flighty, liars - all of them. Even this one, sweet as she was, had mentioned nothing of a husband, despite her wedding band. She was so close he could smell her perfume, the lavender shampoo in her hair, making his heart race. Partway up the street she had stopped walking and held out her hand, "Since you're basically carrying me up the street, I should give you my name." She had held out her hand, slender fingers - she didn't use any polish on her nails, which he appreciated, but they were perfectly clean, tidy and filed. Beautiful.

At the mouth of the alley, he pretended his phone was ringing and asked her if she would mind stopping. She had nodded and smiled, leaning against the wall. He had mock answered the phone, walking down the alley a little and talking constantly. He clicked open his briefcase and removed the telescopic baton from it.

Then he moved quickly.

She turned just before he reached her, her eyes widening in surprise. They were never expecting it. He caught her as she fell, lifting her into his arms like a bride being carried over the threshold. She barely weighed anything in his arms, her head rest against his chest, and he leaned down, burying his face in her hair, feeling the softness of it on his cheek. He placed her gently in the car.

"I'm Hannah," she had said earlier.

He had shaken her hand, "David. Your Prince Charming for the night."

He opened his eyes now and pulled out the pendant, a Tree of Life. Hannah had been almost perfect. She had lasted longer than he thought she would, a fighter after all. He turned the car on and headed to his next appointment. It was important to stick the schedule; he would leave next week as planned. To leave earlier could raise suspicion. And he would make a dinner date with his niece and her husband before he left. The best place to hide was in plain sight.

CHAPTER 26

Rosie had slipped away to call Kate and ask her to mind Lucy another night, and sent Dee a quick text to say she was fine and would be staying with June. She felt oddly like when she was young and would lie to Kate about being at Dee's, and Dee would tell Meg she was staying at Rosie's house. They would head off to a party, sipping too strong drinks and walk home as the sun crept over the horizon. She supposed that was some sort of rite of passage for teenagers. She said this to James when she came back out onto the deck, taking up residence on an old outdoor recliner.

"I never did that," he said.

"You were a good boy, then?" She teased. She was almost finished her second beer and felt the tension in her shoulders relaxing.

James burst out laughing, "Hardly! My folks just didn't care where I was. There was no need to lie. Besides, drinking is a full-time hobby for St Clairs. They would probably have been more alarmed if I said I wanted to take up volunteering."

"God, Kate would have had a stroke if I had of told her half the things Dee and I got up to. She was always fretting about me getting hurt or something happening."

"That's nice," James said.

Rosie cut eyes with him.

"No, I mean it," he insisted. "She cares about you. She wouldn't worry if she didn't care."

Rosie took another sip of her beer. Funny, she had always felt like it was more that Kate cared about herself, that she couldn't bear it if something happened because of how it would affect *her*. She shrugged.

"I guess she cares," she admitted.

"Trust me," he said, "No one was looking out for Brooke and me except the housekeeper. She basically raised us - and she was the one I lied to about where I was and what I was doing."

"Do you still keep in contact with her?" Rosie asked.

"She died around the time Violet was born actually; she was six weeks old. Breast cancer. I think she held on just so she could see Violet."

"I'm sorry."

"Me too. She was a good woman."

They were silent for a moment.

"We have had very different lives," Rosie remarked.

"Indeed."

James stood up, "You want another beer?"

Rosie squinted into the top of her bottle, then finished off the last sip, "Sure. Why not? I'm not driving."

James went back inside, and Rosie leaned back and closed her eyes to the last of the sun rays that peeked over the top of the hoop pines. It was peaceful here. A light wind played over her face, soft like a caress, a balm on all of her raw nerves after the last few weeks. She wondered what James would say if she told him about spirits and shields. She shook her head; she wasn't going to think about that now, not here. She opened her eyes and found that the sun had nearly set. She heard a rustle of leaves, and a bird landed on the lower branches of the tree beside the deck.

"Oh!" Rosie breathed.

It was an owl, looking at her with its big eyes. She was afraid to move but felt her hand reach automatically in front of her as though reaching for a phantom camera.

"Hi," she said softly.

The owl blinked at her. They looked at each other for a long time; it seemed. Rosie had never seen one in the wild before, and it felt almost like a messenger, like a sign that everything would be okay.

James stepped outside, and the bird took flight, sweeping away silently, as quickly as it came.

"Are you okay?" he asked.

She looked up at him, opening her mouth to tell him about the owl but stopped, it felt strangely personal somehow. Instead, she just nodded and smiled. The wind picked up, and she shivered.

"Come around the other side; there is an outdoor heater," he said.

He showed her around the side of the deck and turned on the large outdoor heater which sat close to a huge round bed.

"A bed?"

"A *day* bed."

"It's massive."

James lay down on it, pumping some cushions under his head.

"It's very comfortable. I sleep out here sometimes. It's a bit like camping except the deck roof keeps the rain off, and it's way comfier than a sleeping bag on the ground."

Rosie lay down beside him. In front of her was a clear view of the night sky, which darkened by the minute, the stars seemed to turn on one by one like fairy lights.

"You know, I come and sit outside with my neighbour almost every night. Except *I* bring the beer. He brings the cigarettes."

James feigned shock, "You smoke! Rosie, I'm scandalised!"

Rosie snorted, "*A* cigarette. *One*. A few times a week. But yeah, I should probably just stick with the beer."

"So, should I be jealous of your neighbour that you're hanging out almost every night?"

"Ahh, no," Rosie said, "Mr Thompson is like a surrogate grandfather. He talks about his late wife and I talk about... you know Lucy, work, Dee, my impossible mother... and Ben."

James nodded and was silent for a few moments before he leaned back on his elbows, "So, how did you and Ben meet?"

Rosie laughed and took a sip of her beer, "I yelled at him."

"Pardon?"

· · ·

She settled back on the cushions, falling into the familiar tale.

"I was running late to shoot a wedding down the coast, and my GPS had just died on me. And everything was going wrong. My maps weren't working on my phone and my room-mate at the time had a white cat who sat on the black pants I had laid out on the bed while I was showering. I couldn't find a lint brush; the heel broke off my shoe, and my second shooter had come down with the flu. I raced into the electronics store and was ready to spend as much as it took to get a GPS and get out of there in record speed. But this *idiot* would not stop talking to the salesman about digital cameras. So, I'm standing there, trying to make hard eye contact with the salesman and send telepathic messages to this stupid customer so he would realise I was waiting. Finally, I can't take it anymore, so I just say, 'Look, I'm really sorry, but this is an emergency, and I need a GPS *right now*', and the idiot says sarcastically, 'A GPS emergency?' And I say confidently, that *yes*, it was a GPS emergency. He responded that in that case, *he* had a camera emergency. I pointed to one of the shelf that would do all the rubbish he was rambling to the salesman about and said, 'That's the one you want. Now, I'm late to shoot a wedding, and I really do need a GPS' - and then I think I channelled my grandmother and clapped my hands at the salesman who scurried off and grabbed one. Then I paid and left."

James found himself laughing, marvelling at the way Rosie told a story, using her hand expressively, and acting out everyone's expressions until he felt like he had been right there with her.

"And the idiot was Ben?"

Rosie nodded, smiling, "The idiot was Ben."

"So, did you give Ben a business card or something that day?"

"No. After I left Ben decided he wanted to track me down, so he started searching Brisbane photographers and asking about one that looked like me. He finally found my website. He booked himself a shoot."

James let out a low whistle, "Wow. He was really keen. You must have knocked him off his feet that day."

Rosie said nothing, lost for a moment in the fairy-tale beginning of her and Ben. Usually her memories of him, even the happy ones left her with a bitter aftertaste. This was the first time she could remember speaking of him and having there be nothing but what it was. A beautiful time in her life. She smiled to herself and looked out to the stars.

James looked at Rosie, every part of him wanted to lean over and kiss her, but this thing they had going right now - whatever it was - seemed so fragile. He couldn't risk messing it up. The light from the outdoor heater shone off her hair, as though it were living flame. Rosie turned over towards him, her face inches from his, so close he could have counted the freckles on her nose. The look seemed to last forever; he couldn't have torn himself away if he had tried. *I love her*, he thought suddenly, shocking himself with the truth of it. Rosie's eyes widened slightly, as though she had heard him think it. *She will leave*, he thought, *she doesn't want this*. She sat up on one elbow, and he prepared himself for the way she would let him down gently, make a kind excuse to go. But instead, she leaned forward and placed her hand on his cheek, her thumb grazing over his lips. He heard her breath catch a little in her throat as she tilted her face towards his with a slow deliberateness, an almost defiantness, as though she dared the universe to make her regret it - and her lips met his.

Rosie had expected that when she kissed him, she would suddenly feel every cell in her body scream at the wrongness of it.

It's too soon. It's not Ben. A mistake.

But none of those things happened. Instead, she heard nothing but the chirp of the crickets, the wind in the trees, and the steady beating of her own heart. What surprised her most wasn't the differences; it was the familiarity. How it clicked. As though she had already kissed him a hundred times. It felt as though suddenly, what was happening was always meant to have happened. As though every time they had spoken, every phone call, every text message, had been one more pearl in the strand that would lead them to this moment. When he ran his tongue along her bottom lip, her skin broke out in goosebumps. When he slid the strap of her shirt off her shoulder, she felt herself lean into him. When he moved his fingers to the waistband of her pants, she unbuckled his belt in response. And the whole time he kept asking her if she was sure, if it was okay, if she wanted this, and she found herself answering yes and yes. God, yes. Please. *Yes*.

CHAPTER 27

Rosie lay back under the quilt James had pulled from a box beside the day bed. She slipped her bare leg out from the covers to feel the breeze on her skin.

"This is a good bed," she remarked.

"It's a day bed, but yes. It is good. It's actually my favourite bed now."

He ran his fingers along her arm, and she snuggled in closer to him, resting her head on his chest and enjoying the warmth of his skin; the comforting sound of his heartbeat. She felt like she could stay right here forever.

"I do hope your uncle hasn't come home, though."

"Why is that?" James asked. "The house is pretty far away. He couldn't have seen anything."

"No," Rosie agreed. "It's just... well, sound carries at night."

James bit back a smile, "That's true."

Rosie leaned back on the pillows and looked up at the stars, "You know, I saw an owl before."

"Did you?"

"James?"

He looked over at her; something in her face had changed.

"Yes?" He asked.

"Do you believe in ghosts?"

He put his arms behind his head and let out a breath, "Oh, wow. I don't know. I guess I do. There was this one time when Brooke and I were young - maybe seven or eight. We were playing down the creek not far from here. Just mucking around, you know? Splashing each other, and knowing we were going to get hell for it later because our clothes were drenched. Then all of a sudden Brooke freezes and goes white as a sheet. I thought our dad had come down from the house and was about to belt the both of us - except it would have been a miracle if he had left his study. She is staring behind me, and I turn to look, but there is nothing there. Brooke turns and bolts back to the house like the devil himself was after her, and me running after her asking what she saw. We finally get back in sight of the house, and she sits down on the grass - just over there, actually," James pointed in the direction of the tree Rosie had seen the owl in. "I asked her what had freaked her out, and she said she saw a little girl playing behind us, but she didn't look right. Then Brooke said that the girl had just disappeared, like she had blinked out of existence. I didn't see anything myself, but the way Brooke said it made me break out in goosebumps. We never did play down there again."

· · ·

Rosie had chills hearing it. She looked over to the forest that had seemed benevolent until a few moments ago and wondered whether Lucy would see that girl playing in the creek too.

"Why do you ask?" James questioned. "Have you ever seen a ghost?"

"No," Rosie said, then hesitated. "Well, yes. I guess I have. I just can't remember it."

James frowned, "What do you mean?"

Rosie took a deep breath and began at the beginning, telling him about the shield slip in the car on the day of the accident, the girl in Lucy's room, the dirt that kept appearing from nowhere, and the fire. She told him about Frank and June and retold their stories to him. She talked until she felt drained and unburdened at the same time. When she finished, James lay silently. Rosie was afraid to look at him, certain he was going to think she was certifiably insane.

"That..." he began, "that's a lot to take in."

"I know."

"You think the fire in Lucy's room was started by a spirit? One of these Others?"

Rosie sat up, pulling the quilt up to cover her breasts, suddenly feeling more naked than she had a few minutes ago.

"I don't know. Well... yes. I guess I do believe that."

James nodded, "And your dad, he went basically crazy from being unshielded? But he gave it to you, and now you can't see them, but Lucy can because the women in your family have some kind of 'sight'?"

"More or less."

"Wow." James stood up and walked to the edge of the deck, and Rosie was momentarily startled by his nakedness. He turned to her, "This spirit can touch Lucy?"

"It seems so."

"But it can't touch you?"

"No. I'm shielded."

"Yeah, but June said your shield is basically like Swiss cheese."

"Yes?"

"So, what if it, I don't know, *reaches* through one of those holes, or something?"

Rosie sat stunned for a moment. It had never occurred to her that she might be in any danger due to her torn shield, and she wasn't sure it had occurred to Frank or June either. *Could an Other reach through the holes? No. Otherwise, I would have seen something. Right?* The truth was, she had no idea. She wasn't sure what the rules were here. If there were any rules, at all.

"I'm going to get us another drink," James said. "And then we can try to work out how to get this Other thing out of your house."

"You want to help me exorcise a spirit from my house?" she asked.

"Rosie, this is - believe me - the very weirdest post-sex conversation I've ever had in my life. But, yes. If you have a ghost problem, I will help you evict it from your house. I'm 'all in', baby. However, I really am going to need whiskey for this."

"I take mine neat," she said.

He bent down to kiss her, "You're perfect."

· · ·

They sat wrapped in quilts on the edge of the deck, dangling their feet over the side, and watching the trees sway, black silhouettes against the deep indigo of the night sky. Rosie and James talked over what they knew from June and Frank and what might possibly have come into the house that the spirit could be tethering to.

"Rosie, could Lucy have brought something in that you don't know about?" James asked.

"From where? Plus, I unpack her bag," Rosie stated, "I would have noticed."

"Hmm," James mused.

Rosie looked at him, "What is it?"

James cleared his throat, "Well. You said Lucy had been taking things from kinder... maybe she took something that didn't belong to her... she might deliberately avoid you seeing it."

"She has hidden it, you mean?"

James nodded.

Weeks ago, Rosie would have dismissed this thought completely. But now she had to admit that she didn't know everything about Lucy - any more than Kate had known everything about her. It was a hard revelation to wrap her mind around, how this human who had come from her body was slowly growing away from her into a person in her own right.

"I've been thinking about something," she said slowly.

"What's that?"

"Frank gave me his shield, right? When I saw you at the fuel station earlier, I was wondering about giving it to Lucy."

James blinked, "You can't be serious? Rosie, your dad is, by your account, totally off his rocker because of doing exactly that. We absolutely need to protect Lucy, and we *will* find a way to do that, but not by sacrificing you."

Something about the way he said 'we' made Rosie's shoulders relax, as though since Ben left she had carried the sole responsibility for keeping Lucy safe and now someone was offering to carry it for a while.

"Frank was never meant to be unshielded though," she argued. "I could be perfectly fine."

"Yes, you could be, but I would try something else first."

"You would?"

"Yes."

"Even if it were Violet getting hurt?"

James looked past her thinking it over before he reached for her hand and squeezed it, "You're right. If it were Violet? I would be tearing the shield off me myself."

Rosie nodded and looked out to the trees.

"So," James said. "How do we remove your shield?"

"I guess I'll ask my father."

"And once it's off, you can see the spirit? So you can... move it on or whatever?"

"I'll have to try."

Rosie woke the next morning to the sound of birds. She opened her eyes, she and James had slept out on the day bed under a pile of quilts. The sun was beginning to rise, turning the sky a beautiful pink. She looked over to James, who was sleeping on his stomach, the quilt was down around his waist, and his back was bare. She traced the freckles along it, making constellations out of them. They had fallen asleep in the early hours of the morning, she couldn't have gotten more than three hours of sleep, but she felt more energised and rested than she had in months.

He stirred and opened his eyes, sleepily.

"Hey," he said.

"Hey."

He groaned, "Ugh. Why are you awake so early?"

She smiled, "Force of habit. Plus, I have a shoot this afternoon, and I'm going to go over to Kate's and collect Lucy this morning. I want to try to figure out what I'm looking for before I start going through her room."

James sighed and raised himself up on his arms, "Then you're going to need caffeine. I'll put the kettle on."

———

James dropped Rosie back to her car, and she drove over to Dee's house to shower and eat breakfast before heading to Kate's. When she pulled in the driveway, she realised Dee wasn't home either and felt both relieved and slightly disappointed that she didn't have to face Dee. She felt certain her friend would have seen everything that had happened in the past twenty-four hours written all over her face. Part of her wanted to sit with Dee and go over every second with her. To examine single words and phrases like they would have done back when they were both teenagers, and boys were strange creatures that neither of them understood. Discussing what happened with James would mean discussing what had transpired with Frank and June though, and she wasn't sure she had the strength to explain the whole thing again right now.

· · ·

Tiny leapt off of the dog-bed Dee had placed for him on the verandah as she approached the gate, joyously wagging his tail, his feet dancing on the spot. He let out one bark and then thundered down the stairs to greet Rosie as she entered.

"Hello! Hello! I've missed you!" Rosie said, vigorously patting him. "You're looking for your breakfast, huh? Come on. Let's go inside."

Rosie let herself inside with the spare key hidden under one of the planters and greeted the cats that began winding their bodies around her legs. She went into the kitchen and began dishing food into bowls. After she fed the animals, she put her phone on to charge, before going up to the bathroom and turning on the shower. Standing under the spray, she closed her eyes and let the water run over, feeling calmer and more focused than she had in weeks - despite the fact her life had become infinitely more complicated. She rubbed her wrist, feeling the slight tenderness from where Ricky had grabbed her and frowned. She *would* have to go to the police about him, but that was a job for tomorrow. When she and Dee had gotten home that night, Dee had taken photos of the bruises before wrapping her wrist.

"In case you change your mind," she had said.

Today though, she had a plan, and as she shampooed her hair, she went over it in her mind. She would pick up Lucy and talk to her about what she might have brought into the house to see if she could determine what was tethering the spirit. Then, she would drop Lucy to June and head to her shoot. Once she got back she and June and Frank could talk about unshielding her - surely Frank would know how to do that, he had done it himself, after all. They would set this spirit free, or 'move it on' or whatever, then she could report Ricky, and they would all move on with their lives.

A nagging part of her brain reminded her that unshielding might not be that simple, that it might come with a cost that she would have to bear... but against the possibility of Lucy getting hurt, there was only one decision she could make. Hadn't James said he would make the same choice himself? She poured conditioner into her palm and thought about James, barely believing she had opened up to him about all of this; and the even more surprising fact that he hadn't run a mile when she did. *I'm all in, baby*. What did that mean?

Tiny nudged the door open with his nose and whined at her, clearly finished his breakfast.

"Okay, okay. I'm getting out," she rinsed the last of the conditioner out and turned off the taps. "God, you're worse than Lucy."

After Rosie collected Lucy from Kate, she drove to a nearby park and stopped the car. Lucy peered out the window from her car seat, questioningly.

"I thought we were going to see Grandma June and Grandpa Frank?" she asked.

Rosie winced a little at Lucy's familiar term of Frank, but pushed aside her feelings, "We will. I just wanted to have a talk. Come sit in the front with me for a moment."

Lucy eyed her suspiciously but unbuckled her seat and climbed over the centre console into the passenger seat. Rosie smiled ruefully at her.

"Lucy, I owe you an apology," she began. "When you said there was a girl in your room, I didn't believe you."

"But then you said you did," Lucy interjected.

"That's true. I did say that, but I didn't really know what to believe. I just want to say that I *do* believe you. It was wrong of me not to; you should always be able to talk to me and have me believe whatever you tell me."

Lucy nodded, bored with the conversation, looking towards the playground equipment.

"Lucy?" Rosie said. "There is also something else we need to talk about. Awhile back, your kinder teacher told me you had been taking things from the classroom."

Rosie paused, and Lucy shot her a look full of guilt but shook her head in denial, "I never."

"Lucy, we can't have lies and secrets between us. We need to be honest with each other. I need you to tell me the truth about the things you took. Grandma June and... Grandpa Frank, they were talking to me about seeing things that no one else can see. Grandma June is like you; she can see them too. Both of them think the girl might be... sort of stuck on something in the house. Maybe trapped on something we have brought in."

"Grandma June can see them?" Lucy asked.

Rosie nodded. If she wanted Lucy to be honest with her,

she had to be honest back, "It's like a gift. Like how you have the same colour hair as daddy. This was passed down to you."

"Can you see them?" Lucy asked.

"No. There is something around me that makes it so I can't."

"That light thing," Lucy said, nodding wisely.

God, Lucy can see the shield, Rosie thought, shocked. There was so much about her daughter that she didn't know.

"Yes, that's right. It means I can't see them. Lucy, we need to know if you have brought anything into the house that maybe Mama doesn't know about. Please. It's very important, we can make it so the girl isn't in your room anymore," Rosie asked.

Lucy pursed her lips and looked out the window again, "They are playing out there," she said, nodding at the park.

"Who?"

"The girl and the boy. You can't see them, Mama."

Rosie shuddered, how many times had she been out with a Lucy and thought she was staring into space when her daughter was really watching spirits?

"I took a ring," Lucy said finally, breaking Rosie from her thoughts. "Violet showed me, she said it was at her house. I took it from her bag."

Rosie scooped Lucy into her arms and held her, "Thank you for telling me. Where is the ring now? Where in your room?"

Lucy looked up at her, "It's in my dollhouse. I was using it for a crown."

"Thank you, peanut. Let's go to Grandma's house now, okay?"

Lucy climbed back into her seat, and Rosie twisted around to help her with the buckle.

"Mama?"

"Yes?"

"Why did Violet have a trapped girl?"

Rosie shook her head, "I don't know, Lucy. But I'll find out."

CHAPTER 28

Rosie had dropped Lucy to June's house and said she would be back after the shoot.

"I have something I want to talk to you about later," she had said once Lucy was out of earshot. "We will stay here tonight, and after Lucy goes to sleep we can talk. I think I know what the tethered item is, but there is too much to go over now."

"She will be safe here with Frank and me," June had said, clasping Rosie's hands in her own. They were warm and dry, and Rosie felt as though she could almost feel the strength and calm of her grandmother pass to her in their touch. She had to admit that being with June was probably safer for Lucy right now than anywhere - June and Frank could at least see what Lucy saw. They were more capable than Rosie was to protect her daughter. *But not for long*, Rosie thought, determinedly, *once I am unshielded, I can make sure she is safe.*

She drove out to the state forest, casting a longing glance up the road that led to the St Clair property, and the cabin where she had stayed with James. She wondered if he was still there, maybe standing on the deck in his jeans with a cup of coffee. He could be looking out to the very forest she was now driving past. She was surprised to find herself almost giddy at the thought of seeing him, that heady feeling of freshness and possibility that came with the dawning of a new relationship. *Not that we are in a relationship*, she reminded herself. Still, something was happening; she couldn't deny that what she felt for him was more than lust. Opening up the way she had with James was something she couldn't have imagined herself doing a few short weeks ago. Opening up to anyone was unthinkable.

She tried to imagine herself making a life with James, how would Lucy feel? She and Ben had been so close before he died. Ben had always been a better parent than her, Rosie always felt that she was learning how to be a mother on the fly, but Ben seemed to instinctively know what Lucy needed. She felt a wrenching of her heart when she thought of him, how starting something new would mean finally giving up the last part of their relationship that still remained - her grief. Being with James almost felt like choosing somehow, and yet, James didn't seem to mind her talking about Ben. He asked questions, listened when she spoke of him. Ben didn't sit between them, but he was there and not forgotten, like a photo on the wall.

She shook her head to clear it; she needed to focus on one thing at a time, which meant that right now, she needed to put on her business hat. Turning up the dirt road that led to the clearing where she shot, she mentally went over the poses she wanted to get, the clients' names and information they had given her about their family. Rosie rolled to a stop and cut the engine, pulling her camera bag from the back of the car and shut the doors, locking them behind her. She tapped her pocket to check her phone was in there and then headed towards the jacarandas to set up. Nerves fluttered in her stomach, no matter how many shoots she had, the time before her clients arrived was always full of nerves for her, as though she would forget everything she knew about apertures and shutter speeds. She feared she would end up standing there, camera in hand, unable to remember how to take a single shot. Then, as soon as she lifted the camera to her eye, the whole world slipped away... reduced down to only the rectangle of the viewfinder, time disappeared, and the world beyond her lens ceased to exist. Now, when she felt the nerves coming, she tried to just ride them out, waiting for the moment when it would all return to her like magic.

This time of year, there were no flowers on the jacarandas that shaded the clearing. Their branches spread out above her like arms, as though they were reaching for each other. She set down her bag and took out her camera, sliding a memory card into the slot and raising it to her eye. Inside she checked the light meter, made adjustments and took a test shot. She checked the LCD. The sparseness of the Jacaranda was causing very dappled lighting. *Fine now, but not when there are people in the shot*, thought Rosie. She walked around, checking the lighting from different angles. By the shed was nice, of course. That would work. She wandered closer to the edge of the hoop pines. Maybe she should take them into the forest a little way? She weighed the options in her head; snakes were always a possibility any time of year, the risk was decreasing the closer it got to winter, but it was never zero. Rosie looked down at her jeans and knee-high boots, *better I check it out myself first*, she thought, reluctantly.

Rosie picked up a big stick and whacked at the undergrowth, waited a few seconds, and began walking in. She stomped her feet and occasionally hit the stick against the ground or a tree. *God, I hate snakes*, she thought, gritting her teeth, *let it never be said that I don't suffer for my art*. After about ten minutes, she realised she was heading downhill, and at the bottom, the trees opened up to a creek bed.

"Oh, wow," Rosie said.

The water was low now but she could see that sometimes it must flow quite high. At some point the water had carved a bank, one she stood on top of now, the tree roots holding it in place. Below her, was a stone lined shore, and beyond that flowed a crystal-clear creek, passing amongst large granite boulders. This must have been the creek James told her about, the one he and Brooke had played in when they were young. She thought about the girl Brooke had claimed to have seen and felt slightly uneasy, - but in the golden light of the afternoon, the creek looked like she would be more likely to encounter fairies than a long-dead ghost. *And besides*, she thought, *I am shielded*. There was nothing for her to fear. Apprehension gave way to excitement.

"This is amazing!" She virtually shouted, and forgetting

her fear of snakes; she searched for an easy way down the embankment.

Near one tree was a kind of natural step. Rosie checked her watch, still thirty minutes, she had time. She grabbed hold of one of the trees lower branches and stepped down on to the first 'step' in the side. The next one was a bit bigger; she would have to jump a little, there was nothing to hold. She briefly wondered if her clients could manage this without too much difficulty, but most clients were fairly adventurous with locations. *We can lift down the kids*, she thought. Rosie jumped down on to the rocky shore and picked her way to the water. The water was fairly shallow in most places, mid-shin perhaps, with a few deeper spots that might have been thigh deep. Rosie stepped gingerly on to one of the larger rocks to see if she could find a way to to the other side. Rock to rock, she made her way to a huge boulder in the centre that had a flat top like a table and was just as large. She stood on top, like a triumphant conqueror, sweating and panting. Lifting her camera, she took a few test shots from different angles. "Perfect," she breathed.

The wind lifted her hair, cooling the back of her neck, bringing with it the smell of decaying leaves and grasses from the creek, and the vague smell of something foul. Rosie wrinkled her nose. That would certainly put a damper on her beautiful creek shoot.

"Maybe a dead possum," she said aloud.

She clambered down from the boulder heading toward

the other side of the creek bed, and the smell increased as she moved.

"Okay, that is really bad," she said, covering her nose with one hand. Rosie looked at her stick, dubiously, "It would be nasty... but I could try to cover it up a bit."

She climbed through the grasses on the other side of the creek, heading up the embankment, which was less steep than the one she had come down. She could hear the sound of buzzing flies. *Maybe I should just go back to the shed near the jacarandas; this is so freaking gross.* Even as she thought it, she ploughed on, unwilling to give up her new prize location.

Rosie headed towards the sound of the buzzing, the smell of rot hitting her nostrils and making her cough and cover her nose and mouth. A vague sense of unease settled in her stomach and was increasing with every step.

"Go back," she whispered to herself. Except she couldn't, she had to see what her instincts were now screaming at her.

She found her nestled beside a fallen tree trunk, partially covered by the forest dirt and leaves. Her blonde hair covered her face. A cloud of flies lifted from her skin as Rosie walked up. That was all Rosie saw before she stumbled backwards, her vision tunnelling, a roaring filling her ears. She tried to run back towards the creek, her legs feeling unwieldy, stumbling, falling forward on to her knees and vomiting on the leaves.

Hannah. Hannah.

She picked herself up and looked back where she came,

suddenly fearing she was being followed, but the forest was still and quiet behind her.

She climbed down the embankment carelessly. Her lens smashed against a rock and Rosie heard the glass shatter as she sloshed across the creek, slipping on rocks, the cold water entering her boots. She ran through the forest, emerging back into the clearing with the jacarandas, panting. She saw her camera bag and sprinted for it, ripping it open and pulling out her car keys before racing to her car and getting inside and locking the doors. She sat there a moment, surveying the forest she had just come from, certain that any second someone would burst forth. There was a sobbing sound, and Rosie looked around the car wildly, before realising the noises came from her. She pulled her phone from her pocket with hands that shook violently. She had nightmares sometimes where she was trapped in a dark room, trying to call for help. In those dreams, her fingers would press the wrong buttons, and she would keep cancelling the call and trying again - always calling and never being heard. As she pressed the buttons now, she tried to steady herself, praying her fingers would cooperate. She lifted the phone to her ear; the ringing seemed far away, a sound too civilised, too normal.

"Triple zero, what service do you need? Police, fire or ambulance?"

Rosie opened her mouth, but nothing came out. *What service? Fucking all of them.*

"Hello? What service do you need? Police, fire or ambulance?"

Rosie took a deep breath, "I need the police. I found a body. I think I found Hannah Avery."

Michael hated this. He was filled with a despair. For days, he and his colleagues had told each other they wouldn't find Hannah Avery alive, trying to prepare each other for what they all knew deep down. But hope was a tenacious companion; you always wished you would be wrong. Occasionally, he would imagine himself finding her - that she had run away, that she had an affair, a secret pregnancy that wasn't her husbands, or even that someone had taken her, but he reached her in time. He stood here now, watching his colleague Jim, who was questioning Rosie Parker. Rosie had that shocked look in her eyes that he recognised from other scenes, car accidents and assaults. She would be seeing Hannah Avery for the rest of her life. Of course, they didn't officially *know* it was Hannah. But it was Hannah. Michael knew. The paramedics had arrived on the scene, and a blonde woman was squatting down beside Rosie. Her eyes were filled with concern and empathy as she spoke to her in a low voice while she unpacked a bag beside her.

Jim made his way back to Michael.

"Fuck this job," he said.

Michael sighed, "Yep."

"She's told me the same story three times now, looking for a shoot location and smelled something up the creek, stumbled across the body."

The pair made their way back to the scene, a trail had

been worn into the forest now, and the way through was easier. As they got closer to the scene it buzzed with activity, a small gazebo had been erected nearby, and the area was flagged so no one contaminated the scene, workers in white suits were searching the area, photographs were being taken.

One of the techs came over to him, "There seems to be a trail that comes from the road to this area, it's not very defined but some broken branches, trampled ground. And the ground seems harder there, more compacted."

Jim's eyes followed the direction the tech was pointing in, "So, we have a trail from where he dumped the body, then. That gives us an idea of where he may have parked at least."

The tech shook his head, "No, this trail has fresh markings, but it's well worn. Also? It doesn't actually lead to the body. It ends over there." He indicated to a spot twenty-five meters away from where they were.

Michael frowned, someone had been coming out here often enough to wear a trail in the forest, likely the same person who killed Hannah and dumped the body. But why would the trail end over there? Realisation dawned on him and Michael felt nausea rising in his stomach.

"There is more than one," he said. "Hannah isn't the only one here."

The tech nodded, "That's what we are thinking. But whoever is buried over there... he must go there a lot."

Jim swore and began stalking over to the spot the tech had pointed out, "He's been visiting her."

CHAPTER 29

Rosie lay curled on her side on Dee's couch when suddenly she sat bolt upright, "I need to call June! She's expecting me to collect Lucy."

Dee soothed her back down, "I already called June. Remember?"

"Oh. Yes. That's right."

Rosie had been taken to the hospital by ambulance to be treated for shock, a sweet-faced female paramedic, holding her hand and speaking softly to her - words that Rosie couldn't remember.

At the hospital, Dee had blown in like a hurricane, holding Rosie to her so hard that Rosie felt her bones would snap. Dee had smelled like cinnamon and vanilla, the scents of baking caught in her hair, and the simple familiarity of them had grounded her for a brief moment. Dee took her back to a time before Hannah Avery had gone missing, erasing the smell of decay that she felt had been trapped in her throat since the moment she found Hannah. *Dee.* A solid lifeline that kept Rosie tethered in this world when she felt she might begin screaming and never stop. Dee had patted Rosie down, searching for signs that she was still here and whole, like a mother examining a child after they had suffered an accident. She had taken command of the situation, speaking with doctors. She stood toe to toe with detectives who had arrived to talk to Rosie again, demanding they leave her be, until Rosie had feebly called out that it was fine. She found herself hoping if she simply gave in and repeated her horror again, she could erase it from her mind and never have to think of the dirt in Hannah's hair and how all the beauty and cleverness, all of the memories that lived within her, had been snuffed out and were somehow gone.

Dee had asked if they had looked into Ricky, recounting the night of the vigil, showing the police the photos on her phone of the bruises on Rosie's wrist. They had taken a statement from Rosie about the assault too. That was the word they had used, assault. Rosie had felt her stomach lurch at it, feeling small and pitiful, like a victim herself. She had thought of his hand on her wrist and wondered if those same hands had grabbed Hannah's wrist and bile rose in her throat as she leaned over and delicately vomited beside the detectives' shoes. Finally, Dee had bundled her up and driven her back home, where she lay on Dee's couch, Tiny laying down beside her like a guardian. In the hospital, as she told the detectives again, Dee had covered her mouth as Rosie went over finding Hannah, tears slipping from her eyes - and Rosie had known that for Dee it was as though she was finding her too, empathy rolling towards Rosie like waves.

. . .

Dee came back in now, holding a glass and helped Rosie to sit up. Rosie expected it to smell of the earthy aroma of steeped herbs, but the glass was cool, and the sharp scent of alcohol hit her nostrils.

"Brandy," Dee said.

Rosie nodded, sipping it, feeling it burn the back of her throat, warming her.

"Slowly," Dee urged, biting her lip, "you have nothing in your stomach. I could make you something. A light soup? Even toast?"

Rosie shook her head, the thought of food making the brandy sit uneasily in her stomach.

"Do you think they've told Bryan?" Rosie asked.

"I think so, honey. I don't know."

Rosie nodded and finished the brandy, getting shakily to her feet, "I think I'll have a shower."

Dee followed her up the hallway, grabbing a fresh towel from the linen closet. She turned on the taps of the shower as Rosie removed her jewellery, and began to undress, pulling off her jeans. The bottoms of them had dried stiff, leaving dirt and bits of leaves on them, souvenirs from her run through the forest back to the car.

"Will you sit outside the door?" She asked Dee.

"Outside the bathroom door?"

"No... outside the glass door of the shower? Is that okay?"

Dee nodded, her eyes filled with sympathy and concern. Rosie stepped into the shower and closed her eyes and wondered how it was possible that she had been standing in this same spot only hours before. She methodically scrubbed at her skin, washing her hair, and cleaning her face, until her flesh was bright pink. Sliding to the bottom of the shower, she sat with her back pressed against the cool tiles, pulling her knees to her chest. She stayed there until the water began to cool, reluctantly standing to turn off the taps.

Dee handed her a soft towel and Rosie followed Dee down the hall to Rosie's room, where Dee had laid out a pair of track pants and an old t-shirt earlier. Rosie found herself wobbling on the spot, barely able to keep herself upright all of a sudden. She sat on the bed and allowed Dee to dress her like a child, letting herself be helped back into the bed, Dee pulling the covers up to her chin, before lying beside her.

"I can sleep here," Dee said. "You won't be alone."

Rosie's eyes drifted shut, and she registered the dip of the bed and Tiny jumped on to the end of it, his feet padding the quilt as he found comfort and lay down to continue his guard.

"I wonder if Frank hadn't of shielded me if I could have been able to see her," Rosie murmured.

"See who?" Dee asked.

Rosie opened her eyes, "Hannah."

Dee looked confused but then shook her head, "Honey, you're tired. Go to sleep now. Tiny and I will be here all night."

Rosie reached out and took Dee's hand and slipped into a deep, dreamless sleep.

. . .

Rosie slept and woke, slept and woke. At times the sun would be up, and then she would drift off, and when she woke again, it would have set. Periodically, Dee would force her to sit up and press a glass of water to her lips, or spoon soup into her mouth, and Rosie would obediently open and swallow like a baby bird. Finally, when it seemed as though her body had slept enough; she woke alert in the darkness. Tiny was snoring softly at her feet, and Dee was curled on top of the covers, still dressed in a patterned wrap-around skirt, a tank top and cardigan. Her braid trailed over her arm like a snake. Rosie shifted out from under the covers and pulled a blanket over Dee's sleeping form. She went to the toilet, unable to remember when she had last been, and then into the bathroom to splash some water on her face and rinse her mouth. She wandered through the empty rooms of the house, the clock in the kitchen told her it was three in the morning. *But of what day,* she wondered and searched until she found her phone charging on a small table in the dining room. She read the date and gasped, three days had passed. How was that possible? Where was Lucy? Was she still with June? Had James called? Kate would be beside herself.

"Everyone is okay," came a voice from behind her. Rosie turned around to find Dee rubbing her eyes sleepily.

"I was sleeping for so long!" Rosie exclaimed.

Dee shrugged, "You needed it. Christ, I wouldn't have blamed you if you had slept the rest of the year away."

Dee wandered into the kitchen to put on the kettle, peering out the window, "So this is what three AM looks like. I had wondered if it had changed since I was eighteen and coming home from nightclubs. Turns out, no, it's still awful. However, we *are* awake so let's get something into you. I swear you look thinner."

Rosie felt lightheaded and frail, like the time she had come down with a virus when she was thirteen and when she finally got out of bed, she found she could barely stand on her own two legs. Kate had laid cool, wet washcloths on her head and pressed the back of her hand against Rosie's ruddy cheeks, to check for when her fever had broken. Suddenly, she missed her mother in a way that was almost painful. Kate, broken and anxious though she may be, had an absolute reliability. No matter what time of day or night, Rosie knew exactly where her mother would be.

Sliding into a chair, she called to Dee, "Where is Lucy?"

Dee came back to the dining room, bearing a hot cup of tea, and placed it down in front of Rosie, "She's still at June's. I called Kate and broke the news to her, she was hysterical obviously, but she has calmed down now. James has called you several times. I answered the last time; I just couldn't let it keep ringing, it was giving me anxiety. He had heard the story from his sister; he wanted to check on you."

Dee gave her a funny look which made Rosie realise Dee knew something had happened between her and James. Dee went back into the kitchen and began pulling out bowls and pans, and Rosie sipped at her tea while she listened to the comforting sounds. The smell of cooking tomato and onion made her stomach complain loudly. A short while later, Dee slid a plate of scrambled eggs and toast in front of her and she began to wolf down the food.

"You might want to slow down," Dee said, raising an eyebrow. They refilled their teacups and headed out to the porch, where the light had begun to rise in the east.

Dee took a deep breath, "Ricky didn't kill Hannah. The police investigated, and he was up north at the time of her disappearance. He's been cleared. He is obviously still absolute garbage, however, and the police have said they will pursue the... attack... if you want to."

Rosie nodded, "Maybe. Yes. I will. Just... not today."

Dee reached across the table and took Rosie's hand, "There is something else. They found more bodies. They aren't releasing names yet, but probably the other girls that were missing."

Rosie's hand went to her mouth, and she closed her eyes. She had been right there with all of those women. My god. What if he had come back and found her?

"They *will* catch him," Dee said, confidently.

Rosie said nothing, watching the fingers of dawn break through the night sky, reaching across it in widening rays.

"Rosie? You don't have to tell me, but if you want to... I can tell there are things on your mind. I will always be here to listen."

Rosie looked at Dee, "I don't even know where to begin."

Dee reached over and linked her fingers through Rosie's, sitting silently, leaving space for Rosie to start talking. Did she start with Lucy's girl being real? Or before that, when Lucy had stolen the ring?

Finally, Rosie swallowed, "You remember the girl in Lucy's room?"

The sun had risen by the time Rosie had finished telling Dee everything. They sat and watched as Tiny stalked around the yard, inspecting all of Dee's herbs that sat in pots in a way that should have been disorderly but appeared as though they were meant there.

"You told James all of this?" Dee questioned.

"I did."

"You told him about Lucy and June and Frank and shields... and he didn't immediately run off into the hills?"

Rosie shook her head.

Dee rocked back in her chair, "Well, that's impressive."

Rosie looked over at her friend, "Do you feel like running into the hills?"

"Absolutely. What you have said is bonkers, it's bananas. You should all be locked up. In saying that, of course I believe you. One hundred percent. I wish my mother were here; she would *love* this story."

"I'm not sure I share Meg's enthusiasm."

Tiny spotted a finch hopping along the fence line and began following it enthusiastically, the finch allowing Tiny to get within meters of it before flitting quickly just out of his reach.

"Hey?" Dee said, "what day did you say Lucy started seeing the girl in her room?"

Rosie thought back, "The day I had the car accident. I must have seen her too, just afterwards I had a shield slip."

"Hmm," Dee said, musing.

"What are you thinking?" Rosie asked, standing up and clapping her hands to bring Tiny back, away from the finch.

"Well. Lucy finds a ring, starts seeing a girl that June and Frank think is a tethered spirit, caused by violent death or inability to move on? Then we find out days later about Hannah going missing... I'm just wondering, Rosie. Have you given thought to the fact that your girl might be Hannah?"

CHAPTER 30

Rosie spent the next two days in the garden with Dee. They worked side by side, pulling weeds and harvesting tender tips of herbs that Dee used in her teas. Rosie had never liked gardening, but she found something soothing about putting her hands in the dark, cool earth. It was mindless and meditative. She phoned June several times but hadn't gone to see her yet. She saw no hurry, Lucy was safe where she was, and Hannah - if she was the one in Lucy's room - was not going to be worse off for waiting, time was meaningless to the dead.

After her conversation with Dee, she kept trying to recall the moment after the accident, the slip of the shield, but it was almost as though whatever made the shield stop her from seeing spirits, also obscured her memories of it. She wondered if that was the reason she had so few memories of the time before Frank shielded her.

· · ·

The last two nights James had come to Dee's house and sat with her on the front porch, the two of them not touching, chaperoned by Dee who had hovered nearby with offers of tea and muffins. They had talked about the weather and music and food, everything except spirits and Hannah and what had happened between them at the cabin. Those things sat between them, almost painfully obvious, in the silences in between words. Rosie wondered whether he came to be polite, regretting the time they spent together. She felt so horribly broken and wondered if this was how Kate felt all the time. Then last night, as he stood to go, he reached out and took her hands, pulling her up and into his arms. She lay her head against his chest and listened to the sound of his heart. He nuzzled his face close to her and spoke into her hair. The setting sun was at her back, warming her with the last of the day's rays and she felt safe and secure for the first time in a long while.

"I know you are hurting. I know you have things you need to do. I love you," he said this with a conviction, as though he dared her to question it. "I will be here when you are ready."

Then he kissed her softly on her forehead, and pulled away, walking down the steps and out the gate.

Dee came out and stood in the doorway, "Well?"

Rosie wrapped her arms around herself, trying to trap the last of the warmth left my James's arms, "He said that he loves me."

"Yes. I think that is true."

Rosie turned to her, "I don't remember the last time that

I said that to Ben. Or that he told me that. I can't remember if we said it that morning, or the day before, or if it had been weeks. If I had of known it would be the last time, I would have savoured it, bottled it up and stored it away."

Dee came out on the porch and knelt to scratch the ginger cat between the ears.

"Can I tell you something?"

Rosie waited, Dee would tell her whether she wanted her to or not.

"I always thought I would never get married," Dee said. "Because here is the thing about marriage, either it ends when you split up - or, if you are very lucky - a successful marriage ends when one of your dies, which seems like not that much of a success to me. I always thought I would rather leave men when the going was good, beautiful little romances that I could string together like pearls on a string. Do not laugh at me; I know you want to."

Rosie did not laugh, Dee often talked about her relationships boldly, making Rosie blush, but she didn't talk about love.

"Anyway," Dee continued, "I just thought I wasn't really cut out for it. How could I give my heart to someone knowing that loss was inevitable? To truly love someone, you have to lose them sometime. I can barely breathe when I think of losing my mother or my siblings. Or you. Lucy. *God*, I couldn't stand it. When you lost Ben, I thought, 'well, there you go, Dee, see what love does, you were right'. Then there was James. Not to put too much pressure on you, but I need you to love again because it gives me hope. I think your love of Ben can sit alongside your love of James. Or not James. Someone else. Mr. Thompson, for all I care. You just can't let it break you."

Rosie smiled, "There will be someone you love one day."

Dee stood up and rolled her eyes, "Not in this lifetime." She broke into a laugh, "But there is still sex. Which is something."

Rosie swatted Dee, and they went back in the house to dish up dinner.

"I'm going to see June tomorrow," Rosie said.

Dee lifted a spoonful of sauce to her mouth, tasting it, "Mmm? Lucy will have missed you."

"I just need to start pulling my life back together. I need to get us home, which means I have to do something about the girl in the room, whether it is Hannah or not."

"I should come," Dee said.

Rosie shook her head, "No. There is nothing you could do and... if I do get unshielded and, you know... something happens to me? I need you to take Lucy."

Dee stared at her open-mouthed, "You cannot be serious."

"I am."

"Rosie, no. If it's this dangerous, you shouldn't do it."

Rosie held up her hand, forcing a confidence into her voice she didn't feel, "I need to do this. This decision is not up for debate. I've spent days thinking about this; I'm doing it. I just need to know that Lucy will be looked after. June is too old to be running after a kindergartener and Kate... I need you."

Dee swallowed hard, "Okay."

Rosie hugged her, "Thank you."

Dee shrugged her off, "I swear to god, if something happens to you I am going to be so pissed off."

Michael raked his hand through his hair as he stared at the board in front of him. He was on his fourth cup of coffee for the morning and still felt foggy; sleep had been eluding him since they found Hannah Avery. He had tossed and turned so much that he ended up creeping out to the lounge with a blanket so he wouldn't disturb Brooke. The board in front of him blurred, and he rubbed his eyes. So far, they had found the remains of four women, including Hannah Avery. Beneath the crime scene photos was a list of things they found with the bodies, pitifully little to go on. Scraps of decaying underwear that had seemed to be used to tie up the victims, one woman had a purse but no identification in it, there was no jewellery. There was nothing to do until they had confirmation of identity from dental and DNA. Tiarna Hunter's father was calling constantly, and Michael couldn't blame him. Michael and Jim had been going through lists of sex offenders in the area to try to narrow down someone that was active during all the disappearances.

"You think staring at it is going to solve it?" Jim asked. "Come give me a hand with these files; it's like searching for a needle in a really depressing haystack."

One of the crime scene guys came in excitedly, bouncing the door off the wall.

"We found another one," he said.

"Well, that's not exactly good news, Hodgins," Jim said, looking up from his desk.

"Sorry," Hodgins blushed a deep scarlet. "It's just, this one was wearing jeans."

"So?" Michael said.

Clothing was different from the other bodies, but a nondescript garment like jeans wasn't exactly going to break the case.

"She had identification in her pocket!" Hodgins said.

Jim stood up, "He left ID on her?"

Hodgins nodded. Jim looked at him expectantly, and Hodgins continued to grin at them.

"Well?" Jim burst out.

"What?"

"He is wondering what the ID said, Hodgins," Michael said wearily.

"Oh," Hodgins said, "Her name is Amelia. Amelia Davis."

"Oh god," Michael breathed. "Are you sure?"

Hodgins nodded, "She had a photo in her wallet too. Woman and a kid, might be the victim."

"Do you have them?" Michael asked. "The photos?"

Hodgins nodded, and Jim looked at him strangely; years of working with Michael had made him more sensitive to the almost imperceptible tremor in Michael's voice. Hodgins logged into a laptop on the desk, pulling up a file that had been updated with the recent crime scene photos, finding the two that showed the items found on the body. He stepped back to let Michael get a better look, but he didn't need one. He already knew what he photo was; he had seen the twin of it before in James's wallet.

Michael had broken the rules and phoned Brooke and asked her to collect Violet. She had asked why and he had simply said, "Just go and get her for me, Brookie. Please." His niece didn't need to be there when this went down. Brooke had called around and offered Violet a sleepover and Michael knew she would have been jumping up and down in excitement before James could question anything. Michael could not tell James himself, but as a favour, they had let him ride along. He had passed Brooke's minivan on the road leading out of James's street. He knew she saw him, her eyes meeting his as they went by.

James was in his workshop, sanding back a frame when they came in. At first, he had smiled at them. A slow realisation dawned on him as he took in the group of police, and his face had dropped - and for a second, and Michael was ashamed to admit it, he thought, *was it you?* Then Jim had walked over and said the words. James had crumpled like a sheet of paper, shocked, and the look in his eyes told Michael that it couldn't be James.

"No," James said, "Amelia left, she is gone. She's gone. She isn't dead."

Jim lead him up to the house, his arm steadying James, who tripped over his own feet.

Rosie searched for her handbag in the living room of Dee's house, picking up cushions and quilts. The last quilt had an assortment of items on top, buried beneath the folds and as she lifted it, things fell to the floor, keys, remotes and one of Tiny's dog toys.

"Shit," she muttered, picking up the items and throwing them back on the couch. Her hand grasped for the television remote, accidentally hitting the on button as she picked it up, the tv flicking to life.

"-here at the scene for the sixth day today, and confirmation that another body has been found. Sources have stated that this is the first victim to be found with identification. This morning police have been to the home of a local man who they hope will be able to assist with the investigations."

Rosie fumbled at the remote to switch it off, she and Dee had agreed to a media blackout since Dee had confided that Rosie's name had been leaked to the press regarding her discovery of Hannah. Suddenly, James's house appeared on the screen and Rosie couldn't comprehend what she was seeing for a moment, unable to put together the words of the news reporter with the video in front of her.

She rapidly hit the off button and stood there, staring at the black screen. In her head, she heard Lucy's voice saying that she had taken the ring from Violet's bag. Violet. She went to sit on the couch, missed and slid on to the ground, no longer able to feel her legs. Pieces of the puzzle were rapidly fitting together; Lucy took a ring from Violet that had a spirit tethered to it, one that had met a violent end, days after Hannah went missing. The body, the creek that backed on to the St Clair property, and James who had told her about the creek. God. Oh, my god. She thought about the night she had spent with him, his lips on hers, his hands... she shook her head. This wasn't possible. Something was missing. Something was wrong.

. . .

"Dee!" She shouted. "Dee!"

A few seconds later, Dee came barrelling into the room from the garden, dirt on her hands, her cheeks reddened from the cool autumn air. She stared wildly at Rosie.

"What? Are you okay?" She bent to Rosie, still sitting in the floor, confused as though she expected her to be injured.

Wordlessly, Rosie turned the television back on.

"- heir to the St Clair realty fortunes." The scene on the screen showed James being lead out of his house to a police van; his face was pale and shocked.

"Oh, my god," Dee breathed.

"I have to call him," Rosie said suddenly.

"You can't!" Dee exclaimed.

Rosie renewed her search for her handbag, "I have to! He didn't do this!"

Dee looked at her, agape, "Rosie, he is with the police. He can't get a phone call from his girlfriend. I'm sure they will come to talk to you soon enough."

"I'm not his fucking girlfriend!" She exploded.

"Well, you're acting like it! You're acting insane, as a matter of fact."

Where the hell is my handbag, Rosie thought, throwing a couch cushion across the room.

Dee began pacing, "The ring, holy shit. You said Lucy took the ring from Violet?"

Rosie came over and took Dee by the shoulders, shaking her, "Stop it! I know. I know it looks awful. I just know he didn't do this. He didn't."

Rosie spied her handbag peeking out from behind the couch, and reached for it.

"What are you doing?" Dee asked.

Rosie opened the door, "I'm going to fix it."

She stalked down to the gate, Tiny at her heels.

"Where are you going?" Dee called after her.

Rosie unlatched the gate, letting Tiny out where he ran to stand next to her car, his tail wagging, leaving Dee standing at the top of the steps, staring after her.

CHAPTER 31

Rosie pulled into the driveway at June's, bumping up the curb in her hurry, hearing the undercarriage of her car scrape along the concrete. She threw the car into park, pulled on the handbrake and let Tiny out before slamming the door shut, not bothering to lock it. Rosie ran up the path that led to the back of the house, as though if she moved fast enough, she wouldn't change her mind and she could outrun any fears she had. She took the three steps to the back door in one giant leap and flinging open the door she pulled up suddenly in the kitchen, Frank and June who were seated at the table wearing identical expressions of shock.

June stood abruptly, "What happened?"

Frank looked startled at the appearance of Tiny, but quickly recovered, offering him a biscuit from the plate in front of him.

"I need you to remove my shield," she panted.

"Absolutely not," Frank said.

June placed a hand on Frank's, "We knew this wouldn't

work, I told you as much. She has a right to be unshielded; it was wrong to have done it in the first place."

"No, *you* felt it wouldn't work. But it has worked, perfectly fine, I might add, for twenty-five years. If Lucy had been a boy, we would never have had any issue at all," Frank argued.

June sighed, "Until what? The next generation. It's not a curse, it's-"

Rosie interrupted, "I'm sorry, can you both just shut up? I get this has been an issue between you for years, but I truly could not care less. My daughter is in danger. James is being questioned about a string of murders he didn't do, and it's possible that Hannah Avery is trapped, or tethered or whatever the hell you call it, in my house. And here is a hot tip - if James didn't commit these murders, *someone did*, and they're still out there. If I can speak to Hannah, I will know who did this; there will be a clue somewhere, I can call in an anonymous tip, and then Hannah moves on, Lucy is safe, James goes free, and a killer is caught."

June and Frank sat silently, each turning this over in their brain while Rosie looked from one to the other waiting for a response.

Finally, Frank spoke, "Who is James?"

"James is Violet's daddy. She's my friend." Lucy stood in the doorway to the kitchen, clutching a doll.

"Oh, Lucy!" Rosie exclaimed and bent down to open her arms. Lucy ran into them, clinging to her. "I missed you so much!"

She cooed over the new dolls that June had bought her

and looked over her sore arm, which had healed faster than Rosie would have imagined.

"I think you look bigger," she teased, "Did you grow while Mama was at Dee's house?"

Lucy nodded, then frowning she said, "Grandma said you were feeling sick. Are you better?"

Rosie nodded, "I am. Why don't you go and play for a few moments while Mama and Grandma June have a chat?"

Lucy nodded and began walking away then came back and whispered to Rosie, "Don't be mean to Grandpa Frank. He is a nice man, Mama."

Rosie sighed, "Okay. I'll be good. Cross my heart."

"Rosie," June said, as Lucy left the room, "Sit down. Start from the beginning."

Rosie sat down and filled them in on the ring and James, tactfully leaving out exactly what had happened at his house, ending with what she had seen on the news.

"I had decided to ask to be unshielded before that. But now it seems we need to do it as soon as possible. He didn't do this."

Frank nodded, "I'll do it."

Rosie sighed with relief, "Thank you. Once I'm unshielded-"

"No," Frank interrupted, "I'm not unshielding you. I wouldn't even know how. I mean, I'll go talk to Hannah. Same result, but without you putting yourself at risk."

Rosie put her face in her hands, "That won't work. I need to do this. It's not just that I want the shield off, I want you to put it on Lucy."

She looked up, tears in her eyes. She remembered the

fear in Lucy's voice, and it tore at a part of her heart. Little children should be safe, not terrified of spirits in their bedrooms. *She* had given this to her. June was wrong, this was a curse, and for the first time, Rosie felt she could understand exactly why Frank had done what he had.

Frank reached out his hand to pat Rosie on the shoulder but hesitated, his hand hovering awkwardly in the air for a moment before he placed it back on the table.

He cleared his throat, "There is another hope for Lucy. During my time away, I travelled around. I was mostly running from the Others, keeping my distance from places with a lot of people...but I was looking for something too. A way to *make* a shield. A spell of some sorts. I had heard rumours it was possible years ago. I'm really close, Rosie. I've got most of the information. There is a text I need to find, it's rare, but I've got some leads I'm chasing up."

Rosie shook her head, "You want to manufacture a shield? And what? Use my kid as a guinea pig? How do we even know that's safe?"

"I was going to test it on myself first," Frank said, defensively.

"No," Rosie said. "No way."

"I'm inclined to agree with her," said June.

"And you agree with me on becoming unshielded?" Rosie asked.

Both Frank and Rosie looked at June expectantly.

"I do," she agreed.

Frank swore under his breath, and Rosie nodded. She just needed someone to 'take it off' now. Frank might not know how to do it himself, but someone had done it for him. She could find the same person and get it done. Frank had said it cost him, but she had a little money, and she would borrow from Kate if she had to.

"Okay," said Rosie. "So, who performed your removal?"

Her father shook his head, "Rosie, please, you don't know what you're asking. It's not like having a Band-Aid taken off. There is no telling what pulling the shield off your soul will do to you. Look at me."

Rosie stood up abruptly, the chair screeching loudly along the floorboards, feeling anger bubbling inside of her, "How can you say that to me? What choice do I have? Lucy is being hurt by something - probably Hannah Avery, who was a good woman and would hate that she hurt a little girl - and I can't help either of them because I can't see what is happening. You did it for me. You of all people should understand why I have to do this! So, I'll ask you again, who removed yours?"

Frank looked into his mug, "It won't help you."

"I can't believe-"

"No, Rosie. It won't help you because he's dead. He was an old witch, lived out at the end of Charles Avenue, that run-down house near the river. He looked ready to give up the ghost when I found him. He performed the spell, but he's long gone."

Rosie slowly sat back down, the anger draining from her and despair settling in.

Frank spoke softly, "If you give me a bit of time. I'm nearly there with the manufacturing of a shield. Another three months maybe and I'll have it. We can trial it on me and then use it on Lucy. I will go help Hannah."

Rosie looked over at him, "What are we supposed to do for three months? Not go home? It's not an option. I need help now. James needs help now. And I'm sorry Frank, but you haven't exactly been a pillar of strength when it comes to brushes with the supernatural. If Grandma June is right about the energy of a poltergeist, then I think it might really send you over the edge. I'm sorry."

"I agree with her, Francis," June added. "You aren't strong enough to brush up against this kind of Other. I'm afraid it would break you."

Frank stood and went to the sink with his mug, rinsing it out.

"Well, aren't you both just full of confidence in me?" he said sarcastically.

June smiled ruefully at Rosie, "I would do it myself, love, but I don't have the strength I once did. That kind of energy. I would likely not survive it myself. You would all be back to square one. I'm sorry."

Hearing her grandmother admit to any kind of fragility made Rosie feel bruised, she leaned over to hug her and whispered that it was okay.

June cleared her throat, "There is another option. We have the spell already. We just need to get another witch to perform it."

Rosie burst out with a laugh that she would have thought impossible a few minutes ago, "That would be great if we knew any witches."

June smiled at her, "Honey, you've known one almost your whole life."

Meg turned up still in her yoga pants. When Rosie had called the retreat, they tried to tell her that none of the guests could be disturbed while during meditation, until Rosie had cried down the phone and said it was a family emergency. Rosie could find no easy way to ask Meg to perform serious magic on the phone, so she simply said she needed her and asked her to please come and Meg, bless her, had left immediately. Lucy had fallen asleep in the back room and Tiny lay at the door, his head on his paws, still and quiet as though he knew something was about to happen.

"What does it feel like," Rosie whispered to Frank.

Frank looked at her as if contemplating a merciful lie before he answered, "Like nothing you can imagine. It's like... a tearing of the fabric of who you are."

"Does it hurt?"

"...yes."

Rosie nodded slowly, "I see."

Frank took her by the hands and looked deep into her eyes, "There is still time to turn back. This is dark magic, Rosie. This spell, it was never meant for good. People aren't meant to be unshielded unless they're born that way. It's a curse. Do you understand? This magic was meant for harm. In days gone by it was used as a hex, to turn people insane. Any good magic you've ever felt, this is its reverse. It's the opposite of love. It isn't just the pain; when you have dark magic flow through you, it's hard to feel clean afterwards."

Rosie felt cold all of a sudden and shivered. Fear ran through her. She tried to swallow and found her mouth was dry. *But what options do I have?* She thought. There was no one but her. Only she could do this. Maybe.

"I understand," said Rosie. "But I was never meant to have this shield. It wasn't meant for me. it was meant for you. And with it on I can't help Lucy, or James, or Hannah. Whatever the cost... I have to do this."

In the other room, Meg and June were getting ready for the stripping of the shield. Frank and Rosie came in, and as Rosie looked around, she began to feel unmoored. Her grandmother's sitting room still looked like an alternate reality version of itself. The photos on the walls still showed Rosie in various incarnations, a gap-toothed eight-year-old, a lanky twelve-year-old, her wedding day... but the couches had been pushed against the walls, and Meg had pulled the long table from the kitchen into the room and on it was an altar of sorts. The room was heavy with incense, and seven white candles were lit. A bowl of earth, one of water, various herbs, some she recognised and some she did not, silver cord, an ornamental knife and various other items that Rosie couldn't name. Meg was dressed in a white dress, her greying hair unbound and loose down her back.

"Are you ready?" Meg asked.

Rosie reached for Frank's hand without thinking, and he squeezed it gently. She nodded.

June came and kissed Rosie on the cheek, "I will go stay with Lucy in case she wakes. You will be fine, my girl."

Rosie took a deep breath and turned to Meg, "What now?"

Meg came around and looked deep into her eyes, "You should know, I can't give you any guarantees. This is a kind of magic I've never performed. I have no idea what will happen. And to be honest, this incantation? I'm not even sure I'm pronouncing these words correctly."

Rosie took a deep breath, "Okay. I understand."

Meg had her lay upon the table in front of the items, and began to chant, calling forth spirit guides to protect the space. As she welcomed elements into the circle, she threw salt around the room, and the Rosie could barely hear her over the sound of her own heart thumping and the blood rushing through her ears. Meg began the incantation, strange words and guttural sounds. A cool wind blew over Rosie's skin, raising it in goosebumps, she heard whisperings from all sides as though the room were filled with people. The candles began to flicker, and then the flames shot up longer than the candles themselves.

Suddenly, Rosie felt like someone had reached inside her and was rummaging through her insides, dirty fingers probing into her head and into her heart as they grasped at parts of her she didn't know existed. A vast emptiness opened inside her, and it felt like she was floating through a river of despair and fear. Alone. Unmoored. A deep darkness, blacker than black. She felt a heat under her skin like sunburn on the inside. It grew warmer and warmer until suddenly, a white-hot pain shot through her entire being, a pain that was more than physical, as though her very essence was being ripped apart. Her back arched unnaturally, a scream curdling in her throat and then... blackness.

CHAPTER 32

Rosie woke up to Meg, June, and Frank all standing over her as she lay on the table. Their faces peered at her with various mixtures of fear, trepidation and anxiousness. A wave of nausea rolled over her, and she tasted bile as it rose in her throat. Gagging, she turned on to her side and retched on to the carpet.

"I'm sorry," she gasped, laying back and closing her eyes.

"It's fine," June said soothingly. "Don't worry about it."

Meg scampered from the room and returned with a cold washcloth, placing it on Rosie's forehead. Frank had retreated to a corner of the room and was moaning and muttering to himself. Rosie felt a thread of annoyance at him; her head was pounding. However, as the nausea began to abate, she found she felt strangely... unlocked... as though someone had left a window open inside of her and now a cool breeze was blowing through. She felt exposed and raw. Changed. It felt oddly similar to the surreal feeling of change she felt after she gave birth to Lucy. *Lucy!*

. . .

She sat up suddenly, her head spinning. Slipping sideways, she fell onto the floor, landing hard on her elbow. Meg and June let out identical cries and rushed to her to help her up, fussing and patting her.

Rosie swatted away their hands, "I'm okay! I'm fine!"

She climbed to her feet unsteadily, and for the first time, she noticed a strange shimmer that seemed to float around Meg. It shone like mother of pearl, shifting around her as she moved. Rosie stared, transfixed, it was beautiful. Unthinking, Rosie reached out to touch it.

"A shield," she breathed.

Her fingers slipped through as though it were water, a slight resistance, but permeable. It felt vaguely warm, and her fingers tingled at the touch. Meg looked at her curiously; June smiled. Frank stood abruptly and left the room, his footsteps echoing down the hall where he closed the door roughly to his old bedroom.

Ignoring him, June clasped Rosie's hands, "Don't be afraid. I will help you learn to use the sight."

Rosie looked at her grandmother, but she looked as she always had. There was no shield there.

Rosie turned to Meg, "Do you have it? The shield?"

They could go right now and put it on Lucy. Surely putting one on had to be easier than removal. She wondered if it would hurt, but reasoned it hadn't hurt her having Frank's put on; she couldn't remember it at all. With luck, Lucy would never even remember having seen anyone in her room at all, like Rosie didn't recall her Old Man from her childhood. The memories came to her now, almost like the thinnest of dams had begun to crack, the stooped way he would slip past her room, the way she would bury herself in her stuffed toys trying to hide. Kate reading to her at night. Frank coming in from work smelling of the heat of the day, his hands calloused, holding hers. She glanced back up the hallway after him. Her dad. Would Lucy forget everything? Would she forget Ben? *It's too late to turn back*, she thought.

June and Meg exchanged a look.

Rosie felt her stomach drop, "The shield? Where is it?"

Meg shook her head, "I'm so sorry, sweetheart. It didn't make it. It broke right apart as I removed it, just scattered to the wind like dandelion fluff. We couldn't save it for Lucy."

Rosie sat down heavily in one of the sofas that had been pushed against the wall. "So, we failed. It was for nothing?"

June came and sat beside her, "Not for nothing. You can still move the spirit on. You can still prove your young man is innocent."

"What will I do about Lucy?"

June smiled into her face, "The same thing my mother did with me. You will teach her how to walk with one foot in each world. You can't see it now, Rosemary, but this is a gift."

June followed Rosie's eyes that had drifted back up the hallway to where Frank was, "Not for him. No. It will always feel unnatural for him, painful even."

Meg quietly began gathering up her supplies, packing them into bags and shifting furniture back to its place.

"Thank you, Meg," Rosie said. "Thank you for trying."

Meg took a little bow, "Always. Now, I'll be going home to see what my daughter has been up to since I was away. Shall I take Lucy? Dee and I can mind her."

"No," Rosie said. "It's probably best if she stays with June and Frank. As long as she is unshielded, she needs people who can see what she sees. At least until... I guess, until we know how to manage it."

Meg kissed her on the cheek and said her goodbyes, calling out up the hall to Frank, who stayed stubbornly shut inside.

Rosie and June made their way back into the kitchen, Rosie unsteady on her feet. June set about making her a hot chocolate and pushed a plate of biscuits in front of her.

Rosie stomach recoiled, "Oh, I don't think I could eat."

"It will make you feel better if you do. Like morning sickness, you tend to feel a bit better with something in your stomach."

Reluctantly, Rosie picked up a biscuit and nibbled at the edges. To her surprise, she found she began to feel a bit better. She finished the biscuit and picked up another, sipping tentatively at the hot chocolate.

"Did Lucy wake?" Rosie asked. "During the removal?"

"No. She didn't even stir. I thought she might, but she slept through the whole thing."

Frank appeared at the doorway, looking at Rosie sceptically, assessing her.

"You look pale," he said.

"I'm okay," Rosie assured him, and to her surprise, she found that she wasn't lying. The nausea and the headache had retreated, and she felt steadier by the moment.

"When I was unshielded, it was like having my nerves exposed. The shields, the imprints, everywhere I turned there was... too much of everything. I left, got as far away from people as I could. Of course, there is rarely a place where there isn't energy, but it seems to fade over time, the energy gets lessened, I suppose. Some places are better than others."

Sitting down, he went on to recount the places he had been and lived. The first years he spent floating from place to place, fruit picking or doing odd jobs in the country for cash in hand, finding places where the Others weren't - or were at least more tolerable.

"I met a guy one day on one of the farms, I could see right away he didn't have a shield, and I could tell he noticed that I didn't too. We didn't talk at first, just watched each other - sizing each other up, I guess. At the end of the job, the boss put on a campfire, brought down a couple of cartons of beer, and we all sat around talking. Eventually, only he and I were left. He told me he had been seeing a girl down south, it had gone bad, and her family had removed the shield. Witches, he said they were."

Frank reached out and picked up the salt shaker, turning it to and fro as he spoke. June took a seat and took his free hand and gave it a little squeeze. *What would it be like if he hadn't of left*, Rosie wondered. Frank had missed his father's last years. He never got to say goodbye. *Would he have made the same decision if he knew what it would cost him?* She couldn't be sure.

"So, the woman's family? They cursed him?" She asked.

Frank shrugged, "He didn't say it, but I could tell straight up that her family had good reason to do what they did. He was a real asshole, would kick the dogs if they got too close. He told me he had heard rumours of a shaman out west that could create a shield, make one from energy, basically. I didn't know if he was telling the truth or not, but I decided to go find out. I thought, if I could fix myself I could come back, you would have been maybe twelve years old at the time. I thought we could start over."

He glanced over at her, as though to confirm that she might have accepted him back, "It was like a wild goose chase though. One lead, to another, to another. In the last few years, when I would come into a town, I would go to the library and use the internet and check on you. I would look at your photography. I didn't know you had a daughter though; I had no idea until I found an old news story about your husband, it said he left behind his wife and little girl. I had to come back, to see if you were okay... if Lucy was okay."

Rosie felt her heart soften at the thought of him checking her photography; he had thought of her. All these years, he had been thinking about her.

"Thank you," Rosie said, reaching over the table and took his hand.

June sniffed and wiped her eyes. Then straightening herself up, she cleared her throat, "Now, what do we do about this Other?"

They sat talking at the table for an hour, until the sun began to fade. Lucy awoke, and the conversation halted while she was given afternoon tea. Afterwards, Rosie took her to the front garden to pick flowers for pressing. Rosie squinted at the people walking past with their dogs on afternoon walks,

Frank was right, the shields were distracting. Lucy looked at her.

"You're different," she observed.

Rosie nodded.

"What happened?" Lucy asked her.

Rosie debated what to say, but Lucy lost herself in chasing down a butterfly. She wondered what life would look like for her and Lucy after today. Both of them learning how to manage a gift they hadn't asked for.

Afterwards, they came inside and ran Lucy a bath, dressing her in her pyjamas. June had made Lucy chicken schnitzel with vegetables and allowed her to eat it in front of the television.

Rosie drifted back to the kitchen, "Alright. I guess I'll get going now."

"Remember to keep your distance. We have no idea what you're walking into," June said.

"I will. I'll go in, speak to Hannah. She needs to tell her story, right? Well, that's what I need to."

"It's not that simple, Rosie," June said. "Tethered spirits can be unsteady, talk in riddles or go from being normal to harmful in the blink of an eye. The longer they stay here, the more the energy builds."

"What choice do I have?" Rosie asked. "I have to do this."

"I'm coming," Frank announced.

June looked at him with pity, "Frank, you can't."

"I'll stay outside if I have to. I can't let Rosie go alone; it's dangerous."

Rosie shrugged, "It's your call."

Privately, she felt a little better about not walking into the house completely on her own. Frank may not be able to do much, but any company was better than none, and he had been in this world longer than she. They left by the back-door, Tiny running after them. Rosie tried to push him back inside the yard, but he stubbornly refused to move, and she wasn't strong enough to force him.

"Fine, whatever. Get in the car then."

The drive to Rosie's house was full of awkward silence and tension.

"What sort of dog is that, anyway?" Frank asked finally.

"An Irish wolfhound."

"It's nearly as big as your car."

"He's actually quite small for his breed," Rosie said.

Frank made a noise, "Mmph. Well, I wouldn't want to see a big one."

They pulled up out the front of Rosie's house. It looked strange to her after spending so many days away - like she had never truly lived there. It felt like it crackled with a strange energy, and Rosie shivered, telling herself it was just her imagination. She and Frank stepped out of the car, releasing Tiny from the backseat.

The neighbour across the road wheeled her bin out to the road, and raised her hand in greeting, "Evening!"

Rosie returned the wave.

The woman looked both ways and quickly crossed the street. Rosie found it difficult to look at her, the opalescent shimmer of her shield almost glowing in the gathering dusk.

"You've been away for a few days?" The woman asked. She seemed to be inspecting Rosie's face, and Rosie wondered if she had seen the news and heard about Rosie finding the body of Hannah.

"Uhh, yes," Rosie said.

The woman nodded, "Thought so. Listen, love. Your cat has been making an awful racket in there. It's none of my business, but you might want to consider having it put in a cattery next time you go away? Or get a pet sitter. It kept me up all night last night."

Frank and Rosie exchanged uneasy glances.

"Oh!" Rosie faltered. "Uh, yes. Yes, of course. I'm sorry it disturbed you."

The woman waved a hand, "It's okay. Just for next time, hey?"

She walked back to her house and disappeared inside.

Frank turned to Rosie, "I'm guessing you don't have a cat?"

"No, I do not."

Frank took a deep breath and let it out in a whoosh, "That's great. I'm thrilled. Let's go inside."

Frank turned towards the house. Rosie's stomach lurched, and she felt as though her knees would give way.

"Hold on," Rosie said. "Can we... can we just sit in Mr. Thompson's backyard for a few minutes? I'm just..."

Frank looked at her for a moment and nodded, "Yes. Of course. Let's go sit down. That girl isn't going anywhere."

They reached the seat where Rosie and Mr. Thompson would sit outside at night. She and Frank sat down side by side, while Tiny danced around the yard, sniffing all the familiar smells.

"He probably misses Mr. Thompson," Rosie observed.

"How long is he gone for?"

"Only another few days, he went to see family with his daughter."

"They're close then?"

Rosie nodded.

"That's nice," Frank said. "It's good to have family."

Just at this moment, Rosie realised she could not have cared less about family or backyards, or dogs. Rosie took deep breaths, trying to control her nerves.

"What's going on, Rosie? Talk to me," Frank urged.

"I'm scared," she admitted.

She was terrified of what she would find in the house, of the force of the energy, of what effect it might have on her, of going mad, of losing Lucy. All of it felt too big, too much.

Frank sighed, "I'm scared too. But, as much as I hate to admit it, June was right. This was meant for you. It's a part of who you are as much as your red hair or your photographer's eye. You'll see."

They sat side by side, the minutes ticking on as Rosie gathered her strength, Frank telling her stories of when he was a child, mindless chatter to occupy the silence. The longer they sat, the more Rosie realised she would never feel 'ready' for this. The waiting was worse, and there was only one cure for that.

She stood up and called Tiny to her, "Okay, let's go."

As they made their way back towards the gate, her phone

vibrated in her pocket, startling her so much she felt like her whole body was tingling.

"It's Kate," she said, frowning at the display.

"Leave it," Frank said. "Call her back afterwards."

"No," Rosie said. "You don't understand, this is a mobile number. She never uses it because she doesn't go out. It just stays charged on the bench. I keep telling her to get rid of it because it's an unneeded bill."

If Kate was calling, something was wrong.

She hit the answer button, "Mum?"

Frank watched as the colour drained from Rosie's face, he reached out and grabbed her by the arm, "What is it?"

"I'll be right there," Rosie said, hanging up, her hands shaking.

"Rosie?"

"It's Grandma June. She's in hospital. Kate is there with Lucy."

CHAPTER 33

Rosie and Frank stood in the grassy courtyard across from the hospital, both of them still. Frank looked pained and frightened. Rosie was agog.

"Oh my god," she breathed.

It was almost midnight, but the front of the hospital was full of people. Some milled around absently. Other strode with purpose. None of them were really there. They blinked in and out of existence. Rosie began to walk forward, but Frank remained rooted to the spot. She turned to look at him questioningly.

"I can't," he said helplessly.

"Are you serious?"

"I really can't. This is nothing compared to inside. I just —" he turned and began retching into the garden bed, clutching at his head as though in pain.

"Are you okay? What is happening?"

"It's when they're all together like that," he sank down on to the grass and rubbed at his temples.

"My head starts pounding, and I feel nauseated. There

was a reason I avoided cities for twenty-five years. And this," he gestured towards the hospital, "has too much energy. I wouldn't make more than a few feet inside before it would become too much."

Rosie took a quick mental scan of her body, checking for any signs she was sick or in pain, but everything seemed in order. Frank, on the other hand, was suffering unshielded. She felt a twinge of guilt that this had been for her. He had told her, but seeing it was different.

"I'll go," she offered.

Frank nodded and waved her off wanly, placing his head between his knees.

Rosie strode towards the building as a light rain began to fall. She hesitated as she got closer to the imprints. One passed through her, and Rosie felt a bolt of energy run up her spine. She gasped before she could help herself. It wasn't painful, exactly, but unexpected - like one of those zappers kids would buy as a gag gift.

"Holy crap," Rosie breathed.

At the sound of her voice, one of them turned to her and spoke.

"Can you see me," a woman asked.

She couldn't have been more than twenty-two. Rosie, startled, found she couldn't even speak. She had assumed these would all be imprints, but of course, the hospital would have newly passed on spirits too.

The woman began to walk away, muttering. Rosie glanced towards the hospital doors where June was waiting inside. She wanted nothing more than to run inside and find her family. She bit her lip and sighed.

"Wait," Rosie called. "I can see you."

The woman turned around, and Rosie noticed June had been right, there was something 'off' about the woman. She was different, somehow. Less than human and more than human at the same time. No shield hovered near her. The air didn't move her hair.

"I can see you," Rosie said again. "What's your name?"

The woman raced to her, taking hold of Rosie's hand, sending a strange vibration up Rosie's arm.

"Oh, thank god! I'm Daisy Dahm. I need to get home. I... I don't know what I'm doing here. I was home just a moment ago, and then I guess I blacked out. My husband must have brought me here, but I can't find him. Can you help me?"

"Daisy," Rosie began and then faltered.

How did she explain to her that she had died? June and Frank hadn't explained any of this to her. She had expected that they would know what happened, not that they would be clueless and confused. It also suddenly dawned on her that she had no way of knowing that Daisy was a new spirit. She could just as easily be stuck. *Violent and erratic*, June had said. Ben flitted through Rosie's head, had he known? Had he materialised beside his car and realised he had left them?

A woman in a dated nurses uniform that looked like it came from the 1960's suddenly appeared to Rosie's left and began walking towards her, Rosie jumped to get out of the way of the imprint, goosebumps rising on her arms.

"Daisy," Rosie said, "can we move somewhere quieter?"

She guided them towards the building, and around the side away from the imprints, and out of the rain, which began to fall more heavily.

"Can you take me home?" Daisy asked. "I don't have my purse but I can pay you for your trouble when we get there. There are so many people."

Daisy peered around the corner at the imprints, "None of them would talk to me."

Rosie looked around, Daisy was right. The pavement in front of the hospital was crowded.

"What was the last thing you remember, Daisy, before you blacked out?" She asked.

Daisy looked off into the distance as if trying to recall, "We were doing the dishes after dinner. Sean, my husband, was making some popcorn. We were going to watch a movie. I got a headache, a sharp pain in my head and then... nothing."

A stroke, Rosie wondered, *or maybe an aneurysm?* It didn't matter really though; it mattered that she somehow explain to Daisy that she had died.

"Daisy, look around, see all those people around the corner? Doesn't that seem strange to you?" Rosie showed Daisy the time on her phone, "It's 12:16 in the morning. This place should be empty."

Daisy followed Rosie's gaze.

Rosie continued, "And look at me. Look at the rain on my skin. Can you feel it on you?"

"What are you trying to say?"

Rosie reached out and held Daisy's hand, ignoring the prickles running up her arm, "I'm so sorry, Daisy. I don't know what happened to you tonight, but you didn't... you have died."

. . .

Daisy stared at her and there was a panicked look in her eyes, like an animal caught in a trap. *She does know*, Rosie thought, *she just doesn't want to know.*

"No." Daisy said. "You're crazy."

She wrenched her hand out of Rosie's and began storming off, "I'll get home myself. Stay away from me."

Rosie stared after her; she couldn't leave Daisy like this. She needed to make her see. She thought about Daisy wandering through the streets, lost and stranded and shuddered. Rosie fumbled her pocket and pulled out her keys.

"Daisy!" She called.

Daisy wheeled around, and Rosie threw her keys to her. Daisy automatically put up her hands to catch them; the keys sailed through her hands and landed on the ground below. Daisy jumped back, staring at the keys on the ground. She slowly bent and tried to pick them up, her fingers grazing along the ground uselessly. Realisation coloured her face, and she sat down on the ground.

Rosie picked up her keys sat beside Daisy. The ground was wet and soaked into the seat of her jeans immediately. She shivered involuntarily.

"I really am sorry."

"But I touched you," Daisy murmured.

"I'm... different."

"How?" Daisy asked.

"I don't know how. I only know that it happened."

"What about Sean?"

Rosie took a breath. She knew first-hand what Sean was

feeling. She knew today was the worst day of his life and that for him, everything had changed and would never be the same again. Grief altered the fabric of who you were.

"Sean will be okay. Not today and maybe not for a long time. But one day, he will be. He will always miss you, but he will be okay. We will all be okay."

Daisy sat there, telling Rosie strange, disjointed things about her life and things she had left undone. Her favourite movie, a book she was in the middle of reading. She told Rosie about the way her husband slept curled on his side, the smell of him. Rosie listened, saying nothing, and letting Daisy pour the details of her life into her hands. The rain stopped, but Rosie's cheeks were still wet with her tears. *Life is unfair,* she thought, *nothing here is fair.*

Finally, Daisy looked at her with tears in her eyes, "What happens now?"

"You just... let go. It's like, you just accept things are as finished as they will ever be. And you release."

Daisy nodded, "I think I'm just going to sit here a moment."

Rosie got to her feet, "I have to go. My daughter and grandmother are inside. But if you're still here when I get back out, we can talk some more if you need to."

Daisy nodded, but Rosie could already see her leaving, she had begun to fade like a photograph left in the sun. Rosie turned and began to walk towards the entrance of the hospital, moving around imprints as she went.

. . .

Entering through the automatic doors, a roaring filled Rosie's ears, and her stomach dropped. The energy felt like static in the air. All around her people blinked in and out of existence, making it difficult for her to discern what was real and what wasn't. She stumbled forward, falling through imprints, and each one felt like an electric shock. Gasping, she reached for the wall. She shut her eyes tightly, trying to make it all become background noise the way June had explained.

Someone touched her arm, "Are you okay?"

Rosie opened her eyes, in front of her was a nurse, her shield wavering around her. *Real*, she thought.

"My grandmother. She had a stroke. My daughter is with her," Rosie managed.

The nurse's eyes filled with sympathy, "Let's go find her."

Rosie watched her feet as they walked, trying to keep her balance. She felt like she was drunk.

The nurse went over to a computer and asked Rosie for June's name.

"She's been moved to the third floor. Room 327. Do you want me to take you?"

Rosie shook her head, "No, I'll find it. Thank you."

Rosie walked away, focusing on the ground, trying to look normal and wincing at each touch of an imprint. *I'm okay, I'm okay*, she chanted, stepping into the elevator. The doors shut, and she was alone. Suddenly a little girl blinked in beside her, bald headed, with a bear under her arm. Rosie closed her eyes, *oh god, please no, don't make me have to explain to this little girl she has died*. She reached out tentatively; her fingers passed through, the girl didn't look up. *Imprint*, Rosie thought, gratefully. And with dismay, she wondered how many times this child had ridden this particular elevator in order to imprint here. The doors opened, and Rosie stepped out, hurrying to her grandmother's room. She pulled the door open and shut it behind her roughly, leaning against it as though she could shut out the Others on the other side.

The room was softly lit. Her grandmother was a small, sleeping figure in the bed, a bright white bandage on the left side of her forehead. Cords attached to her body lead to machines that circled around her, one of them beeping rhythmically. Kate sat in a chair beside June, holding her hand. On her lap was Lucy, sleeping. Kate stood slowly, transferring a sleeping Lucy back into the chair and coming around the bed to her daughter. Rosie had expected to find Kate anxious and distressed, but she seemed surprisingly alert and vibrated with an energy. Her shield pulsed around her, flecks of calming blue. Kate reached for Rosie, pushing her rain-soaked hair back from her face and scanning her as though searching for something.

"Something has happened to you," she said slowly.

Rosie swallowed, "I'm okay, Mum. I'm alright."

Her mother took her hands in hers, and the warmth of them grounded Rosie, easing the unsettled feeling that had run unchecked inside her since she entered the hospital. The roaring of energy dulled to a soft buzzing.

Kate led Rosie to the bed and filled her in on June's condition, relaying medical information that Rosie barely heard.

"Lucy called me when it happened. Mine was the only

number she knew by heart. She had already called 000; she's a clever cookie," Kate said, proudly.

"You came? You left the house?" She knew it had happened because they were here together, and yet she could barely wrap her mind around Kate outside. Kate explained how she had called a taxi and arrived at June's house as the ambulance was loading June into it. Then she and Lucy had followed behind in June's car. Kate made a joke about driving being like riding a bike.

"I'm glad there was no traffic, though," a smile curling in the corner of her mouth. "Also, my license expired some time ago."

"Thank you, Mum," Rosie said, squeezing her mother's hand.

Kate shrugged, "Lucy needed me. Of course I came."

Memories rose to the surface of Rosie's mind. All the moments she had missed with her mother blooming like roses. She wanted to pick them up, to examine them. But she knew Kate had always done the best she could. Those moments had been lost to Kate too. She thought about what she had said to Daisy about letting go and realised she needed to take some of her own advice.

Lucy stirred in the chair, "Mama?"

"Hey, honey," Rosie went to her and pulled Lucy into her arms.

Lucy leaned back and looked at Rosie.

"It's so loud here," she said grimacing.

"I know," Rosie smoothed Lucy's hair and kissed her forehead. "Maybe Nanna can take you back to her house now? Is that okay?"

Lucy nodded, and Kate held out her hand.

"I'll take June's car back to my house," Kate picked up her handbag.

Rosie looked at her grandmother, pale under the small light above the bed that illuminated the room, "I can stay with Grandma June for a while. I'll come by in the morning, Lucy, okay?"

Rosie kissed both her daughter and her mother goodbye.

"I'm not sure when I'll get to drive a car again," Kate said as she reached the door. "It's surprisingly invigorating."

As Kate and Lucy left, Rosie sank into the chair beside June and picked up her grandmother's hand. She had never realised how frail June had become. The skin on the back of her hand was creased like tissue paper and just as fragile. She ran her thumb softly over it, feeling the bird-like bones beneath the skin. Her grandmother had been a constant in her life. These hands had been the ones that had put Band-Aids on her grazed knees when Rosie was small. They had knit blankets and planted flowers. They had baked birthday cakes and held endless cups of tea. It was unfathomable to Rosie that she may one day have to navigate life without June. She didn't know how to live in a world where her grandmother was not.

"Rosie?" June croaked.

Rosie looked up, her eyes filling with tears, "You're awake!"

She laid her head upon the bed, crying as she pressed her grandmother's hand to her cheek.

June groaned, "Oh, I hate the hospital. When can I go home?"

Rosie laughed and sniffed back her tears, "Probably not

for a while. You had a small stroke, they think. And you broke your pelvis and hit your head pretty hard when you fell. Lucy called an ambulance."

"Oh, poor Lucy! She must have gotten a fright."

"She's okay. She's tough."

"Of course she is. She's her mother's daughter."

June touched the bandage on her head and winced.

"Banged myself up pretty good." She looked over at Rosie. "How are you handling the hospital?"

"It's hard," Rosie admitted. "Overwhelming, really. There is a lot of energy. Frank couldn't come in. He started vomiting before we even got properly on the hospital grounds. He wanted to though."

June nodded, "You see how difficult it is for him. He made a mistake when he did what he did and we have all paid for it, but he did it out of love, Rosie. He loves you."

Rosie nodded.

June leant over, "You should go. Go help the Other in Lucy's room. Find out who hurt those girls and get your young man out of trouble. I have a good feeling about him."

Rosie burst out with a laugh and wiped her tears away, "Oh, really?"

June took both Rosie's hands him hers, "I have to tell you something, Rosie. I couldn't before now, and it's weighed on me."

Rosie squeezed her hand, "Okay."

"I saw Ben," June said. "It was after the accident. At first, it was the night of the accident at your house - you remember I came and stayed with you for a week?"

Rosie nodded, barely breathing.

June continued, "He stayed for so long, I was scared for him. He stayed until after the funeral. I didn't speak to him;

I thought it might make it harder on him if he thought he could get a message to you, and I couldn't tell you, of course. He would just sit with you, sit with Lucy. I would walk past your room while you were sleeping, and he would be lying beside you in bed. Then, after the funeral, I saw him go. He just slipped away after the service while you and Lucy walked to the car. He loved you two so much, Rosemary. He would have stayed if he could, but he knew he had to let go. He knew he had to move on. I just wanted you to know; he would understand you moving on too."

CHAPTER 34

Rosie made it back to Frank and reported that June had woken and, while frail, seemed like she was going to be okay. Frank seemed to sag in relief, and Rosie helped him to the car.

Forty minutes later, they were standing back out the front of Rosie's, Tiny back with them after Rosie released him from the yard. She had reservations about bringing him at all, but something about the dog's presence made her feel more grounded somehow.

"I'm going to go in with you," Frank said.

Rosie looked at him sceptically, "Are you sure you can?"

"No. But I'm going to try."

Rosie nodded and moved towards the house, her key slipping in the lock. Tiny whined beside her. The door swung open. The air smelled stale in the kitchen and faintly of smoke, still not aired out after the fire. Apart from that, though, things looked relatively the same.

"Where is the room," Frank asked, his tones were hushed and reminded Rosie of when she and Dee had tiptoed up the hallway to take the photo, wondering if they would capture a spirit. She thought of the Polaroid she had taken, the way it had been totally blown out, as though too much light had gotten into the image. It had been like taking a photo of the sun, and she wondered how much energy one of these tethered Others gave out. She pointed up the hallway and began walking towards it.

Rosie and Frank moved tentatively up the hall. From the bedroom, Rosie could hear a slow scraping as though the furniture was being moved slowly. The light in the hall flickered. *Oh god,* Rosie thought, and fear twisted in her insides. Unthinking, she reached for Frank's hand, and he squeezed it gently, *I'm here*. Every fibre in Rosie's body was screaming for her to turn around. She imagined just moving out, her and Lucy living with Kate, and bugger the house. It could stay haunted. It was the thought of Hannah that pressed her on. More than protecting Lucy, because if needed, she could remove Lucy from the situation. More than helping James, because surely the evidence would show he had nothing to do with this. It was the thought of Hannah, here, trapped, unable to move on until she told her story and someone listened. She walked on for Hannah.

The hairs pricked on her arms as she got closer, the energy running through her before she even got close to the door. What June had said about trapped spirits was true, the energy multiplied, it pressed against Rosie, snaking through her. Frank began to breathe heavily and stumbled.

"Are you okay?" She whispered.

He looked at her, his face pale and slick with sweat, but nodded.

The door to Lucy's room was shut, under it, a light flickered on and off. The air smelled of pine needles, dirt and on top of that, like the smell of sparklers. *Sulphur*, Rosie realised. She reached out with a trembling hand and turned the knob, the door swinging inwards.

Inside, the room was in disarray, clothes and toys were strewn on the floor, furniture moved and knocked over. On the bed sat a woman. Rosie recognised her from the car on the day she had the accident. All of her memories that had stayed trapped behind the shield suddenly rushing forward to greet her, as though they had been there all along.

Long, dark hair, pale. She turned to face Rosie as she walked in; her green eyes made Rosie feel as though she were naked. Rosie let out a small noise. This wasn't Hannah. She didn't just recognise her from the car. *That was why she was familiar to me when I saw the photograph*, Rosie thought, *I had already seen her in the car days earlier when I had the shield slip.*

The spirit stood up, turning towards them.

Rosie stepped forward, "Hello, Amelia."

Amelia lurched towards them, grasping, and Rosie instinctively took a step back, bumping into Frank. Tiny whined and turned circles in the hall.

"Christ," Frank said, making retching noises.

"I'm not here, I'm not here," Amelia chanted.

She turned abruptly and paced back and forth, her speech wavering from one tone to another, by turns she was happy, then furious. Unstable, erratic. Had this been what she was like with Lucy?

"I said I was happy to be with you! With Violet! Why do you always have to think the worst of me!" She wailed. Then she sat down and began to talk in whispers as though cooing to an infant.

"What is she doing?" She whispered to Frank.

She glanced back at him; he was half crouched over, one hand pressed to his head as though in pain, "Past conversations. She is talking to people that she used to know."

"How do I make it stop?"

He shrugged and groaned in response.

"Amelia?" Rosie said, she began to walk into the room but stopped herself, unsure how close she should get.

Amelia turned to her, "Yes?"

Rosie was so surprised to get a response that she hadn't thought what to say next. *Do I tell her she's dead? Ask what happened? How much does she know?*

"Uhh, my name is Rosie. I'm a friend. I live here," she began.

"I live here," Amelia repeated.

"Yes... well, sort of, I suppose. I think you meet my little girl? Her name is Lucy."

Amelia began to rock, "I have a little girl. I dressed her. I... where is James? Where is my little girl? *Where is she?*"

Pine needles rained on to the floor, and the smell of

sulphur grew stronger; Rosie wrinkled her nose and wracked her brain for a way into the tangled maze of Amelia's thoughts.

"I can help you," Rosie said. "Do you... umm... remember what happened to you?"

"I spend my time watching. I count my fingers."

Rosie turned back to Frank, "This is useless. She is totally mad."

Frank sighed, straightened a bit and stumbled forward a couple of paces. "Amelia?" He asked.

She ignored him, plucking at her fingers.

"Amelia? I lost my little girl too," he said softly.

She stopped moving and muttering.

"I wanted to find her," Frank continued. "And I searched all over the country for a way back to her. I bet you have searched all over for your little girl?"

Amelia nodded slowly.

"Where was the first place you searched for her? Maybe we can go back there, start from the beginning. I sure would like to help you find her."

Amelia looked up, her green eyes flashing, "In the forest."

Frank nodded, "Right. In the forest. That would be hard. Lots of places to look in the forest. We could go there, all of us, and have a look around."

"What are you doing?" Rosie hissed.

Frank turned to her, "It's something I heard while I was away and travelling. Sometimes with tethered spirits like this, you get no sense out of them, but if you can bring them to their bones, then it grounds them. We need to bring her back."

"But her bones aren't there," Rosie pointed out, "The police removed them."

"Part of her will be... in the soil. Decomposition." Frank looked vaguely embarrassed as though he had just had to talk to her about reproduction.

Rosie pulled a face, "That's horrible."

Frank shrugged, "Dust to dust."

Rosie cleared her throat, "Amelia? I'm going to come in and pick up your ring, okay? Then we will go look for your daughter. We will go to the forest."

Before Rosie could blink, Amelia was in front of her taking her by the hands and energy coursed up Rosie's arms like she was holding on to an electrified wire. She gasped, and Tiny began to bark. Frank made a move to grab her and pull her away, but she managed to hold out a hand to him.

"It's okay. I'm okay. It was just a shock."

And she realised this was true. The initial touch had been startling but not painful. Now it felt as though the energy was moving through her, alighting her from the inside, she felt giddy and vaguely high, almost as though she herself could reach out with her mind and turn on lights simply by thinking it. Amelia released her and Rosie felt the energy slowly melt away. She shook herself off and went to the dollhouse, peering inside where Lucy had said the ring was hidden.

Like everything else in the room, the dollhouse was a mess, it had been flipped on its side, and all of the little felt animals and tiny dolls were bundled in a corner with furniture and miniature clothes. She rifled through them, searching through small shoes and tiny dishes, before her fingers grazed something cold and hard. She pulled out the ring, a delicate gold band with a red stone in it.

"That was mine," Amelia said. "He liked to carry it. He said it reminded him of my hands. He always liked my hands."

Rosie cut eyes with Frank who wore a look of sadness and horror on his face, one she was sure was mirroring her own. She pulled herself up.

"Let's go," she said.

CHAPTER 35

Rosie edged the car as close to the forest as she could. Amelia's ring sat in the pocket over her breast, and Rosie could feel a vibration emanating from it. Unshielded, this would be impossible to lose; she felt it on her keenly. Amelia had chattered incessantly for the drive, whispers and shouting. Intermittently, the electrics in Rosie's car would act up, the hazards coming on at one point, and sometimes the windscreen wipers would slide across the dry glass with a high-pitched squeak. Rosie had grit her teeth and pressed on, praying for the trip to end, so they could get some space between themselves and the spirit.

As they had gotten closer, Amelia had gotten quieter, until now as Rosie looked in the rearview mirror, she saw Amelia looking back at her with almost sanity in her eyes. In the backseat, Tiny whined, his body was pressed against the door edging away from Amelia, and in the passenger seat, Frank sat looking sick and stressed. *This is taking a horrible toll on him*, Rosie thought, and she worried what sort of strain this was putting on his body. *Could it kill him*, she wondered in alarm. Contact with the Others made Rosie woozy, and she felt currents of energy, but she seemed to be becoming better at pushing it to background noise. Frank, on the other hand, looked like he was actually deathly ill. It wasn't difficult to imagine him collapsing, and Rosie thought of herself alone in the forest, with a ghost, an Irish wolfhound, a dead father, and a possible serial killer nearby and shuddered.

"Maybe you should stay in the car?" She suggested, reluctantly.

Frank looked at her sharply, "I am *not* going to leave you. Not again. We will do this together."

Rosie felt relief wash over her, "Okay," she nodded. "Then let's go."

Rosie got out and released Tiny from the backseat, who bounded out and over to Frank, butting against him.

Frank ruffled his fur, "I'm okay, buddy. You go stay with our girl. Go look after Rosie, go on."

Tiny looked from Frank to Rosie and padded obediently back to Rosie's side. Rosie led the way through the undergrowth, the moon was not quite full but illuminated the forest, dappling the ground with moonlight that filtered through the branches. Amelia soundlessly followed them, disappearing and reappearing ahead or behind - but always within a certain radius of where Rosie walked, carrying the ring that tethered Amelia to this world that she no longer belonged in.

"I always hated when people did this sort of thing at night in movies, you know?" she said to Frank. "It would be dark and spooky, and the main character would decide to go check out the graveyard instead of waiting until it was daylight and not absolutely terrifying. And now, here I am."

Frank chuckled, "Sometimes the only time to do things is right now."

Rosie nodded, "That's true."

In the darkness, without the noise of birds and other animals, she heard the call of the creek and veered towards it.

"It's steep getting down the embankment," she warned Frank, and he grunted in response.

Rosie edged towards the embankment and eased herself down, showing Frank which tree to hold on to. Amelia appeared at the bottom in the blink of an eye.

Frank snorted, "Easier for some, I suppose."

Amelia looked at him, expressionlessly, "My first trip here was a hard one."

Frank nodded, "I imagine it was. Point taken. Let's keep going."

They picked their away across the creek, following Rosie's path from when she found Hannah. The creek was different now though; it showed the signs of being disturbed from the foot traffic of police and searchers. The grass was flattened along the far side, a clear path that led the way to where the women had lain.

Amelia hummed a tune Rosie recognised as a lullaby and wished she wouldn't. What was Amelia thinking now? Was she remembering her daughter? Did her thoughts even work that way? Without warning, Frank leaned over and began retching into the undergrowth.

"Close," he managed, wiping his mouth.

Rosie realised they *were* close. She wasn't far from where she had found Hannah, but more to the point, she could feel the vibrations of spirits. It was different though, less present, like when she sat down on a chair that had recently been vacated and could still feel the warmth of the person left behind.

In a short while, Amelia pulled up abruptly.

"I am here. I was here."

Tape circled the trees where police had cordoned off an area. Rosie lifted it and ducked under, holding it up for Frank and Tiny to pass under, silently hoping the police hadn't posted someone to guard the area - she wasn't sure what excuse she could come up with. They followed Amelia now, who led them to an area that had been recently dug up. Rosie's feet crunched on pine needles as she edged closer to Amelia who sat beside the ground, her hand hovering over the soil.

"This is where you were?" She asked gently.

Amelia nodded.

Rosie sat on the ground beside her, "Amelia, can you tell us what happened?"

The story came out of Amelia in bits and pieces, Rosie and Frank occasionally interjecting to ask a question. And slowly, the more Amelia talked, the more lucid she seemed.

When she had been pregnant with Violet, James had been

making only a little bit of money. Amelia had gotten a job working reception for a while, but the pregnancy was making her more tired than she imagined it would. Her skin, which had always been pale, seemed translucent, her hair began to fall out. In the evening, she would fall asleep before dinner, rousing only when James placed a dish into her hands, which she would pick at listlessly. She had worried the baby wouldn't get the right nutrients, and her anxiety seemed difficult to manage. She had no family or friends to share her worries with, and she didn't want to bother James, who was trying so hard to build a home for them. She had felt like she was walking through a fog, and she began to make mistakes at work.

"They fired me after the third time," she said. "I couldn't tell James. So, I just kept getting up and going into the city and then spending my days walking through the mall. I knew I needed to tell him soon, my pay wasn't going to go in the following week, and I didn't know what we were going to do. He barely made enough to cover the rent, we wouldn't have enough to pay the bills, and we had bought nothing for Violet. I was twenty-eight weeks pregnant, and I was scared."

One day in the city, she had been sitting at the mall on one of the benches, picking at an apple when David had spotted her and come over to say hello. He offered to take her to lunch, and she had been hungry for the first time in weeks, so she agreed. There, in the restaurant, she had broken down and confessed to David what had happened.

"He offered me some money," Amelia said. "I knew I shouldn't take it, because James wanted to make it ourselves.

David said we didn't have to tell him. It could be a loan, and I could pay him back. In the end, I agreed."

She had met David for lunch most days for the next two months, since she was travelling into the city to pretend to go to work. He slipped her cash - hundreds each time, and she had purchased things for Violet, some new clothing for herself, and a couple of tools that James had needed for work and been borrowing from Mr. Goldman.

The first time David had kissed her was the day she went into labour. She had gone to kiss him on the cheek as she was leaving after lunch, and he had taken her hand, and turned his mouth to hers. His lips meeting hers, his tongue sliding between her teeth.

"I was so shocked; I didn't know what to say. He played it off like it had never happened. I went into labour that night, and for a few weeks, I didn't see him at all. Things were going so well. Violet and I would have coffee with James in the morning, and during the day we would lie on the day bed we had in the sunroom, and I would count her fingers and toes."

Rosie felt a pang in her stomach, remembering those early days with Lucy and thinking how similar her and Amelia were in some ways, but she could go home and hold her daughter, and Amelia never would.

Amelia continued, telling them how when Violet was a few months old, they had been having some money troubles. Mr. Goldman had been sick; James had been managing the store on his own, and their car had broken down. James was getting up to cycle to work in the morning, and Amelia was feeling lonely and isolated. Violet had been colicky, and she was exhausted. Brooke had shown up and offered to mind Violet for a few hours so Amelia could go out for a bit. She had taken the train into the city and turned up at David's office to see whether he would spot her the money to fix the car. David had invited her in and shut the door. When he kissed her that time, she had kissed him back. It felt so long since she had felt like herself. She and James had both been so tired that they hadn't touched each other beyond a kiss goodbye in the morning since before Violet was born. When David touched her, she felt like she was a person again, sexy and desirable and wanted. He had taken her underwear down, and they'd had sex up against his office door. Afterwards, he had given her two thousand dollars.

"Anytime you need anything, let me know," he had said as she left.

It happened more often, a day here and there, sex and money. The more often it happened, the more trapped she felt, the more she hated herself, and the more she pulled away from James, because of her shame. Her anxiety got out of control, and David began giving her Valium as well as cash. She spent the weekend with him, David drinking expensive liquor, and Amelia got a hold of some drugs from an old contact. And then there was the time she just didn't come home. She kept meaning to, she kept thinking of Violet... but the thought of her made Amelia feel so unworthy of the sweetness of her daughter that she just needed one more hour, one more day. When she had finally come back, James had been furious. He had grabbed her by the arms and shook her until her teeth rattled in her head. She had lashed out, raking her fingernails down his cheek, before grabbing her handbag and storming out. She had no cash; she had blown it all.

She had wandered barefoot through the streets, crying, hating herself. She needed to get straight, to come clean to James. She was scared and humiliated and sick. She had hitched a ride to David's house with a balding man who leered at her and tried to run his hand up her leg, his fingers grazing the inner seam of her jeans, making vomit rise in her throat. By the time she knocked on the door at the St Clair estate where David was staying, she had been hysterical. She was shaking with fear and shame, crying and saying that she needed to tell James, she wanted to stop, it had been a mistake. David had pulled her into his arms, and she had cried against his chest.

"I thought he understood. It felt like comfort."

But then he began kissing down her neck, trying to put his hands under her t-shirt and she had pushed him away.

"He became so angry. He was shouting that I owed him a lot of money, that he loved me and I had used him; calling me a bitch and a whore. I started for the door, and he screamed at me that he would kill me. And I didn't believe him," Amelia looked at Rosie. "But I should have."

Rosie stood a little way from Amelia, who remained in the same spot near her grave, and whispered to Frank, "What now?"

Frank shrugged, "Usually when they tell their story they move on. There has got to be something else. Something she's left out."

Rosie grimaced, "I don't know how much worse it could get. She seemed to tell us everything. I don't usually use the word hate, but I really hate this guy. He played her when she was vulnerable and groomed her. Violet has missed five years with her mother because of him."

She looked over her shoulder and scanned the forest, and shivered, "Also, I really would like to get out of here, the St Clair estate isn't far... and James said David stays there when he is in the city."

The stood in silence, remembering when Amelia had last been in those rooms.

"Can we call the cops and let them deal with it?" She asked.

Frank looked at her with one eyebrow raised, "And say what? A ghost told you that it wasn't your boyfriend that killed her but actually his uncle?"

"He's not my boyfriend."

"Not really the most important thing right now, Rosie."

Tiny pressed close to her, and she ran her fingers through his fur. *I'm not sure this is what Mr. Thompson had in mind when he asked me to mind him*, she thought.

Amelia spoke, startling Rosie, who jumped a mile at her voice. Frank lay a steadying hand on her back.

"We need to get the others," Amelia said.

"The other what?" Frank asked.

"The other girls. They're still there."

"The other women he killed?" Rosie asked.

Amelia nodded and stood, "They're stuck here. He keeps us with him."

Rosie could not think of anything she wanted less than to go looking for more tethered spirits. Still, they had come this far.

Rosie looked to Frank, "We can check the house out, if it looks like he is there we come back later, find whatever is tethering them and release them."

"I think we should just call the cops," Frank said.

"You just said we *shouldn't* call the cops!"

"Right. But it's preferable to us walking into the house of someone who has killed multiple women. We can do an anonymous tip, they can find the items that belonged to the women, and that's evidence David did it."

"It's James's house though," Rosie pointed out. "David just stays there. Also, what happens when the police take those items into evidence? Those women go with them. I can never release them. They stay here, tethered. That's awful."

Frank sighed and nodded reluctantly. Rosie knew he understood better than most; Frank had lived straddling two worlds for years, and he knew what the torture of forever would be like.

"Okay," he conceded. "But we are careful. And if it looks like he is anywhere nearby, we bail. We come back when it's safe."

"Agreed," Rosie said. She turned to Amelia, "Show us the way."

CHAPTER 36

Rosie and Frank stood with Tiny in the trees on the edge of the St Clair property. Out on the manicured lawn, Amelia stood in the moonlight with no fear of being spotted, looking hauntingly beautiful. From here, Rosie could see the dark outline of the cabin James had taken her in the distance, and she felt a wistful pull, remembering the night they had spent there before everything had changed.

"What do you think?" Frank said.

Rosie shook her head, "It's impossible to tell. It's three in the morning. Even if he is in, we can't expect to see a light on. Although, when James and I came here before, there was a car parked in the driveway. James said the automatic door wasn't opening on the garage. I don't know if it's been fixed though."

Quietly, Frank pulled away from her and walked along the tree line towards the garage. Rosie watched as he slipped from shadow to shadow towards the garage and peered into the glass in the doorway. He turned towards her and shook his head, motioning her over with his hand. Rosie began walking across the grass, the dew wetting the hem of her jeans, Tiny staying close to her. Frank, Rosie and Amelia reached the front door, Frank and Tiny keeping a wider birth from Amelia than Rosie. Frank took a deep breath, and Rosie looked over at him.

"I'm okay," he said, and tried to smile, but it looked more like a grimace to Rosie. If what Amelia was saying was true then inside she and Frank were about to find four more tethered spirits, she had no idea how that would affect Frank, or herself for that matter. She reached out a hand and turned the knob. Locked. Of course it would be locked; she was an idiot to think they would just walk in.

"It's locked," she whispered to Frank.

He looked behind her to Amelia.

"I think she's got it," he said, gesturing with his head.

Rosie turned back to Amelia, who put her hand near the handle, and there was an audible click as the lock sprang free. Rosie tried the handle again, and the door swung inwards silently. Amelia stepped forward and led them inside.

They tiptoed into a large entrance room opposite a set of stairs. The house was horribly silent, and every move they made seemed to echo off the marble floors. Still, it crackled with a presence somehow, a vibration that Rosie was coming to be familiar with. Tiny whined, his nails tapping on the floor as he moved behind Frank. Standing in the house now, Rosie could understand why James didn't want to live here with Violet. She didn't need to use her sixth sense to understand this place had a bleakness to it. The St Clair house had been haunted a long time, well before spirits moved in.

Amelia led them down a long hallway to the right, the lights in the hall flicking on as she passed. Rosie glanced back at Frank and Tiny assuring herself they were still following. The passed rooms, some with doors open. Rosie peered into one to see a stern-faced man sipping scotch by a window and jumped back into Frank, letting out an audible squeak.

"Imprint," Frank said, looking past her into the room. "Just an imprint of some old guy."

Rosie nodded, feeling foolish and remembered James talk of his father in the study. She glanced back at the imprint, noticing similarities between him and a James, the straight nose, the hairlines - except James held himself with a casual confidence, and this man made her feel slightly intimidated, even if he was just residual energy. She would not have wanted to meet Henry St Clair in real life.

She swallowed, her mouth suddenly dry, "Right, okay. I just got a fright."

Amelia turned back to her, "That one isn't here. He's just a shadow."

They continued on down the long hall.

"How big is this place?" Frank grumbled.

Amelia disappeared into a doorway at the end of the hall, and Rosie hesitated, unsure what she would find on the other side. She was holding up against one tethered spirit, but would she handle more? Even June had said there were places she wouldn't go because the energy was too strong, and she had far more experience than Rosie. She glanced back at Frank for support, his face so pale, it almost seemed to glow.

A small girl blinked into existence at Rosie's side, and Frank stumbled back in shock, his hand scrabbling for purchase on the dark wood panelling. She looked about Lucy's age and wore a white dress with a pale blue ribbon tying the waist. She looked so much like Violet that for a moment Rosie looked around for James, then she realised the girl's eyes were differently shaped, her mouth a small bow, where Violet had Amelia's full lips. Around her neck was a small heart-shaped locket.

"Hello," the girl said. "My name is Sophia."

She wore no shield. New as she was to this world, Rosie knew this child was dead. And worse, that she was tethered.

Rosie's eyes filled with tears, "Hello, Sophia."

Behind her, Frank swore, "A little girl?"

The mother in Rosie ached. She could not imagine the agony of losing her child. She wondered if Frank was thinking of her at this age. She turned back to her father now, who looked worse than ever and for not the first time she wondered if he would survive this. Sweat was pouring down his face; she noticed his hand hovering near his chest.

Sophia held out her hand, "I can take you to them. They're this way."

Rosie took her hand. The electricity ran up her arm, but this time it felt as though it were charging her, releasing her fear. It felt as though she was truly unshielded, as though her whole life she had lived in a state of fear so commonplace that it had become a part of her and now she was finally throwing it off. She could hear Frank lagging behind, the sounds of Tiny's whimpers, but they came from a place far away. She entered the room and met the women David had taken.

She recognised Sarah Yarrow, Madison Brown, Charlee George and Tiana Hunter from the news articles she had read. There were six other women in the room, who passed their names to Rosie as though it were a prayer, and Rosie supposed, in a way it was. After all this time, someone had come for them. Frank and Tiny waited at the doorway, Frank sagged against the frame, his other hand resting on Tiny. Rosie sat on the couch as the women poured out their stories.

he took me from a street in Melbourne
I was running after uni
he bought me a drink

On and on, who they had been, who had loved them, and what they had left behind. Rosie cried and held their hands and listened to these women curate the stories of their deaths. Time was meaningless here. These women had waited for an eternity to tell their tales.

Sophia stood apart quietly. She had said nothing during the time the women spoke. Rosie did not want to ask. She didn't want to hear the answer, but she was Sophia's only doorway to the other side. There was nothing else to be done.

"Sophia? Did you want to tell me something?" Rosie whispered.

Sophia shook her head, "He was my brother. I don't know why he did it. We were swimming in the creek."

Amelia reached for Sophia and folded her into her arms. *So there was that at least*, Rosie thought, *Sophia and Amelia had each other.*

Rosie looked around, "Where is Hannah?"

Amelia looked at her sadly, "With him."

Sarah spoke up, "He carries something with him, from us. We have to go where the item is."

Rosie looked aghast, "You mean Hannah is tethered to him while he has the item. She is stuck with him right now?"

Sarah nodded, "He usually took Amelia. She was gone so often. When he lost her, that's when he took Hannah. He never takes Sophia."

"I stay in the house," Sophia said.

Rosie imagined Amelia forced to walk beside the man who murdered her day after day for years and broke into a cold sweat. No wonder Amelia had been near insanity. That would be hell for anyone.

"Where are they?" She asked. "The things he keeps?"

Amelia let go of Sophia and took Rosie to the fireplace, indicating at one of the stones on the hearth. Rosie knelt down and tried to pry the stone up, but it was too heavy. She looked back to Frank for help, who grimaced but pushed himself up and he and Tiny made their way into the room.

"Can you step back please," she asked the spirits, "My dad is sick. He can't touch any of you."

The women obliged, moving away.

Frank looked at Rosie gratefully, "Thank you."

Together Rosie and Frank pulled at the stone, lifting it up

and away, revealing a cavity beneath. Inside sat a brown timber box. It was roughly made and unadorned. A simple thing considering what it contained. Rosie lifted it out and opened it. Inside was the locket worn by Sophia, a ring, a charm bracelet, a single pearl earring. Pieces of jewellery from each of the women. She ran her fingers over them. Frank retreated to a far corner of the room and slid down the wall, sitting splayed legged on the ground, Tiny by his side.

"How do I move them on," she asked Frank.

He looked at her, helplessly, "I don't know, Rosie. June might know. I spent the last twenty-five years trying to avoid all this shit. As far as I know, they should just go. They've told you their stories; we know the truth."

"None of that will help James, though."

"It might, if they find Sophia's necklace in here. That had to have happened years before James was alive."

Rosie looked down at the box. Frank was right. They had done all they could; they needed to call the police.

Suddenly, the hairs on Rosie's arms prickled and the air felt charged. She looked up. Hannah was in the doorway, looking surprised and horrified. She was exactly as Rosie remembered her. Before.

"Rosie," Hannah said.

It was almost a plea. She raised her hands in front of her. Hannah was the first Other that Rosie had ever known in the living world, after days of grief over finding her body, to see her now was like a gift. Entranced, Rosie stood, her hands still clutching the box and started towards Hannah.

"Hannah," Rosie said. "Oh god, Hannah."

"No," Hannah shouted. "You have to leave!"

The lights flickered; it felt as though the room crackled with electricity. Rosie pulled up abruptly, the smell of sulphur was overpowering, she coughed and covered her nose with her hand.

Sophia pushed forward and came to Rosie's side, looking at her with wide blue eyes, "He's back."

Rosie looked from Sophia to Hannah, realisation dawning on her face - he had Hannah with him, if she is here, *he* is here.

He's back, she thought numbly.

The air around Hannah shimmered - David walked right through her towards Rosie.

"Hello, love," he said smiling. And raising one arm, he struck her across the face.

Rosie fell heavily on to her side, and the box skidded across the floor, hitting the wall and spilling the contents. Tiny growled and raced to stand between Rosie and David, crouching low. The fur on his back was raised, his teeth bared as he snarled at David. The sight of Tiny seemed to give David pause. He hesitated before leaning over and pulling one of the bookends from the shelf beside him, he tested the heft of the heavy marble for a moment and grinned. Rosie's head was spinning, and blood rushed in her ears. She tasted blood and struggled to sit up. *Where is Frank?* She thought. She looked for her father, but the room spun wildly, and she shook her head to clear it. Around her, the women gathered, silent, watchers, and unable to help.

. . .

David swung the bookend at Tiny wildly, but the dog moved back and snapped at the hand, grabbing a piece of the cuff of the shirt and tearing at it. Behind David, Frank moved quietly, he held no weapon at all, except that David wasn't expecting him. Rosie watched Frank stagger towards David, he swayed wildly, as though drunk. *If Frank could get David to turn around, it might give Tiny the chance to get hold of him,* she thought. Frank lunged at David, grabbing hold of his arm and swinging a right hook towards his face, that glanced off his chin. David stumbled a bit and then shook himself off.

He turned his face back to Rosie, and grinned, manically, "You brought friends!"

Turning back to Frank, David swung out with his hand that held the bookend, smashing it into the side of Frank's head with a sickening crunch, and Frank dropped to the ground in a heap.

Tiny leapt.

He was small for an Irish Wolfhound, but he was still a large dog. The weight of him knocked David flat on his face, the bookend released from his hand, where it slid across the floor, coming to rest against Frank's immobile form. He scrambled across the floor towards the door, but Tiny grabbed hold of his leg, growling and snarling. David turned on to his back, smacking at Tiny with his bare hands.

Rosie crawled towards Frank, "Dad! Dad?"

She lay her head on his chest to listen for breathing. She couldn't hear a thing over the sound of her own heart and Tiny and David, but her head rose with his breath, and she sighed with relief that he was alive. Beside her stood Amelia, who held out her hand and helped Rosie to her feet.

. . .

Rosie walked towards David. He lay bloodied and still, his eyes shut tightly against Tiny, who was snarling inches from his face. She could call the police now... if she wanted to. Seeing him on the ground, beaten, Rosie realised he was just a man. The whole time she had been terrified of what Lucy had been seeing in her room, thinking it was some kind of monster. There were no monsters. The girl in Lucy's room had just been a woman. A mother that was taken from her child and the people who loved her. The person who had done that was just a man. He had no power over her. These women here held power, one he simply couldn't see because of his shield. But anyone could be unshielded. She knew that.

"Tiny," Rosie said, calling the dog away. Tiny looked towards her and back to David.

"Tiny!" She said again, more sharply. Tiny uttered a final growl and stepped back, walking towards Rosie. He lay down and began licking the side of Frank's face. Rosie still held Amelia's hand as she leaned over David.

"David," she said softly. "I don't want you to move now, or I'm going to call my dog back, and this time I won't call him off. Nod if you understand me."

David nodded slowly.

"Good. Listen to me. For twenty-five years, my father walked this earth, seeing what people like you have done. He saw everything, and it nearly destroyed him. It took him away from my mother and me, just like you have taken women from their children and their mothers. I really want you to see them. I'm going to show them to you.... Hold on; this is going to hurt."

She didn't know the spell. She wasn't a witch. But instinct had woken a dormant part inside her mind and she realised now; she didn't need to be one. June had been right, she had been born to this. It was her gift, passed on by generations of women, and Rosie could almost feel them standing with her now.

Rosie squeezed Amelia's hand and nodded to her. Without a word, Amelia reached back and took hold of Sarah's hand, who held on to Madison... and one by one as the women locked hands, Rosie felt the electricity running up Amelia's arm flowing into her. Blood rushed in her ears, the smell of sulphur filled the air, pine needles and dirt rained on to the floor.

Amelia,

Sarah,

Madison,

Charlee

Sophia

Tiarna

AmberJillRachelBriannaCaitlinMelindaHannah...

Rosie reached down and ripped off David's shield.

CHAPTER 37

It was a small thing really, the shield. Shimmering in the palm of Rosie's hand, opalescent and pulsating with its own energy and glow. She marvelled at it, entranced. On the floor, David was out stone cold. She knew from experience he wouldn't be awake for a while. Amelia leaned over Rosie's outstretched palm, looking at the shield.

"What are you going to do with it?" She asked Rosie.

Rosie pulled her eyes reluctantly from the orb in her hand. She hadn't thought that far ahead when she had taken it from David. She had simply wanted to take something from him the way he had stolen something from each of them. She looked over at Frank, who was still unconscious on the floor, with Tiny at his side.

"I'm going to give it to my dad," she decided.

Rosie walked to Frank's side and knelt before him. She didn't know how to... what? Put it on? Install it? She had never seen it done, and Frank had been vague on the details of when he had given her his. Wasn't there something she had to say? A spell of some sort? Not knowing what else to do, she cupped her hands over Frank's chest and opened them slightly allowing the shield to slip through her palms and on to him. She urged it gently with her hands towards him, feeling the energy of it catch somehow on to Frank's. There it seemed to sink into him, stretching and moulding until it began to pulse all around him. She sat back and inspected it. There didn't seem to be any tears like June had described with Rosie's borrowed shield. It was perfect.

Hannah came and sat beside Rosie. Rosie looked at her with regret colouring her face. This should never have happened. None of this should have happened.

"Oh Hannah," Rosie said, sadly, "I am so, so sorry. I wish this hadn't of happened to you."

Hannah reached out and squeezed her hand, "Thank you for finding me."

Rosie felt tears slip from her eyes and brushed them off her cheeks, "I don't know how to move you on. I don't know how to help you all."

Hannah looked up, "I think I'm going to go now, actually. It's time. I'm glad you are okay, Rosie. I'm glad you aren't... well."

Rosie nodded, "What about Bryan? I could try to tell him something..."

She trailed off, unsure how she would even begin to explain to Bryan anything that Hannah told her.

Hannah smiled at her, "No. Bryan knows. I wish I could have had dozens of more years with him, but you know? I don't think it would ever have been enough."

"I know exactly what you mean."

Hannah let go of Rosie's hand, and then, just like that - she was gone.

Frank began to stir, and Rosie reached for him, "Dad? Dad, are you okay?"

Frank tried to sit up and immediately fell back, he lifted a hand to his head, feeling where he was struck, and Rosie noticed blood on his fingertips.

"Rosie," Frank groaned.

"It's okay; I'm okay. We're safe."

Rosie looked around and pulled a throw rug from the couch and pressed it against Frank's head where the bleeding was. He winced and pushed it away.

"You're bleeding!" Rosie protested.

"I'm okay."

Frank reached out and rubbed the top of Tiny's head, "You did good."

Tiny tilted his head to the side, as though contemplating the compliment. *He had done good*, Rosie thought. She would have to give him an extra helping of breakfast this morning. She ruffled his fur in thanks.

Frank raised his head, "The Others are gone. You moved them on."

Rosie shook her head, "Hannah moved on. But the others are still here. You're shielded. I gave you David's shield."

Frank looked at her, alarmed, "How?"

"I'll explain it later. I think I should probably call the cops now."

She looked around for her phone, which had fallen out of

her pocket when David had struck her. She was finding it difficult to focus her right eye, which was swelling shut. She found it under the edge of the couch and pulled it towards her.

David began to make whimpering sounds and opened his eyes before rolling on to his side and vomiting on to the flooring.

"Here it comes," Frank said under his breath.

David raised himself up on his elbows and looked around the room, his eyes widened, and he sat up as though he had been shocked and scuttled back along the floor until he hit the bookshelf behind him.

"What the fuck!" His face went pale. He looked nearly as ill as Frank had before.

Rosie supposed it was worse for him, at least Frank hadn't been witnessing the women he had killed.

It's a curse, Frank had said. For some people, Rosie could see he was right. Freed of his shield, David was vulnerable. He could see the Others now - and for the first time since their last breath, they could touch him. Rosie knew exactly what that felt like.

Sophia ran to him, "Hi David! You can see me now! Do you want to go for a swim?"

David recoiled from her in horror, holding his head. The women surged forward, each of them telling him their stories as they had told Rosie and Frank earlier, talking over one another, reaching for him. David writhed beneath their touch, each one shooting electricity up his veins as their fingers grazed through him.

"Stop!" He screamed. "Stop it!"

"We should go," Rosie said to Frank. "You're bleeding, and you need an ambulance."

He shrugged, "I feel quite okay, really. I haven't felt this good in years."

Rosie helped him to his feet, and he and Tiny went out the door and down the hall, leaving Rosie alone with the room of spirits and David. He was no threat to her now.

The women had begun to disappear; Amelia turned to Rosie as though she was going to say something, but then faded from sight. Finally, only Sarah remained. When Rosie called for the police and an ambulance to the St Clair property, the room was quiet except for David's sobs. Hanging up the phone, she looked at Sarah.

"Sarah? Are you going to move on?"

Sarah shook her head, "I've been with David a long time. I'm waiting to watch the arrest. I've earned that. He carried me with him when he took some of them. I was there when he killed Amelia, helpless, trapped. I need to see this. I want to hear the click of the handcuffs."

Rosie nodded, "I'll leave you to it, then."

She turned and walked away.

Michael really didn't know how to describe what he saw at the St Clair house. He had arrived on scene to Rosie Parker with a black eye, a man that claimed to be her father but looked like he was homeless sporting a head injury, the biggest dog he had ever seen - and David St Clair incoherent in the back study. On the floor was jewellery he recognised from the hours he had spent going over every detail from the cases of the missing women. David was ranting about Sarah Yarrow as though she was right there in the room. And Rosie had no decent explanation for how she, her dad, and a dog that looked like a horse had ended up there in the first place.

Daylight was beginning to break as David was taken in the police car for questioning, and teams of crime scene investigators descended upon the property. Michael's partner Jim explained to Rosie and Frank that they would have to come in to make a full statement later that day and told them they could leave. There wasn't a car in sight, but the pair just set off down the driveway, the hound at their side, arms linked around each other's waists.

"This is the strangest fucking scene I've ever been to," Jim said. "There is dirt and shit all over that study. It looks like half the forest is inside it."

"You're not wrong," Michael replied.

"How are you going to explain to Brooke that her brother is innocent, but it looks like her uncle's a serial killer?"

Michael ran his hand through his hair, "Shit."

"Yep. That's what I thought too."

CHAPTER 38

Three Months Later.

She pulled on her jeans and a t-shirt as the first fingers of dawn slipped between the blinds. Tiptoeing towards the front door, she heard the floorboard creak behind her and turned around to see Dee in an oversized t-shirt and a sleep messy braid.

"You're going now?" Dee asked.

Rosie nodded, "I don't want to be late."

Dee stood silently for a moment and then crossed to wrap her arms around Rosie.

"It's been every day this week, honey. You don't think, maybe..."

"Just once more," Rosie said as she pulled away.

She pulled up two houses down from her and Ben's old house

at 6:45 in the morning. The morning air was cold, but she turned off the car and waited, the warmth of the heater disappearing. Goosebumps rose on her arms. It was 7 o'clock.

The front door didn't open. He simply materialised in front of it as though he had walked straight through it. He walked out a few steps and before pulling his keys from his pocket and pressing the button to unlock the car. Rosie watched as he continued down the driveway to a car that didn't exist. He opened a door made of air and turned to the house. In her mind, she could see Lucy and herself standing at the threshold waving him off. She could almost hear Lucy calling goodbye. Ben's mouth moved as he called back, his hand rose in a wave... and then he was gone.

The first day she had seen Ben, it had been by accident. Rosie had been up shooting the sunrise over the beach, and on her way back, she had driven past the house just as he walked out. Rosie had hit the brakes, stopping dead in the road, grateful for the empty street because she couldn't have moved if she had wanted to. She couldn't breathe, watching him wave goodbye as he had done every morning before he died. She had managed to pull over to the side of the road before doubling over, gasping for air as though she had been winded. *It's just an imprint*, she had heard June saying in her head, *they attach to people, places or things.*

. . .

Of all the regrets Rosie had over the loss of Ben, the greatest had been that she had never known it was 'the last'. You never know. You wake up, and you drink a coffee, and you kiss your husband goodbye like an afterthought. It's quick, as if you had another forty years of kisses - a forgettable kiss. You throw out an 'I love you' as they get in their car, like to love and be loved isn't the most important thing in the world. You say it like you'll hear it again. You don't know that the last time you touched them would be *the last time.* You don't know that the last goodbye, would be the final goodbye. She hadn't been ready. She had not been prepared. So, every day that week, Dee had spent the night so that Lucy wouldn't be alone while Rosie had waited for Ben to say goodbye. And each day she came home and realised she still wasn't ready. It still wasn't enough. Today she knew she would never be ready to say goodbye. It wouldn't have mattered. Here is what she knew...that there isn't always going to be a reason why; somethings will never make sense. And that she could have had those forty years of kisses and still not have been ready. Grief didn't have an end any more than love had an end. She would never be ready, but somehow, you have to learn to live anyway.

She smiled, "Goodbye, love."

Rosie turned the car on and drove away. Fifteen minutes later she pulled up, and before she could stop to think about what she was doing, she ran up to James's door and knocked. He had called her after David was arrested, and she had asked for more time, she had so much on her mind between Frank and Lucy and what had happened at the St Clair property. She just felt as though she needed to process it all. She and Lucy had stayed with Kate for two weeks while she gently worked to get Lucy to come back to the house, promising there was no one in her room anymore. Frank had moved in with June to help her after her stroke; he had just gotten a job at the local hardware store. He looked better, Rosie thought he looked like ten years had been taken off him. She had attended Hannah's memorial and had her heart broken all over again, watching her family grieve for her. Bryan had stood up and said, "Hannah lived a big life," and went on to talk about all the things she had fit into her twenty-six years on Earth. *A big life*, Rosie had thought. She wanted that.

Inside the house, she heard tiny running feet before James called from somewhere inside.

"I'll get it, Violet, you need to go and get ready for kinder."

The door opened, and there he was, standing in boxer shorts despite the cool temperature. His eyes registered surprise, and then pleasure.

"Rosie! You must be freezing, come inside."

She shook her head, "I can't stay. I have to get home for Lucy. I just wanted to say something."

He stayed silent, waiting for her to continue.

Just say it, she thought, *just jump.*

"I'm ready," she said, before hurrying to add, "And it's okay if you aren't, or if you don't want to, I would completely understand."

"If I don't want to... what?"

"Try. To see if we can try to do this. You and me."

He smiled, "You're ready?"

"I am," she nodded.

He pulled her to him and wrapped his arms around her, "Me too."

ALL GIFTS COME WITH A PRICE...

Penny's life was normal. She had a fiancé, she was working in a steady job, and visiting her grandfather in his nursing home.

Then, everything changed.

Penny's mother had been 'gone' for years when she began receiving emails from her written years beforehand. For nine months, every week, they chronicled her mother's downward spiral as she fought against mental illness. Then they stopped as suddenly as they began.

When Penny meets an elderly man with a gift of seeing beyond time, he begins giving her clues to her mother's whereabouts, and

Penny thinks she might finally have the answers she has been hoping for.

What she learns is that all gifts come with a price.

Penny discovers a tangled web of family lies - lies that expose threads of truth in her mother's letters, and nothing is as it seems.

As she follows the trail of breadcrumbs that lead to her mother, Penny hopes to find out what really happened.

But who will be waiting for her at the end?

ACKNOWLEDGMENTS

I began writing Shielded in 2015, but it had lived in my head for years. I believe the veil that separates what we can see in this world from everything else is thinner than we think. Sometimes, people talk about mediums as having a second sight. I like to think that we all have that ability, but few of us see past what we expect to be there.

As I wrote this book, Rosie talked to me. She spoke to me as a mother, who would risk everything for her child. Sometimes, as I sat there, I felt like the story was writing itself, and I was just the hands that were typing. It's easy to see how the concept of muses was born.

Still, no woman is an island. And Shielded would not be here if I didn't have a team of amazing cheerleaders at my back.

So...

Firstly, I want to thank the women in my life who have

supported me with all of my dreams. Massive thanks go to Kelly and Danielle for your unwavering support, and for going through Shielded chapter by chapter to break it down with me. Thank to Netra, who blew through my first draft in a night, and helped me puzzle out where to go when I accidentally wrote myself into a corner. I also need to thank the Birdman, Ákos, for his wisdom on owls - they fly silently, did you know? For Sarah and Darla for offering to read through my draft, and helping me with punctuation and sentence structure. And, finally, I need to shout out to my friend, Shannon, who was the inspiration for the spirit of Dee - kind and calming, loyal, and a little bit magic.

A big thank you to the writing community on Instagram, who have cheered me on during the 'work in progress' stage, and commiserated on the difficult days. You know who you are, and I could not have finished this without you.

For Jessie and Markus, who sat with me during some of the challenging chapters, and read them as I was writing, offering pieces of wisdom and humanity to the scenes I was creating.

For Isabella, who will tell me if a chapter is boring, and how to fix it.

For Clint, who has more faith in me than I have in myself, and celebrated every sentence when I would offer up my word count tally for the day. Words are inadequate when it comes to you. You have my whole heart.

For all my children, who ask a question and have to wait

patiently beside me while I finish a sentence before I respond. My brain always has too many tabs open, I apologise. I love you.

And lastly, for any girl who has discovered she has gifts, and is learning how to navigate the world with them. You were meant to be here. You are supposed to do something important. You are worthy.

ABOUT THE AUTHOR

Liss Brewer lives in Brisbane, with her partner, her children, and her cats. Her first title, The Curator: A Memoir of Motherhood, was published in 2020. Shielded is her second work and first fiction title.

Liss enjoys hot cups of tea, reading, playing in the garden, and daydreaming. Her books are available in paperback worldwide via selected sites, or via her website for Australian distribution. Ebooks are available on Amazon worldwide.

You can find her on Facebook, Instagram, Twitter, and Pinterest.